THE CUSTODY BATTLE

ELLIE MONAGO

THE CUSTODY BATTLE

bookouture

Published by Bookouture in 2024

An imprint of Storyfire Ltd.
Carmelite House
50 Victoria Embankment
London EC4Y 0DZ

www.bookouture.com

ISBN: 978-1-83790-813-4
eBook ISBN: 978-1-83790-812-7

*

I never imagined it could end this way. Not only because it was beautiful at the beginning and in the middle, and even the beginning of the end, but because I thought I knew us. What we were capable of, the lines we would never cross. At the very least, I thought I knew myself.

All I can say is, I'm sorry. Sorrier than I knew a human could be.

There's that expression: I was driven to it. That's how it felt, like I couldn't steer, I couldn't swerve, I couldn't get off this road. But I would never want Lola to use that excuse. A person who blames others, who blames the world... what kind of person is that?

Solomon threatened to cut the baby in half, and the threat was enough to reveal who the real parent was. If only we'd had his wisdom in our corner.

Everyone knows divorce can be hell, but no one ever told me that custody could be murder.

DISSOLUTION

SIX MONTHS EARLIER

ONE

MADELINE

"Even though you'll have two homes now, we're still one family," I tell Lola. "Daddy and I both love you more than anything. That will never change."

"Never," Greg says fiercely. He's fighting back tears. He's always been the sentimental one, and it doesn't help that this wasn't his doing, or his choice. I appreciate that he hasn't made it any harder on me than it already is, but I do wish that he were able to contain himself. As parents, we should be the ones comforting Lola, not the other way around.

Her eyes dart back and forth between us like fish in a bowl. She's reading. Anticipating. Practically every parent says how smart their kid is but mine really is as sharp as a ten-year-old gets. I'd know, being a pediatrician. But physically Lola looks so small, hunched over and dwarfed by the embroidered chair that Sidney—my best friend/interior designer extraordinaire—insisted we buy during the most recent (unnecessary) redecoration. I liked our old living room furniture better, preferring the sectional configuration to all the stand-alones. But every few years, Greg and Sidney gang up on me and insist on a refresh. Well, they used to gang up on me. This is my house now.

"Wait," Lola says. She stands up and walks out of the room.

Greg and I exchange identical glances of worry and confusion from where we're seated side by side on the silk sofa. We peer after Lola, who's gone downstairs. To her room, presumably. Is she coming back? Should we go after her?

Despite my professional acumen, despite the books I've read on separating with dignity and co-parenting peacefully (books I asked Greg to read as well though I suspect he hasn't cracked a single spine), this is uncharted territory for me. Unless you count what I went through when I was a kid, and I try to never think about that. I certainly don't relish breaking up my own family.

No, it's not broken. It'll be a new configuration, another remodel. We'll always be family.

Greg and I are silently and nervously staring out the floor-to-ceiling windows, in no state to appreciate the view of the bay and San Francisco beyond. When Lola returns, she's clutching Blob, her stuffed raccoon. It's from Aunt Sidney, her godmother, and it's one of the few lovies that survived the purge that Lola did two years back.

She perches on the chair again and says, "So what's going to happen to me?"

Now I have to fight back the tears. I see in my peripheral vision that Greg has already lost that battle.

"We love you more than life itself," Greg says. "You know that, right?"

"I know," Lola says, with a touch of impatience. Cut to the chase, she's telling us. Kids are naturally egocentric. She wants to know what a divorce will mean for her, in practical terms.

"You're going to be here with me, mostly," I say. "The rest of the time, you'll be with Daddy. You love one-on-one time, and now you'll get lots of it. You'll have our full attention."

"Where will Daddy be when I'm here?"

I glance at Greg to see if he wants to field this one. He looks incapable of speech, his handsome visage ravaged by grief. I wish he could step up but I can't blame him. He doesn't want this; I do.

"He has a three-bedroom right on the water at Jack London Square," I say. "You love it there, Lo. That's why he picked it." Well, why I picked it. "On Sundays, the farmers market will be right outside your window."

Lola looks at her dad. "Will I be with you every weekend?"

"Every other weekend," I say.

"Daddy?" Lola's voice is tremulous. It's like she's concerned for him more than for herself.

I elbow him gently. "Tell her," I say. "Tell her how great it's going to be. That the three of us will always take care of each other, no matter what."

"It's true," he manages, though he's less than convincing.

"You'll still have all your things here, and your own room at Daddy's. Sidney's already furnished it."

"But I can also buy you anything you want," Greg adds.

He's always had a certain Disneyland Dad quality, probably because he works such long hours as an architect to the mega-rich. When he gets to spend time with Lola, he wants to spoil her. But now he'll have to learn to truly parent without me as a foil.

Lola seems a bit mollified at the idea of having everything she wants.

"Your favorites can go back and forth with you," I say. "Like Blob. He can sleep with you here and at Daddy's."

Greg is starting to pull it together. "Blob could even have his own bed, if you want. I got you bunk beds."

"So I can have friends sleep over at your place?" Lola is brightening, probably imagining the possibilities. All that she and her friends could do without my supervision. Greg will let them decide their own bedtime, food, entertainment...

"Yes, you can have friends over as much as you want," Greg says. "It's going to be great!" His voice goes up at the end, like that old ad with Tony the Tiger talking about some sugary cereal. Which his cupboards might soon be full of.

I take a deep breath. This'll be good for me: learning to relinquish control; becoming more adaptable. "It'll be different in some ways but we'll all adjust," I tell Lola. She's studying me closely with her dark-blue eyes. Greg's blue eyes. They're gorgeous, and potent.

"Uno is better as a two-person game than a three-person game," Lola says.

I smile at her. I knew she'd be resilient.

Greg gets to his feet suddenly and rushes over to the guest bathroom, slamming the door, like he's about to be sick. But this is going so well, he must be able to see that. We just need to set the right example. Now Lola and I are the ones exchanging worried looks, as if we're the parents and Greg's the child.

While Lola has Greg's eyes, she has my everything else. Her blonde hair started nearly white and has darkened over the years until it's the same honey color as mine. Hers is almost to her waist and she's just recently started brushing it, realizing that it's an asset. That her beauty is. I'm not sure when that happened for me, when I succumbed to a practical sort of vanity. I put money and effort into my appearance because it's currency, not because it's fun. Lola is still free.

"Daddy's going to be fine," I say, "once he sees that you are. And I know you will be. Maybe not right away but over time."

I give her an I've-got-this smile, the one I successfully deploy at work with other people's children. "You're going to see him more than you do now since he'll be picking you up at school every Wednesday. And on his weekends, you'll have him all to yourself."

I'm keeping it upbeat but I do feel some trepidation. We are talking about the dissolution of a marriage, the cessation of a certain kind of family that I always meant to have and that I'd hoped to provide to my child. Greg and I both intend to be kind and respectful, to cooperate and collaborate, and above all, to make this as easy as possible on Lola. Yet while I've made it 100 percent clear to him that I don't want to reconcile, I have no choice but to be less than truthful. It would kill him to know that I've fallen in love with another man, and Lola needs her dad alive. Though sometimes keeping that secret—and keeping a distance from the one who awakened my heart—feels like it might kill me. That's why I can't let this drag on.

In the state of California, you can file for divorce immediately upon separation but it won't be finalized for six months. I wish it could be quicker than that in order to drive the point home for Greg, who's frankly always been prone to a certain degree of denial. He's the dreamer, I'm the pragmatist.

It's not like I'm cold, or inured to his pain. I hate seeing him like this. I just can't skate on the surface anymore. I need to feel intensely, too. For so long, our friends have thought of us as a golden couple because of how we look and how we live. Superficially, we're a perfect match. But there's been an emotional disparity for as long as I can remember.

We're just such different people. Take this house, for example. Designed by Greg, it's a showpiece in the Oakland Hills with spectacular views of the bay from every room. A glass palace terraced into the hillside, it's a significant architectural feat by all accounts. There are multiple decks, one with an eight-person hot tub, but a sheer drop and no yard. It can feel like the end of the world.

Greg couldn't be prouder; my feelings have always been mixed. It's ironic that I'm the one who'll be staying but it makes sense since Lola will be with me 70 percent of the time. I don't want to change too much at once when this is the only home she's ever known. But I'd be lying if I said that I didn't some-times dream of moving out of Greg's dream house.

Mark my words: In half a year, this divorce will be final, and I'll be free.

TWO

GREG

I'm hiding out in the bathroom—the guest bathroom, I'm now officially a fucking guest—because I couldn't take another torturous minute. I know what I have to do. I need to appease her, follow her lead, let her be the general while I act like a good little soldier, because that's the only way I can win this war. It's the only way to win her back.

I'm aware that I'm not always the easiest person to be married to, as passionate as I am about my work. I've probably taken her for granted a little, leaving her to run the whole domestic operation, but I also pay for everything. There's no way we could afford this lifestyle on a pediatrician's salary. Sure, I work long hours, but my office is right downstairs. I've always been here for her.

Why didn't she tell me how unhappy she'd gotten until she claimed it was too late, that she wasn't in love with me anymore and would never be again?

I'm a never-say-never kind of a person, particularly where love is concerned. I can turn this around. I have to, for my sake and for Lola's.

Listen, I've put that woman on a pedestal since the day we

met. Was that a decade and a half ago? I'm lousy with dates. What I do know for sure is that I haven't let myself go, haven't let our relationship go. I'm forty-one now, but I stopped aging years ago. I get artful Botox and I have a stylist who comes to my office once a month with a tailor in tow so that my clothes perfectly complement the physique that I work for five times a week with a personal trainer. I've got all my own dark hair and I've been told on more than one occasion by complete strangers that my navy-blue eyes are "devastating." But here I am, devastated, while Madeline is cool as a cucumber.

We've always been a study in contrasts, though. She's my better half, and I'm hers. Yin to my yang, and vice versa. We need each other. Soon, she'll see that. She'll have to.

I step on the sink's foot pedals and run cool water into my hands that I then splash on my face. The foot pedals are on every sink in the house. I sourced them from medical supply and then had cabinetry custom built around them. I did that for Madeline, because sanitation is so important to her. I could bring her an entire garden but what she really finds romantic are the things that make her life cleaner and easier. That's part of why I thought she'd love the simplicity of living on a slope.

I focus on the subtle etched flowers on the wallpaper, trying to steady myself. Sidney had pushed hard for the color scheme in here: "Gold for the golden couple." Madeline had been doubtful, said it sounded garish and egotistical to boot, but then Sidney found the most exceptional rose-gold fixtures and it just grew organically from there. Madeline hadn't been able to resist.

That's what I have to remember. She might sound resolute but sometimes she lacks imagination. She admits that herself. It's my job to open up vistas. To show her what's possible.

Once the conversation with Lola is over, I'm supposed to take the packed suitcases that are hidden in our walk-in bedroom closet, put them in the trunk of my Tesla, and drive away to my new apartment. Sidney's already got it furnished, and Madeline said she'll work on getting everything "of personal value" boxed up and delivered to me in the next week or so. Tonight is supposed to be the first night of the rest of my single life.

I dry my face on the hand towel and tell myself that this war isn't over. I'm going to emerge victorious, and when I do, we'll all win. Me, Madeline, and Lola. Lola most of all.

When I'm at the dentist or going through some personal maintenance task, I have this fantasy that some would call utopian and others dystopian. In the future, we'll all have detachable heads and we'll be able to just have things done to us while our bodies are plugged in elsewhere. Then people like me could avoid unpleasantness and tedium and instead be off attending to the important things, like making sure their wives still love them. If only the future was now. Then my head could be next to Madeline for the rest of this conversation and I could be offline.

I have some inkling of what's to come. I did skim those divorce books from Madeline.

Is she going to give Lola that line about how two homes can be better than one? Lola doesn't know any kids from divorced families so she's got no idea what it'll really be like, that we're talking about a tragic miscomputation. In this context, two is infinitely less than one. All Lola's friends' parents, all our friends, have marriages that have endured, regardless of their actual quality. How can ours be the first to disintegrate?

I love this woman, through and through. I'm not trying to stay for the kid, I'm not toughing it out. I'm still incredibly turned on by her, and I could still talk to her all night, if she wasn't passed out by 9:30 after a half hour of Netflix.

I know that deep down, she feels the same way. I can still turn her on. I just don't believe her "I love you but I'm not in love with you" routine. For one thing, that's not how Madeline talks. She doesn't linger on feelings. And if her feelings for me had changed, I would have felt it. Madeline isn't about big gestures (that's my department); her love is steady. She hasn't wavered in all this time, or I surely would have noticed.

But okay, for the sake of argument, let's assume her feelings have changed. There's that saying: Divorce is a permanent solution to a temporary problem. Or maybe that's suicide? The point is, feelings can change back.

Right now, Madeline needs me to be the steady one.

I thought telling Lola would be the wake-up call Madeline needed. It would finally get real for her, because what could be more real than tears streaming down Lola's face? Only Lola's taken it like a champ, just as Madeline predicted. That's even before Madeline tried to get Lola looking at the bright shiny objects, like the pool in my apartment complex with the bay right outside beckoning and the stand-up paddleboarding we can finally try, walking distance to a hundred restaurants, a vacation for Lola, an entirely different experience than living up in the Oakland Hills where you can see but you can't touch. I can practically hear Madeline describing all of it to Lola in nearly pornographic detail. After all, Madeline was the one who picked it out so she's best qualified to sell it.

Agreeing to all her terms (this ultra-efficient move, the way we're telling Lola, the kind of apartment, the visitation schedule she devised) is part of my stealthy counterattack. Be cooperative, kind and loving, and then she'll come to her senses. Sure, it hurts my pride a little. Maybe more than a little. Most men wouldn't be able to put their egos aside for the sake of their families, but I'm better than all of them.

When I exit the bathroom, Lola and Madeline are smiling at each other. I try to find it heartening rather than galling. Lola's not shattered, and in classic Madeline fashion, she's handled it without me. Maybe that means I won't have to be her ventriloquist dummy anymore. I can be done here.

Only I don't want to be done. I never want to leave.

"Everything okay?" Madeline asks. While there's concern in her voice, it's clearly a leading question, with only one right answer.

"I will be," I say.

Madeline looks at Lola. "See, that's what I told you. With time, we're all going to be just fine."

Lola's gaze is hopeful but not free of worry. She needs me to reassure her. So I do what I have to: I lie. "Absolutely," I say. "It's just a matter of time."

Madeline is pleased. She looks at Lola again. "Do you have any more questions for us now?"

Lola shakes her head. I'm not surprised, since Madeline's nothing if not thorough. She must have fully briefed Lola while I was otherwise engaged.

"As we go along," Madeline says, "Daddy and I will try to tell you what you need to know but we're only human. We'll forget things, we'll make mistakes. It's your job to ask questions and tell us what you're feeling. You're our number one priority, always."

"We love you more than anything." I push the words out past the lump in my throat.

"You already said that." But I can tell Lola liked hearing it again. "So you're leaving now?"

I nod, wishing she sounded just a tiny bit more shattered.

"And I'll see our new home on Wednesday?"

Another nod. With my dam threatening to burst, I don't trust myself to speak.

Lola stands up and moves as if to go downstairs but takes a sharp right, into my arms. She clutches me fiercely, and that does it. I'm crying. But I'm not sobbing; I will not break down. "I love you," I say. If you have to be a broken record, that's the groove to get stuck in.

"I know," Lola responds. "I love you, too."

"I'll order the pizza soon," Madeline says, and Lola smiles. Lose a father, gain a pizza—what a trade!

Bitterness will get me nowhere. But Jesus. They're going to celebrate my eviction with pizza?

Once Lola's gone, Madeline stands up and walks toward me. "That went about as well as it could have, I think," she says in a low tone.

"It hasn't sunk in yet. She's got pools and paddleboards dancing in her head."

Madeline's expression is gentle. She feels sorry for me, I realize. "All I meant was, we're off to a good start. Of course it'll be a series of conversations, some of them painful. This is going to be a process."

"That's what the books say." She gives me a very slightly incredulous look, knowing how unlikely I am to have read them.

"I know this isn't what you want, but it's the right thing," she says. "You deserve to be with someone who loves you just as much as you love them."

I've never heard that one before.

"I promise you, I'll always be kind and fair. Dragging this out would only cost us emotionally and financially." Again, just like the books say.

I can't resist, I grab her in a hug. In the most difficult times, I've always leaned on her. She's always leaned back. Only now her body is wooden. She doesn't resist overtly but she doesn't yield. She's a pillar, available to give support, not to receive it.

I release her, and she averts her eyes while thanking me for the "united front." She walks across the open-plan living room and into the kitchen. "I'm having a drink," she says, reaching into the freezer and pulling out the vodka. "Do you want one for the road?"

I shake my head. Then I allow myself just a few seconds of righteous, searing anger.

A few seconds, and no more. Remember, I love this woman.

"I should get going." I can't just sit and have a send-off drink with her, toast the good times and our great kid. Yes, there have been good times and she is a great kid, which is why this separation is so crazy.

"I really think it went well," Madeline says, oblivious. Congratulatory, even? "I hit all the marks. Lola was surprised, of course. She said how you and I never fight, and I told her that it's not about that. People change. They evolve. But we're going to love each other forever, in a new way."

Just when I thought my nausea had passed.

Madeline takes down a martini glass. "She likes the idea of having more time with you than she does now. I said you and I will still sit together at soccer games, and that we'll have family dinners sometimes."

I'd told Madeline that she was welcome at my place anytime; she hadn't echoed the sentiment. But then, she's always been big on boundaries.

"I stayed focused on what it'll be like for her, and how we'll always put her first," Madeline continues.

"That's the plan," I manage. But I can't bear this—bear her —for one more minute.

I head downstairs for the suitcases. They're large, and it takes me two trips. I'm moving slowly, giving her time to regret it. Time to stop me.

But she doesn't. Not when the suitcases are both lined up in what's now her living room; not during the two separate trips out to the carport, or the final trip back in to announce, "I guess that's all for now."

She stays where she is at the counter, drinking her vodka and soda with lemon peel, nodding in grave acknowledgment. "I'll text you about Lola," she says. "Let you know how she's doing. We'll call you before bed to wish you good night."

I hesitate an extra moment so Madeline can say something,

but what would it be? She's already apologized plenty and it's never helped. She's obviously not going to ask me to stay.

I stumble out to the carport and get into my Tesla Model X. I couldn't even say what this emotion is but I'm trembling as if I've got hypothermia. Because I've played this all wrong. I should never have let her exile me to Jack London Square. Possession is nine-tenths of the law. This is my turf.

I've done my fair share of travelling, and I've seen every nook and cranny of the San Francisco Bay Area, arguably the greatest city in the world, yet for me, nothing compares to the Oakland Hills. It's less than fifteen minutes from downtown Oakland but it's like a secluded world away. To get there, you have to drive up steep, winding, unpaved roads with switch-backs and no streetlights. Two-way traffic is allowed but on many streets, two cars can't pass at once. In other words, you have to take your chances, especially around the blind curves. You have to be willing to pull to the side or force the other guy to do so. It's got a *mano a mano* flavor that's hard to describe. Since GPS gets confused in these parts, you really have to know where you're going or you can get hopelessly lost. In its way, it's like the last frontier.

The lower stratum of the mountain features mostly smaller homes that overlook ravines rather than the bay. Snake higher, and it's for the truly wealthy. But it's not insular or protected. There are a surprising number of break-ins. More than that, though, is the primitive quality, like the way deer can suddenly appear and total a car, and the particular vulnerability to natural disasters like earthquakes and wildfires, what with being on a fault line and so much brush everywhere. We were without power in the winter for ten days after a series of record-breaking storms, what was eloquently called "the atmospheric river." There was that time we gathered with our neighbors in the street, watching with fearful fascination as the multimillion-dollar houses on a nearby ridge burned, our survival literally depending on which way the winds blew.

Given the location, plus the ambition of my aesthetic, our house had been nearly uninsurable. But the challenge only spurred my determination.

The Oakland Hills is an anomaly and a contradiction: so close to truly urban areas but also the wild west. There's something dangerous about it. I tamed the terrain, subjugating it to my whim. Sure, some residents weren't happy, initially. They didn't think the style was in keeping with the others, that it seemed more Southern California than Northern California. I wasn't interested in building an Eichler rip-off. In time, though, I won them over.

Surely I can do the same with my wife. But it feels a lot more perilous.

Mark my words: I will get her back, whatever it takes.

THREE

MADELINE

Just one session. Do it for Lola. Please. *Prayer hands emoji*

I sigh. I've told Greg over and over that there's no point to couples therapy, not even for one session. It's a waste of money and more than that, a waste of emotional energy. My mind is made up. Why won't he hear me?

And does he really think it's appropriate to text this during my workday?

And since when does Greg pray?

Lola didn't ask me to go to couples therapy, I text back.

I'm not about to keep up appearances for some therapist, pretend like I'm still invested in my marriage. I used to maintain façades effortlessly (I've played Greg's secret weapon with his most difficult clients, mounting charm offensives at countless Michelin-starred restaurants) but over the past few years, it's been wearing on me. I've always been an introvert masquerading as an extrovert, socially adept while, deep down, small talk exhausts me. I've come to see how shallow the relationships have been with our circle of couple friends, how performative it all is. As proof, those "friends" expressed shock when Greg and I announced our split but it was tinged with schadenfreude. Since then, they've barely managed a text to check on my welfare. After all, what am I really worth if I can't host couples dinner parties in Greg's architectural wonder?

I set the phone to silent and put it in the pocket of my white lab coat.

The door to the exam room opens just as I'm about to grab the knob. I almost collide with Pru, and we both laugh.

"Sorry, Doc!" she says. She's in Minecraft scrubs today, her frizzy hair in a precarious, explosive bun on the top of her head. Babies could not love her more, and I happen to agree with them.

Yet I still haven't told Pru—or anyone else at the clinic—about the separation. I'm not sure if I should tell one of the more gossipy nurses and just let it spread, or take off my rings and let the speculation begin, or do a confessional tour. No, confessional tours are most definitely not my style. I have nothing to be ashamed of. Greg and I have had a wonderful marriage that's run its course and a beautiful daughter who will continue to flourish.

That's my story and I'm sticking to it. But should I tell it?

All I know is that if the whole truth got out, no one here would ever look at me the same way again.

I won't let anything jeopardize my good fortune in working for this pediatric practice. It's thoughtfully managed, which means I have a reasonable caseload and the time to truly connect with my patients, and it's staffed by dedicated, wonderful people. I have a sterling reputation here, and, in part, that's because my philosophy is to treat everyone warmly while maintaining boundaries. I always aim to ask more questions than I answer.

But I'm also acutely aware of how appearances can help, and how they can hurt. My looks have opened doors, though I know that behind closed ones, people are often whispering, rooting for my downfall. It's not something they're conscious of, even. It's just human nature, and I never blame anyone for being human.

I try to be above reproach: perfectly though subtly made up, wearing expensive and well-made clothes (never flashy) beneath my lab coat. I value my femininity, I won't deny that, but I appreciate that the world is moving toward gender equality. I like that Lola has no qualms about beating the boys in PE class and that I sometimes have to remind her to brush her hair. But for me, speaking softly is what commands rather than demands attention. There's steel underneath, and sometimes people don't see that coming. The element of surprise can work in my favor. I make sure it works in my patients'.

Like now, with my patient Clint. He's only seven years old and he's nearly debilitated by asthma. His mother is in tears, describing her interactions with the insurance company and Clint's pulmonologist. I keep my face blandly empathetic but inside I'm roiling. Clint's pulmonologist wants him to have a brand name medication and the insurance company will only pay for the generic; instead of Clint's doctor fighting on his behalf, he's doing the equivalent of a shrug.

"I'll talk to him," I say. "I'll teach him some of my advocacy tricks."

Clint's mother almost smiles. "You have tricks?"

"What self-respecting doctor—what self-respecting woman —doesn't have tricks?" I pat her arm. Up on the exam table, Clint's breathing is more like snuffling. It breaks my heart just to hear it. It should break the heart of his pulmonologist, too, but too many professionals have become desensitized. I refuse to let that happen to me. I turn to Clint. "Don't worry, buddy. The adults have got this."

Or they will. I'll figure out who to talk to at the insurance company myself, do the initial combination of carrot and stick, and then deliver that to the pulmonologist, who I'll make sure to sweet talk/chasten into taking the steps that he should have already taken. As in, I'll do the legwork for him without any hope of compensation. It's galling but it's for the greater good. Too often, the specialists (mostly the men) don't do what's needed because they believe they shouldn't have to. They're not going to work without getting paid, the horror! That kind of ego paired with greed leads to unnecessary suffering but since none of it's theirs, since they don't have to see it, they can put it out of their minds. But as a pediatrician, I'm the gatekeeper, and it's right in my face.

"I wouldn't want to get on your bad side." Clint's mother laughs.

I laugh along with her. "No, you wouldn't."

I never give up on a challenge when I'm in the right. I know that much of life is about not just being tenacious but demonstrating that tenacity: letting people see what they're up against, that there's no way you're going to give up on something this important so they might as well back down now. Who wants to engage in a fight that they're so evidently going to lose?

I have to admit, I don't always feel as much surety as I project. There are a lot of assholes in the world. People who refuse to see reason, who don't feel compassion even for sick kids. But I want Clint and his mom to believe I've got this, absolutely. They deserve that peace of mind, even if it might only be temporary. What I hope they know is that I'll never stop fighting.

We say our goodbyes and I promise to be in touch after I've spoken to the powers that be. I exit the exam room and check my phone, which has been vibrating throughout. More texts from Greg, still going on about couples therapy. He can be tenacious, too, unfortunately.

I don't know how to be any clearer, and I've tried so hard to be kind. Does he need me to be brutal?

FOUR

GREG

"Tell him I'll call him tomorrow," I say.

"You really might want to—" Lucas says.

"I really want to do what I just told you. I'll call Peter tomorrow." I yank the earpiece out and disconnect. I don't normally talk to Lucas like that, I try not to talk to anyone like that, but I'm at the end of my rope. It's my first day working out of my new office in my new apartment, and I'm about to crawl out of my skin. I've texted Madeline an embarrassing number of times, stopping just short of begging to come home.

I miss my house. I miss my family.

Reverse that. Family first, always.

I don't belong in this utilitarian, characterless box, a triumph of function over form. I'm used to quiet and privacy, which is sorely lacking. From my balcony, there are scads of people running and power walking and sauntering along the trails. I'm assaulted by the rise and fall of my neighbors' voices and their footfalls and the shrill train whistles from the nearby tracks. I never even came to see the apartment, I couldn't bear it, and besides, I wanted to demonstrate my trust and loyalty by taking Madeline's recommendation. She'd viewed a number of apartments and said this was the one. "It's not a bachelor pad," she told me. "It's a launch pad. A stop gap until you get inspired and can see your future clearly. Then I know you'll make it happen." Her smile had seemed genuine. Genuinely patronizing.

Do I believe that she really wants me to be happy? Yes, so long as it's without her. And if I'm happy, then she doesn't have to feel guilty.

But she is guilty. She's the one who did this to me, and to Lola.

I look at my laptop screen. Lucas has emailed me documents with no mention of what just transpired between us. He's practically the only person I've told about my situation with Madeline so he's willing to give me slack. I kept it broad strokes since the particulars are so humiliating.

He's the best assistant imaginable and I'll apologize to him soon. I have to stand my ground, though. The last thing I can handle from a state this raw is a conversation with Peter Tramboni, tech scion and noted douche (though he tries to paper over it with philanthropy, which is why so many buildings bear his name). He never stops reminding me that I owe him a great debt since he took a chance on me when I was a nobody. He commissioned me to design the Tramboni Center, a landmark building that transformed the San Francisco skyline and my career.

People often think of architecture as a prestige job and assume it's highly lucrative, but that's not true for the vast majority. Only suddenly, with the Tramboni Center, it was true for me. I was a starchitect. Afterwards, the offers I received were staggering, and I was expecting to stick with commercial and public buildings but then Peter wanted me to replace the architect who'd been working on his new estate. I had a blast enacting my vision—which Peter said was his vision and you never contradict Peter—and from there, all his "friends" were lining up for their own dream palaces.

Working for the titans of Silicon Valley means no limits on my imagination. Even if they claim there's a budget, there isn't. What could be better than spending most of your time enacting flights of fancy? Sure, my clients are typically assholes, but they're insanely busy assholes. It's not like they have the time to micromanage. I've honed my persona over the years so that I'm just fawning enough while still demanding respect. They want to know they're working with someone who's as passionate, driven, and skilled in his field as they are in theirs. They want someone to hold his own. To a point.

It's a delicate dance, and one that I'm not capable of performing right now. Hence, I'll call Peter tomorrow. Lucas will need to think up a satisfactory lie to explain my unavailability. Peter can never think anyone or anything is more important than him.

I pace the office. Sidney's decorated it beautifully but it's still an interior space. No water view, not even a window. Didn't Madeline think what it would be like to go from the sense of expanse I had to this? But then, she works in window-less exam rooms all day long. She probably didn't even give it a thought.

I text her a picture of the office, without caption.

She doesn't respond. She's probably in with a patient. So I add, *I don't think this is going to work.*

To my surprise, I get a curt insta-response: *You'll live.*

It can be hard to tell tone in a text, but I really can't see any way to read that other than her telling me to suck it up. Other than her telling me that she doesn't want to hear what I'm feeling.

She's had it already? I just moved out last night. Out of my dream house, the one I suspect she doesn't even like, deep down. I was the one who worked from home while she went to the office. Yet somehow, she finagled it so that she's the primary occupant. I couldn't make a counter argument, not without looking like a shit dad who's putting my own needs ahead of Lola's.

Besides, Madeline knows best. She's the practical one. She's also the kind one, off ministering to the sick while I minister to the mega-rich. Meanwhile, she handles every domestic task so that I can single-mindedly focus on my business. Madeline is a genius at coordinating the army of professionals (house cleaners, a meal prep service, goat herders to tend to our slope, window washers...) that make our lives run smoothly.

We've always balanced each other out. She certainly balances me out, both personally and professionally. She's the best listener, whether I'm excited or frustrated or furious. She knows how to refocus me when I need it; she's helped me through impasses and talked me off more than a few ledges. Then there's the impact she has on other people, how well she performs at trade events, awards banquets, and working dinners. She makes me look good. Enviable. My clients love the pediatrician thing, that she's both stunning and caring. She keeps the spotlight on their wives, if they have them. Or if they don't, she's good at letting them flirt with her while remaining appealingly demure. She's particularly useful when I wind up with a more conservative client, one of those family-values types. Having her as my wife and helpmate has anchored me in ways that I'm only just now realizing.

So there's the part of me that wants her, absolutely, and then there's the part that needs her. A very small sub-part worries that if she's not around to handle the mundane and to encourage me in low moments and to strategize about difficult clients or even step in to woo them herself, it might turn out that my beautiful life has been a house of cards. That she's the one who kept it from tumbling down.

We've always been a team, communicating with respect

and, I thought, genuine care. But the way she's sounded today, in our texts—I hope that's not the new normal.

I reread our last exchange. Frost is practically radiating from the screen so no wonder her final two words chill me to the bone.

You'll live.

FIVE

MADELINE

"I'm sorry I'm late," I say. "I just dropped Lola off at Greg's, and he was being..." What I want to say is "clingy" but I know he'd be mortified by the descriptor. "It took longer than I expected."

Sidney nods, her eyes limpid. She already has a cocktail in front of her. "The mimosa special, with elderflower liqueur. You definitely need one." She stands up and gives me a hug. I feel sweaty and out of sorts and eminently grateful to have her.

The restaurant is brunch only, painted in varying shades of yellow, sun beaming through the large windows. Despite a careful makeup application, I'm not exactly radiant myself. It's been a very long week. If I'm honest, the struggle wasn't being without Greg; it was being without...

I just have to stay strong and resist my baser impulses. Play it smart, don't rush. He's worth waiting for.

"I know you haven't been eating," Sidney says, "which is why you need to try the lemon ricotta pancakes. They're irresistible."

The server comes by and I order as instructed. Sidney gets an asparagus frittata with a side of sweet potato latkes.

"And she'll have the special mimosa, too," Sidney adds. "Thank you."

Once the server's gone, Sidney pushes her long auburn hair back from her face, making sure that her large hoop earrings don't get caught in the expensive weave of her scarf. As always, she's in simple and outrageously priced designer clothes with bold accessories. In her work as an interior designer to the wealthy (though not uber-wealthy like Greg's clients), she needs to demonstrate good taste at all times. She and her husband are both workaholics with a hedonic streak. They make sure to get away at least once a month to a spa or someplace five-star where they can relax, have gourmet food, and loads of sex. She's been my best friend since college, and is my only friend without kids. Maybe she's my only friend, period. Since I announced the divorce, I wouldn't say it's like I've got the plague, more like I've got a bad cold with obvious congestion and phlegm; everyone still talks to me but from a safe distance.

Sidney puts her champagne flute in front of me. "Drink up. You need it more than I do."

"Thanks." I take a sip, then a bigger one. "It's been stressful, dealing with Greg. I just wish that he'd accept our situation. He's making me reject him all day long."

Sidney's new mimosa arrives. We both drink.

"You've been mentally preparing for this for a lot longer than he has," she says. "He's probably still in shock."

"In denial, you mean."

"It sounds like Lola's pretty much taken it in stride, huh?"

"Thank God for Lola. She amazes me." Talk about adaptable. I'm resilient, but I've struggled with anxiety since I was a kid. The obvious remedy? Hyper-organization. Control everything I can.

That means I'm not as fun as Greg is, but it also means that I keep life easy for Greg and for Lola. Well, I used to. Greg will have to find his own systems now.

I used to wish he would do more of the grunt work in our marriage because then my stress would be lower and Lola could see how much fun I can be, too. But Greg works such long hours and makes so much more money than I do. Besides, despite how supposedly progressive the Bay Area is, wives doing more of the grunt work is still the norm in our friend group. Or what used to be our friend group.

"Lola is amazing, that's for sure." Sidney smiles. "I need to schedule one of our teas." It's a tradition for Sidney to take Lola to San Francisco's Palace Hotel for high tea. They spend hours eating tiny sandwiches and pastries and gabbing. I hate to admit this but Lola opens up to Sidney in ways she never does with me. I'm not sure why, seeing as I've tried taking Lola to opulent settings before, trying to replicate the magic.

"Yes, Lola would love that," I say. "I know you don't usually tell me the details of your conversations," that's part of why Lola feels free to be so open, "but just for a while, if you hear anything concerning, could you give me a hint?"

She nods vigorously. "You're her mother. If Lola's struggling, you need to know so you can get her help."

"You mean like a therapist?"

"Maybe." She laughs. "What's that face? Since when are you so down on therapy?"

"I'm pro-therapy. I recommend it for patients sometimes."

"But you think you're too good for it?" Her teasing is gentle. Over a twenty-plus year friendship, you develop certain roles. I'm the serious one; she's playful. The fun one, just like Greg. But I'm hoping that once I'm not married anymore, I won't be hemmed in. I'll get to show all my aspects.

"That's exactly it," I say, with an eye roll. "I'm too good for therapy."

"I'm just thinking about all those texts Greg sent you. It seems," she hesitates, "don't get mad at me for saying this, but it seems like, this whole time, you've dismissed couples therapy completely out of hand. You haven't even considered it."

"No, I haven't. And you know why." Surely any couples therapist worth their salt would ask if there's someone else in the picture. Greg has never asked that question, which makes me think he'd prefer not to know. If he did ask, I'd have to lie. The truth wouldn't change the outcome, and the last thing I want is to cause him more pain.

Well, if I'm entirely honest, the last thing I want is to cause me pain. If Greg found out there was another man, I don't really know what he'd do. He's not jealous exactly but he is territorial. Over the years, he's made it clear to other men (and sometimes women) that he'd staked out his claim. I was his. All his.

Until now.

"Any contact with...?" Sidney lets it dangle there, and while I appreciate her discretion in public, I realize that in private, she never says his name either. It's as if she thinks he'll be conjured up like a villain in a fairy tale.

"No," I say. I have to bide my time. Whatever's going to happen—and I have a pretty good idea, or at least a fervent hope —shouldn't be tainted by the divorce, and vice versa.

"I'm always here for you, no matter what or who you choose." Sidney leans forward to meet my eyes. "That said, there's still time to reassess."

"I know what I want." Who I want.

"Obviously I haven't always been a fan of Greg's. He can be self-absorbed, and he sometimes takes you for granted. You do the hard stuff and he swoops in and steals the glory with Lola. But he is very devoted. I imagine he'd be willing to do an awful lot to save his family."

Too much, really. "He's been a good husband. This isn't about his efforts. All I want is the chance to love someone as much as he loves me. Shouldn't I have that?"

Sidney leans back a little, as if deflated.

"What?"

"I'm just thinking about Lola, that's all."

"Lola's fine." It comes out sharp so I soften my next question. "I mean, doesn't she seem fine to you? Do you know something I don't?"

"From what I can tell, she's taking it like a champ. I guess I just feel like once you've had a child, if there's any possibility of fixing the marriage, then maybe it's worth trying?" Seeing the look on my face, she backtracks. "Sorry, I know you've said there's no possibility. I need to do a better job of respecting that."

"You and Greg both." But I smile. "Apology accepted."

"I've just got this afterimage burned into my retinas from seeing him yesterday. I'd found the perfect lamp for his office and needed to deliver it, and when he answered the door, he was an absolute shell. He's in such agony, Maddie."

"Don't you think I know that? I feel terrible about it." Just not terrible enough to give in and do what he wants. And how much did the perfect lamp cost? I can't help but wonder. Greg being Greg, he didn't give Sidney a budget, and she loves free rein. They've got that in common. "I can't go through the farce of couples therapy knowing what I know. Feeling what I feel. Stringing him along would be the cruelest thing."

"I hear you." She's fiddling with her earring again. I can tell she thinks I'm making a mistake, that I should be trying harder.

"Divorce isn't a tragedy, if you do it right. The tragedy is staying in an unfulfilling marriage until one of you dies."

I can see that struck a chord with her. "Part of why I never had kids is because I want to preserve the ability to walk away. I want to be able to stay selfish. Jared sees it the same way."

Wait, is she saying that I'm being selfish when I don't have the right to be?

That can't be what she meant. Besides, Sidney and Jared

aren't exactly my role models; I'm too co-dependent to do it their way. I like being needed. I recognize how well it works for them, though, that it's allowed them to maintain their intensity as a couple. On the rare occasions that I see them together, their emotional and sexual chemistry is on full display.

I do want that for myself, just without all the time apart, and I never had it with Greg. People might have seen us as a golden couple, but from my perspective, there's no golden era for us to return to. Greg would disagree (not that I'd ever say any of this to him), which is why he keeps campaigning for couples therapy. All I know is, we can't get back what we never had.

I have no doubt that Sidney will support me fully, no matter what, but maybe a lot of people would consider my decision selfish. I've been telling myself that I'll be a better example and a happier person if I'm fulfilled, which will benefit Lola, but what if I'm wrong?

Would Greg want me to be happier and more fulfilled if it was with someone other than him?

Well, not at first. That's why we have to hurry up and finish this divorce with him none the wiser. Close that door, and by the time my next one opens, Greg will be in a very different place himself. I would be thrilled if he found a new love of his own.

I finish off my drink, battling my unease, and Sidney must sense that because she says, "There's nothing to worry about. You and Greg are reasonable people."

True, we always have been. But the fact is, we do have a lot at stake, should it go sideways. There's a lot of money on the line, and also a lot of debt, most of it Greg's. He's the one with the bespoke everything, and a cadre of professionals including a personal trainer, various consultants, and a tailor. Then there's the $200,000 Tesla. I didn't sign off on any of that. It's always been a given that he has clients to impress so of course those are the essential accoutrements. But what about the $150K home gym that he's not there to use anymore, and the $100K music listening room that he never used? Despite how rarely he entertained clients at home, and despite my protests that it wasn't ethical, he still had the accountant write off those types of expenses on our taxes. Our joint taxes. What could I be liable for down the line in an audit? Those are the kinds of questions that keep me up at night.

California divorce law has basic financial formulas but if a person wanted to play dirty... well, there can be a lot of wiggle room in terms of community property and community debt.

I intend to keep it clean. I'm sure Greg does, too.

"What are you thinking about?" Sidney asks.

"Just how expensive it is to live in the Bay Area. Keeping up appearances. I wouldn't mind downsizing, actually. If I'm not married to Greg, I wouldn't need to spend so much on clothes. He liked showing me off, you know? I don't need to shop at the boutiques that I've gotten accustomed to. I've probably tried too hard to distance myself from how I grew up. I went too far in the other direction."

"Greg didn't grow up with money either, did he?"

"No, that was one of the things we bonded over in the beginning: our humble beginnings." We're both from families with financial challenges; his was intact, mine was divorced. That's part of why we're so aligned about not wasting any of our hard-earned money on a protracted legal proceeding. More importantly, we have to keep this as amicable as possible to spare Lola what I went through.

Sidney's face is pure sympathy. For my past, or my present? Or is she predicting my future?

She doesn't know Greg like I do. She doesn't know *about* Greg like I do. I have ammunition that I hope I never need to deploy. Because if it comes to that, if Greg and I each have missiles trained on each other, then it could very well end in mutually assured destruction.

Not that we'd ever let that happen.

"Greg and I are going to protect Lola from any fallout," I say. "We're completely aligned on that."

"Of course you are." Sidney sounds soothing, but how come neither of us looks convinced?

SIX

GREG

It's a beautiful March day: sunny, cloudless, sixty degrees. I know that, I'm sitting in it, but I can't feel it. All I can feel is this pervasive misery, and I'm trying to drink it away when I should be working. It's just beer, though; I'm not letting myself have the hard stuff.

Even at 2 p.m. on a weekday, the water is dotted with people on their stand-up paddleboards. They're gliding placidly, seemingly without a care. Next to me, a couple is canoodling; on the other side, a group of six is laughing uproariously. I'm the only one who's alone on this patio, and I'd thought that would feel better than being alone in my apartment. Maybe I thought this would feel like vacation (as Madeline keeps stressing), with the awareness that I'll be home soon. But since Plan A hasn't been working, I'm going to need to come up with B. I gesture toward the server and order another.

My phone goes off. Madeline's ring. "Hello," I say, heart racing.

"Hey there. How's your day going?"

"Not too bad." Lying has become reflexive. I've had to alter my initial strategy since it's apparent that she's not about to feel sorry for me. Pity isn't going to get me home. Invoking Lola's well-being hasn't made a dent either, probably because Lola appears to be doing so well. On the surface, that is. Underneath, she has to be hurting. "How are you?"

"Not too bad either. I hate having to ask this but do you have a lawyer yet?"

"No." If she hates asking, why is she doing it? Who's forcing her? Ever since she told me she wanted to separate, she's been behaving as if it's all inevitable. "Do you have a lawyer?"

"Yes. Have you started looking?"

Of course I haven't. I can barely function at work. My call to Peter Tramboni was a disaster, so much so that I had to reveal that I'm having a few issues in my marriage, and Peter was as sympathetic to that as he's capable of being about anything, which is to say not very. But he's been through three divorces himself and he was more than happy to tell me all about them. "I know how women can be," he said, as if Madeline is anything like the gold-diggers he married. At least he let me off the hook. For now.

It's no surprise that Madeline found her lawyer in record time. She's never been able to stand items lingering on her to-do list. There's no point in resenting those sorts of essential aspects of a woman that I love, no point in resenting that she seems to be in such a rush. It must be that she doesn't want to give herself time to slow down and face what she's losing. She doesn't want to feel her feelings. She loves me so much that she needs to do this fast or she'll never be able to go through with it. Which is why I need to slow this waaaaaay down. While still appearing entirely cooperative.

"I've contacted a few attorneys," I lie again. "I have some consultations scheduled for next week."

"Are they from the list I sent you?"

"Yes." What's one more fib?

"So you should have an attorney by next week?"

"Not by next week. That's when I'm meeting them." I'm trying not to sound annoyed but her urgency is unsettling.

"Well, as soon as you decide, please give me the name. And start thinking about whether you want to serve me or if I should serve you. It doesn't really matter who initiates since it's all going to be straightforward."

"Right." Another burst of explosive laughter to my left.

"Where are you?"

"I'm out meeting with a prospective client. I stepped away from the table to take this call." I see the waiter in my peripheral vision. He's caught me lying, which is embarrassing. But that's a pale cousin of the steadily accruing humiliations of this past month.

"Thanks for taking the call. Remember to think about the server question. If you want to do it, or if I should."

"You do it." *Since you're so fucking eager.*

"Okay." Does she sound pleased? "I want to make this as easy as possible for you. Should I hire a process server, or would you prefer that it's someone we know?"

"Sidney," I say, my mouth like a desert. "Make it Sidney."

I have a suspicion that Sidney is on my side—well, the side of the marriage. She hasn't said it directly and we've never really been friends but when she stopped by with a $1500 lamp (as if I give a shit about a lamp at a time like this), I couldn't hide what a wreck I was. I've always had the sense that she thinks I'm kind of full of myself but now that I've been cut down to size, she seems to like me better. And I think she's always been able to see how deeply I love Madeline and how committed I am to my family.

It would be smart to court Sidney, see if maybe she could work on Madeline on my behalf. Plus, I wouldn't mind some company. Sidney's a very bright presence and my life's pretty dim these days.

During Lola's first weekend visit, I felt both better and worse. Madeline was right: Lola does love Jack London Square, and she loves having a new room. She loves everything Sidney picked out for her. She and I went out shopping again, and during the spree, it felt almost normal. I always spend a lot on Lola when I get her to myself. It keeps the guilt of working so much at bay, and she's the opposite of a spoiled brat. She's effervescently grateful for everything.

When I tucked her in that night, she said, "You and Mom are going to be so much happier apart."

"What do you mean?" Is that what Madeline told her? I'd been stroking her hair and my hand stilled.

"Just that this is a good thing."

"I don't see how that can be." It just slipped out; Madeline'll never know.

"You don't see it now." Lola smiled at me so sweetly. "But you will. I'm going to show you."

She must feel like she needs to lead the way, that she has to put on a good face. Which is the opposite of what I want. She needs to show Madeline what a disaster this is. "You don't have to fake it with me," I said.

She was still smiling. "I love you, Daddy." She gave me a kiss and then rolled over. Rolled away. And I was left more alone than I've ever been in my life.

Madeline is just too persuasive. She's convinced Lola of something that's patently false: that a divided family could be better than a whole one.

When Madeline and I got married, I was so sure. Part of that certainty came from our similarities. We grew up without financial security. My parents had a loveless marriage; hers had a hateful divorce that dragged on for years. We both knew what it was like to never have enough, emotionally or materially. After finding one another, we pledged to keep striving together, and never give up. We were going to provide Lola with the stability we'd never had.

She's strayed from that aim, but I haven't. I'm going to hold her to the promises we've made since the beginning. Then when I'm back home where I belong, she'll be the one thanking me.

SEVEN

MADELINE

Esther Kahn has the blackest, shiniest, straightest hair I've ever seen. Just grazing her collarbones, it seems to have its own light source. She also has the most ageless skin. I'm good at spotting when someone's had work done but there are absolutely no tell-tale signs with Esther. I know that she's been in practice for over twenty-five years yet there's not the slightest hint of a laugh line.

I wouldn't say she's humorless, but she is a staunch professional. That's what I'm after: someone who takes her job and her reputation seriously; someone who'll never drop the ball. I don't need coddling or hand holding. I need ruthless efficiency and precision. Get in and get out. Because if I don't get out soon, I'm going to lose my shit. That's saying a lot because I have never been the shit-losing type.

Every day, it gets harder not to text or call him. I haven't allowed an email. But not even I'm disciplined enough to control all my thoughts. All my yearnings. God, it feels sweet to yearn again. It's been so bloody long.

Truth be told, I never yearned for Greg. It's not a truth he should ever hear.

That's the other reason this has to go quickly. If Greg knew there was another man even tangentially involved, even out on the periphery, there's no predicting how he'd react. On the one hand, it might help him accept that our marriage is truly over; on the other, it would add a layer of betrayal on top of the hurt. I've never given him any reason to feel insecure or jealous in our relationship so I can't say what he'd do. He's always been very controlled in his anger toward me but I've heard him go on vicious diatribes about clients when all they did was inadequately appreciate his brilliant designs.

I need to control as many variables as possible. This is a race to the finish line. I've been through one ugly protracted divorce (my parents') and I'm never going through another. Neither will Lola.

"It's good to see you again." Esther smiles at me from across her spotless glass desk. "It's been over six months. I assumed you'd decided to reconcile."

I shake my head. "It just took me some time to work up the nerve. But once I'm resolved, there's no turning back. I'm fully committed."

Esther nods approvingly. "That's my philosophy: Be as committed to the divorce as you were to the marriage." She glances at her computer screen. "During the consultation, you were very clear that your preferred strategy puts kindness, decency, and fairness at the forefront. Preserving your integrity and his, and, above all else, protecting your daughter from discord." She looks at me intently. "Has anything happened between you and your husband to change that?"

"No, absolutely not. Greg's devastated but he's been entirely cooperative. We're on the same page." Literally. I give her a copy of the paperwork that I've created and that Greg has endorsed: joint legal custody (equal control over all health, medical, and educational decisions made about Lola), a 70/30 parenting time arrangement, and a proposed division of assets and debts.

"This is impressive," she says, scanning the document. "He's agreed to all this, including the financials?"

"I don't see how he could disagree. I just followed California's formula. 50/50, straight down the line."

She doesn't look up. "It seems like you're a pragmatic person. Is your husband?"

"Definitely not. But he is a principled person." Well, mostly.

"I hope you're right. Too often, people's emotions drive their decision-making, and you're initiating a divorce that he doesn't want."

She's still not looking at me, and her tone isn't in any way accusatory but still, I feel a desire to defend Greg. "He might not want the divorce but he accepts it." Or he will, soon. At least he's stopped suggesting couples therapy. "I want this to be quick and clean." Surgical. A wound that's instantly cauterized.

"I'll do my best."

"Greg and I have nothing to fight about. I've always kept flawless financial records and California's a no-fault state so..." I trail off as she fixes me with a piercing gaze.

"You're right," she says. "California is a no-fault state, which means that there shouldn't be any need to prove wrongdoing or to litigate marital mistakes. It should be as simple as irreconcilable differences. But once it gets dicey, prior bad acts—and good ones, too—are admissible. It'll become a battle to demonstrate superior—and inferior—character. And the fact that you and Greg are on the same page now doesn't mean you'll stay there. That's why you need to be thinking of impression management right from the start. We don't want any missteps that can be used against us down the line. If you've got any messes, best to clean them up now."

Esther launches into what I assume is a well-practiced spiel about the importance of being dependable and above reproach (driving in the slow lane, not even a speeding ticket; keeping a clean house; no disparaging the ex or fighting in public)—

"I'm sorry to interrupt," I say, "but this really isn't that kind of divorce." I can only imagine what kind of clients she's used to dealing with.

"Very few people start out having that kind of divorce." She must be able to see how perturbed I am because she adds gently, "My job is to prep and protect you. That means I'll never lie to you and you never lie to me. Not because I'd be offended—I've got crocodile skin—but because when I'm surprised, you're in trouble."

"I understand."

As the meeting continues, I answer everything as honestly as possible until we get to one pesky question. "Are there any other parties involved in the split?" she asks, fingers poised on her keyboard.

I barely hesitate. "No."

I decided ahead of time to leave him out of this, since really, there's nothing for Esther to discover. I'm not seeing him right now, I won't see him until this is concluded, and besides, we've never acted on our feelings. No one has witnessed anything untoward. This divorce is about my personal growth, not another man. It's not about what I feel for someone else but, rather, what I don't feel for Greg. What I never felt for him.

Esther's moved on. She's describing all the documents that I'll need to provide.

"That sounds like a lot, given that Greg and I already have an agreement in place," I say. I'm organized so it shouldn't take me that long to gather it all, but still. I hate wasting time.

"You have a proposal. It's not signed or notarized. You said he doesn't even have an attorney."

"He will by the end of the week." Greg hadn't exactly said that but I can prod him. "He's going to pay me the spousal and child support on the first of the month."

Esther looks less than convinced. I feel bad for her, that her line of work has made her so cynical and jaded. Medicine and law are often lumped together but they're actually quite dissimilar professions. My work affirms my belief in humanity (insurance companies and the occasional specialist aside). Hers seems to be having the opposite effect.

"According to this," Esther is looking at my document, "you'll always have Sunday through Wednesday with Lola, he'll pick her up at school that day and keep her overnight, you'll have her every Thursday, and you'll alternate weekends."

"Yes."

"How is Lola handling it so far?"

"Beautifully." I can't conceal the note of pride in my voice. I don't want to. "She's a fantastic kid."

"I'm sure she is." It's almost absent-minded. Esther is back to business. "Regarding parenting decisions, California law is written with the children's best interest in mind. The family court has broad discretion to determine what that is. But hopefully, you and Greg will be able to make all the decisions together. Because once a judge gets involved, it can become very unpredictable."

"Don't worry, we'll keep it predictable. That's my middle name."

She smiles. "What's Greg's middle name?"

I don't quite know what to say.

But she's on to her next riff. It's about how to gather evidence. "The purpose is to either demonstrate your credibility or weaken theirs. If you get lucky, the same piece of evidence can do both."

I need to stop her. I'm paying for every minute of useless information. "This isn't relevant. Greg would never try to weaken me, and I'm not going to weaken him."

"You're a doctor. You know that it's better to over-document than to under-document."

"True," I allow. I've always believed in thoroughness and covering my bases. While I'm (almost) completely sure that Greg and I are nothing like Esther's other couples, my chest is tightening. Because I used to have so little, I'm well aware that Greg and I have so much—i.e. so much to lose if it all goes sideways.

I can't let that happen. Not to me, and definitely not to Lola.

"Best-case scenario, you won't need anything I'm about to tell you. But I'd advise you to take notes. There are a lot of moving parts, and they're not necessarily intuitive."

"I've been recording this whole conversation."

"Perfect. That's the exact spirit I want you to have, going forward."

EIGHT

GREG

Hugh Warshaw wasn't at the top of my list. He wasn't on Madeline's list at all. But after three consultations that went nowhere, three attorneys telling me that they wouldn't do what I need and one going so far as to say it was unethical, followed by calls to ten other offices where I just gave a quick hypothetical for a quick no, I realized it was time to go off-road, so to speak. I'm going to require someone with more imagination.

As soon as I see Hugh's office, it's like, "Hallelujah!" Madeline would hate it. She'd think it was unprofessional and disorganized, with all those stacks of paper—she can be kind of smallminded, subscribing to the idea that a cluttered space equals a cluttered mind—and she wouldn't appreciate all the modernist paintings, especially not the abstract female nude in lurid colors right behind Hugh's desk. But what it says to me is that Hugh Warshaw isn't hemmed in by convention. He's not constrained by other people's notions of propriety. Hopefully, he'll enjoy a challenge like the one I'm about to present.

"Full disclosure: Other lawyers have turned me down," I say. "They want to just cross t's and dot i's for $500 an hour. That's not what I need."

Hugh looks intrigued. He's got a ruddy complexion and his hair is wild and shaggy, Einstein Lite, while his suit is pressed. I think he might be early forties like me but he's got the mannerisms and affectations of someone older. Madeline might find it all contradictory and thus disconcerting but I like contrasts, and people who like what they like, unabashedly.

"I need someone with vision and creativity. For context, I'm an architect who's built dream palaces for some of the world's richest men."

Hugh laughs. His teeth are slightly stained. Smokers' teeth. I appreciate his lack of vanity. I wish I felt free to be less vain myself, but my client base wouldn't allow it. Or maybe I just don't have the bravery of Hugh Warshaw. "What about women?" he asks.

"What do you mean?"

"You build any dream palaces for the world's richest women?"

"Now that you mention it, no." I've never had a female primary client; when I deal with women, it's wives who are generally overruled.

"You think that might be part of what went wrong in your marriage?"

I'm startled, but in a good way. My initial read was correct. He's not afraid to ruffle feathers or be seen as abrasive. Abrasive could be useful. He'd be bad cop to my good. "I worship my wife. That's not the problem."

"What's the problem, then?"

"That she wants a divorce and I don't. She keeps telling me that old story: Somewhere along the line, she fell out of love. I need her to fall back in."

"Ah." He nods. "That is a big problem."

"I've been trying to convince her to do couples therapy with me. She says there's no point, she knows what she wants, but I think, if she's so sure, she'd be able to get in a room with me and a psychiatric professional and have a mature discussion."

"Obviously you've never been to therapy before."

I've decided that if Hugh and I do work together, I'll have to ignore a percentage of everything he says; like now, I don't need to dignify that. It's true, I haven't been to therapy before, but I know my marriage can be saved. "Do you think you could get the court to order couples therapy?"

"Highly doubtful. Judges order co-parenting counseling sometimes. That's if you keep fighting about the kids, especially in front of the kids. Do you have kids?"

"A ten-year-old named Lola."

"Lola. That's cute." He smiles, with difficulty. His natural resting face is cynical. "How's the communication with your wife? What's her name?"

"Madeline. We communicate well on most things but she can't seem to hear me on the most important one."

"She's set on this divorce, huh?" I nod. "So you want to punish her? You want to play hardball?"

"No, that's not it. It's not about punishment, but I want you to delay at every turn. Make everything a negotiation to the point of absurdity. Irritate the shit out of her attorney if you have to. But make it take as long as possible. I need you to buy me time so that I can get through to her. She's living in some kind of bubble and I need to burst it."

"You want me to engage in pointless arguments and run up my fees?" Now his smile comes more easily. "You got it, boss."

NINE

MADELINE

I've been tense all day, I can't say why. I mean, it's all going according to plan. Greg's got a lawyer and he's texting me a lot less; Lola is ostensibly doing great. She's in the backseat right now, humming to herself. It's one of my favorite things about her, how dreamy she can be at times but she's so focused when it matters, like when it comes to schoolwork and soccer. She's the perfect blend of Greg and me.

Really, it couldn't be going better. And yet...

I'm so antsy. It could just be my constitution, that I don't like things being unfinished. Maybe I won't fully relax until the documents have been officially filed with the court, all the informal arrangements made formal. While the divorce decree won't be issued for six months from the date of separation, we can get all the details worked out now. Then it'll be seamless down the line.

But some of my nerves have to be the stress of keeping a distance from the man I believe to be the love of my life. It's strange, feeling so strongly without being able to test out those feelings. I'm not usually guided by intuition, not like Greg. I'm guided by facts and practicalities. Right now, there's a lingering and unquenchable uncertainty.

Did I mention the yearning? It should be delicious but instead, under these circumstances, it's just plain agonizing.

We're almost home, and in my eagerness to arrive, to just be done with this day, I take the remaining curve too fast. It's entirely unlike me, and the correction comes swiftly. I have to slam on my brakes because there in the road, inches from my front bumper, is a doe. You'd think the screeching would alarm her but she must have been immunized from living in this neighborhood.

She stares at me through the windshield, gorgeous and regal and unafraid. How can something that beautiful be that stupid? How has her species even survived, with such a low sense of danger?

"Holy shit," Lola breathes, awestruck.

I should tell her to watch her language, but really, who fucking cares right now? My heart's beating crazily. I can't believe how close I came to killing this incredible creature.

To killing a whole family. That's when I see the two fawns who are lurking in a nearby outcropping of rock. They must have crossed the street just ahead of their mother.

Lola sees them, too. "Wow," she says. "I know there are a lot of deer up here but I never see them."

She's never really been a nature girl and since Greg's not a nature guy, I realize I've just let the part of me that loves getting sweaty in the outdoors go dormant. That can change now. "We should go hiking this weekend."

"Do I have to?"

"I'll buy you a new pair of hiking boots." It's a page out of Greg's book.

The deer are all bounding away now, heading up the rock-face in effortless leaps. Lola and I are both transfixed, and then a horn blares behind me. I do a "sorry" hand wave out the window and continue on.

"That deer mom wasn't very smart," Lola observes.

Even though I'd had a similar thought myself, I say, "She's just making her best estimation. Sometimes you guess wrong. I'm sure she had good intentions."

"Do you think maybe she was kind of hoping something would happen to those guys? Then she could just jump around all day by herself."

"Lola!" I scold. What a terrible sentiment.

"I bet not every animal wants to be a parent. Some deer have to be bad moms."

But murderously bad moms? I decide it's best to go silent.

As I pull into the carport, I'm still a little shaken and I don't know if it's Lola's casual take on infanticide or how close I came to hitting that deer. I can still see that unblinking, beatific stare of hers. Maybe she wouldn't have cared what happened to her babies, or to herself. Or maybe she was never the one in danger. My neighbor Sylvia hit a deer a few years back, totaling her car, while the deer just bounded away, seeming not only unhurt but unfazed.

I've come to really like Sylvia. She's almost seventy, the definition of a tough old broad. She actually gardens on her slope, which I would find terrifying. She was initially cold to Greg and me, like a lot of the old timers were because they'd watched the construction of our house with disapproval. It's sculpted into the cliffside in a way that Sylvia told me right to my face was "ostentatious" and "unbecoming"; her husband called it "asinine." You would have thought there was no coming back from that kind of an initial meeting but somehow, we all warmed. Some of that had been literal: gatherings in the street together, feeling the rising temperatures of nearby wildfires, watching other parts of the neighborhood burn. It exposed how petty our differences were.

Anyway, when it came to the deer, Sylvia had been driving her old Toyota because she doesn't believe in spending money on cars. She was able to get home with just a mangled bumper but the insurance company declared the car totaled. "No one wants to fix anything anymore," Sylvia had groused. "It's just out with the old, in with the new." I wonder what Sylvia will say when she learns Greg's moved out.

No one in the neighborhood knows yet. He'd left with just a few discreet loads in his SUV. Come to think of it, he still needs to get the rest. He's been dragging his feet, asking if he can continue to use the basement for storage. That doesn't feel like a good practice. We need to fully cut ties. Extinguish his hope. Sometimes you've got to be cruel to be kind, right?

But maybe I shouldn't take too much of a hard line about the storage, given how much progress he's made on the acceptance front. He's stopped asking whether he can use the home office and the home gym. I reminded him that his apartment complex has a lap pool.

It does feel a little cruel, me staying in a house I'm so ambivalent about when Greg's so passionate. He originally started drafting the plans for a client who pulled out and by that point, he was so rapturous that he managed to convince me it was a good idea to buy the land and build it ourselves. We'd just gotten married and stopped using birth control and we were standing on what literally felt like the top of the world. I had reservations but I stifled them. I didn't have the heart to bring him down so, instead, I let him carry me away. He's creative, I'm practical; those are the roles we've always inhabited. My job is to coordinate the logistics so that his vision can come to fruition. And Sidney, who knows a lot about real estate from being an upscale interior designer, told me that I'd be crazy not to proceed, especially with the deal that Greg was able to get on the land. When your oldest friend and your husband team up, you cave. Well, I did, anyway.

Because what kind of woman denies her husband his dream (house)? I'd never even wanted one for my Barbies, and maybe on some level, I disdained myself for being so relentlessly reasonable and pragmatic. Compare that to Greg, who's fantastical and whimsical. A visionary. Maybe I married him to see the world through his eyes, but it's time to see wholly through my own.

Back then, when it was just a plot of land, I hoped against hope that I was wrong and that all my misgivings would melt away once I saw the splendor of the finished product. But by the time the house was ready for move-in, I was hugely pregnant. I looked out from the deck and my vertigo was so sudden and acute that I started vomiting over the side. I realized what a terrible mistake I'd made, or rather, allowed Greg to make in our names. Almost five million dollars and an astronomical mortgage and a slope but no yard? Babyproofing would be nearly impossible, all sharp edges and potential shards.

Yet there was nothing I could do. We were in too deep. Greg was in love, like Narcissus with his own reflection, and this would have to be our home.

I told him that the vomiting must have been morning sickness (even though that had actually ended in the first trimester), plus overwhelming excitement. I told him how proud I was of him, and how happy we would be here. He believed me totally.

Over the years, my true feelings about the house have leaked out. He's realized that I don't value aesthetics above all else. It's a smart house in every way, except for how dumb it is to perch your family over a cliff. Why court doom?

While this has been a source of tension at times between us, it's generally remained an unspoken one. We've tended to leave a lot unspoken to maintain our gilded veneer and to keep the peace.

When I'm finally able to leave, I won't really miss this house, despite its opulence. I definitely won't miss this neighborhood. I won't miss run-ins with deer, or humans. With all these crazy narrow two-way roads, someone has to yield. With no clear right of way, certain people (certain personality types) can really intimidate others, driving aggressively as if to establish dominance at a distance, demonstrating their unwillingness to move over. Sometimes I don't see anyone during my drive but when I do, I still cringe at the implied game of chicken.

In theory, I have no problem with yielding. Really, it's a point of pride. I refuse to have a "whose dick is bigger" contest where nothing's at stake.

But lately I can't help thinking about how I wound up here. I mean, maybe I didn't tell Greg directly that my dream house isn't on a hill with a walk score of five but he should have known; he knew me. We discussed having a family on our second date, and surely he could tell that I'm not daredevil enough to push a stroller along these roads. I'd been terrified to drive them with a baby on board.

I yielded to Greg then, but no more. I'm not his deer in headlights.

TEN

GREG

"Special delivery." Sidney's smile is equal parts sheepish and regretful as she hands me the manila envelope.

I gesture for her to come inside the apartment. "You can't just serve and dash." I toss the envelope on the kitchen counter, unopened. It's going straight to Hugh Warshaw, who has his marching orders. "You want a drink?"

It's just after five, and it won't be my first of the day. But I haven't had an entire glass, not all at once. I'm about the nipping, just a little every now and again, enough to take the edge off. The trouble is, the edge keeps coming back.

"I'll have something with bourbon. Or just bourbon." She's very evidently doing me a favor. She doesn't want to be here, and I get it. I'm jilted and pathetic. But I need her, in more ways than one. So I'll take pity. In fact, I'm banking on it.

She's walked over to the glass doors and is looking out at the view. I bring her a bourbon with a splash of sweet vermouth, a lazy Manhattan. "Outside?" I ask. She nods.

We step out and stand in silence, our eyes following a sailboat that's making its lackadaisical way across the water; otherwise, the surface is undisturbed. "It's pretty here," she says.

"Nowhere near as pretty as my old view."

"This is more accessible. From Madeline's house, you're so high up." She must have noticed my wince when she called it "Madeline's house" and adds, "Sorry."

"Don't be. I get how awkward this is, so I appreciate that you bit the bullet. Thanks for serving me."

Sidney holds her glass up higher: "And thank you for serving me." She perches on one of the hand-crafted teak chairs that she picked out, placing her glass on the Carrara marble table. Her manner is unusually diffident. She doesn't know where the boundaries are anymore, what constitutes loyalty. I know the feeling.

I take the seat next to her. "Tell me the truth, please. You knew Madeline before I came along. Was her life better with me or without me?"

She averts her eyes. "Maddie's the only one who can answer that. Have you settled in yet?"

"More or less." Sidney's done her best to make this place homey but I haven't held up my end. The walk-in bedroom closet is full of boxes I don't intend to unpack. That would feel like a defeat, like I'm giving up. I can't let myself get comfortable. "I'll change my whole life if I have to. Is that what it'll take?"

"I really don't know." I'm not letting Sidney get comfortable either. She's practically squirming. But maybe that's just because of the eco-friendly sustainable biodegradable cushions.

"But you do know she's making a mistake."

"That's not for me to say." She does think it, though; I can tell. I'm gratified by how torn she is. She wants to stay loyal to Madeline and she wants to help me. More likely, she wants to help Lola. Two birds one stone. Maybe three birds one stone.

"Madeline needs you to stop her from doing this," I say. "You might have to call her out, for her own good."

"Or you need to start moving on with your life."

"So there's no chance I'm ever going home?"

She stands up. "Take care of yourself, okay?"

Because Madeline's not going to, is that what she means? "Please stay. I could really use the company."

"I'm sorry, but Madeline gets custody of me in the divorce."

"I can't work, I can barely function." My eyes are imploring. "She's all I think about. I have to get home, Sidney."

She stares out at the water, tears filling her eyes. Finally she says softly, "Don't hold your breath."

"She really doesn't miss me at all?"

"For months, I've been telling her my opinion. I've told her I think she should give couples therapy a chance. I've reminded her of what she went through growing up. But I haven't been able to make a dent."

Wait, so Sidney's been fighting for me and for my marriage this whole time? "For how many months?"

"I don't know exactly." Sidney's eyes skitter away, like she regrets what she's just let slip. So Madeline may have been thinking of leaving me for far longer than I knew. Far longer than she's led me to believe.

Her oldest, dearest friend has spent months, plural, telling her it's a mistake to leave me, pointing out what divorce can do to a kid, what it did to Madeline herself, and still, Madeline's remained determined. It doesn't make sense.

"What isn't she telling me?" I ask. "What have I done that's so unforgivable?"

Sidney looks like she wants to jump overboard.

"So there is something?"

"No, not really. Just what she told you." She's clearly lying.

I knew it! I know Madeline, and when she first talked about splitting up, I could see she was holding back. It's almost like she had to leave, like she was compelled by some unseen force. I begged for answers and she said, "There are no answers," but there have to be. There's a missing puzzle piece and when I find out what it is, I'll be able to fit my family back together.

I must have done something, or she discovered something. I don't know what it is, but it's out there, waiting to be found. This is a problem that can be solved. As in my work, when I've seemingly hit a wall, what's required is more creativity. A new way of seeing.

Sidney is still talking. Rambling, really. "Madeline never says a bad word about you. She still feels so much respect and love. But you know the story. She says that you're friends and roommates and co-parents. The spark is gone and she knows she can't get it back."

"Yes, I've heard the story." I just don't believe it.

Sidney's visibly confused by the sudden shift in my demeanor, by how much brighter I seem. Invigorated. She clearly didn't mean to give me hope, but she has.

Madeline's lucky I'm a forgiving person. But she shouldn't try to stretch it too far. All men have their limits.

ELEVEN

MADELINE

"I hate to break this to you but I don't think you and your husband have the same legal strategy," Esther Kahn says. I stare at her uncomprehendingly across her barren desk. "Hugh Warshaw doesn't know the meaning of fairness or decency."

"Hugh Warshaw?" It's the first time I've heard the name.

"That's the counsel your husband retained."

"There must be a mistake. Greg said he was having consultations with the attorneys from the list I gave him."

Esther tips her head slightly. "He might have talked to them but he retained Hugh Warshaw. You and I will need to adjust our strategy accordingly."

"There must be some mistake," I repeat dumbly. Greg wouldn't have double-crossed me.

"No mistake. I spoke to Mr. Warshaw earlier today, referencing the parenting plan and financial plan that you gave me. He pushed back on nearly everything. To hear him tell it, those were all just preliminary talking points. There's no agreement." Her tone is neutral but I feel stung anyway. "His client isn't so sure he likes the parenting schedule; he might want 65/35 instead."

"That's what he said? That his client doesn't like it?" My heart plummets.

"I know you wanted a broad parenting plan that would allow for latitude, but that doesn't seem to be your husband's goal."

"What is his goal, then?"

"I'm not quite sure yet. Unfortunately, we're going to have to get granular."

Granular—as in our attorneys have to hammer out every detail. As in more billable hours. As in burning through time, money, and energy.

"Maybe you misunderstood Greg's lawyer," I say, "or maybe Greg's lawyer misunderstood him. That must be what happened. I'll just call Greg right now—"

"Absolutely not." Esther sounds immovable. "I've been doing this a long time. I don't misunderstand anything."

I refuse to believe that. Refuse to believe what she seems to find so self-evident.

"I need you to stop texting each other," Esther says.

"He's Lola's father!" I'm aghast.

"No, I meant that instead of texting each other, you'll need to sign up for a co-parenting app. You'll communicate only through the app. It'll record all communications in a form that's admissible in court." Seeing my face, she adds, "Just in case."

"Should I record all my phone calls, too, and every interaction we have during pick-ups and drop-offs?"

Esther ignores my facetious tone, saying, "Many people do."

I want to tell her that Greg and I aren't many people but then, that's what I said last time.

"What I'm about to recommend might sound extreme, but I really think it's the right preventive measure to take before the situation degrades further. Co-parenting counseling could help you get on the same page and stay there. An ancillary benefit is that one of the first things a family law judge will consider is how cooperative a parent is being. By initiating the co-parenting counseling, you'll immediately establish yourself as trustworthy in the eyes of the court."

"That's not the plan," I say. "Greg and I are going to make agreements and then the judge will just sign off on them." That's what we said. Well, it's what I said, and Greg never said no.

"I know that's your plan but it doesn't seem to be Greg's."

"His lawyer must be in his ear." This isn't Greg. But if he's willing to throw out everything we discussed on the advice of his attorney, then I could be in real trouble here. I'm losing control, and that's terrifying.

"The other factor the judge will consider when it comes to custody is the level of emotional bonding with each parent. Bonding isn't just the amount of time; it's the quality. It's about attention, caring, responsiveness, closeness," Esther recites. "Co-parenting counseling gives you a chance to prove how much you love Lola to an impartial third party."

"Greg and I both love Lola more than anything. That's not in question." Is it?

"I have to warn you, things can get uglier much quicker than you'd ever imagine. People show a different side of themselves in a divorce when they have both nothing and everything to lose."

"We have Lola. Greg's not going to lose sight of that." Or at least, I thought he never would.

"Then what's he doing, making agreements with you and having his attorney negate them?"

"I don't know," I have to admit. It's getting a little harder to breathe.

"We don't know, but we have to be ready."

"Do you think that in co-parenting counseling, I'd get answers?"

"Possibly." Esther does that head tilt of hers again. I can't tell yet if it expresses incredulity or an unwillingness to speculate. But I'm worried that I'm going to have plenty of time to find out.

That's only if Greg continues along this path, the path that his attorney must be advocating. Maybe I can just get Greg to fire Hugh Warshaw and this can all still proceed according to plan.

I have to force myself to focus during the remainder of the meeting with Esther. I'm externally calm and cooperative—I'm not going to waste a second when I'm paying $550 an hour—but I'm screaming inside.

This wasn't supposed to happen! It was supposed to be quick, clean, and kind! Why isn't Greg sticking to our plan? Why can't we just follow the formula?

Maybe I was being unrealistic, thinking it could all be wrapped up with a bow for a judge to sign within a few weeks and then, at six months precisely, the divorce would be finalized. I wanted to get out of my marriage like a thief in the night, jewels intact, and Esther's been trying to tell me that's not how these things go. A price has to be paid. And she doesn't even know that I have someone waiting for me who might not wait forever.

Could Greg know? Is that what's really going on here?

No, there's no way. Greg isn't strategic; he's emotional. If he'd found out, I would have heard from him immediately.

"Are you with me?" Esther says. "I know this is a lot to absorb."

"I'm with you," I say.

Once I'm back in the car, I text Sidney:

Just met with Esther. Greg's attorney is trying to screw him. To screw us.

You think Greg doesn't know what his attorney's up to?
Attorneys work for the client, not the other way around.

Usually, but Greg's a mess. You've seen him.

True.

He can hardly think straight.

Someone unscrupulous could easily take advantage of that, turning our amicable divorce into acrimony to line his own pockets. It's disgusting. We can't let this Hugh Warshaw character get away with it. But Esther doesn't want me to confront Greg, she made that clear.

What are you going to do?

Esther suggested co-parenting counseling. I could talk to him then.

But it would all be on the record, if the therapist ever has to testify someday. Knowing that, I'll have to be very careful about impression management. Fortunately, Greg won't be. His emotions will get the better of him for sure.

I hate that I'm thinking this way. But better safe than sorry. I mean, I'm already starting to feel sorry.

Yes, do that, Sidney texts. *Go into therapy.*

Greg's been after me to do couples therapy; I'll need to make it clear that this isn't that. But what is it, really? Lola's doing great. We shouldn't have anything to talk about.

I've got a bad feeling, I tell Sidney.

My friends did co-parenting therapy. It really helped.

But why, exactly, do Greg and I need help? I don't understand what's changed.

I'll get the therapist's name and text it to you.

Thanks. I start to text more of my worries and then think better of it. No need to give them any airspace. I'll just convince Greg to get a new attorney and we'll be back on track in no time.

This is totally normal, Sidney texts. *Divorces are always trickier than you first thought and you always need more experts than you expected.*

I appreciate Sidney's attempt at reassurance, but to this point, she's never said anything like that. I wonder if she, like Esther, thinks I've been deluding myself, believing that Greg and I could pull off the world's first genuinely amicable divorce.

And I wonder for the first time just how tricky things might get.

TWELVE

GREG

Hugh Warshaw is after me for "the documentation": vital statistics on me and on Madeline (where we've lived, the colleges we attended, our work histories, our criminal histories); the chronology of our relationship with every important event detailed; major events in Lola's life; major events in our lives that could have impacted Lola. In other words, I'm supposed to account for everything—good, bad, and ugly. I get the impression that Hugh is especially looking forward to the ugly when it comes to Madeline's past experiences and actions.

This isn't that kind of war. It's not about wounding her; it's about stalling for time. I need to figure out what's actually going on, whether someone's told her lies about me or if she's secretly got a brain tumor or, you know, *something*. Because she must have some hidden reason for doing the seemingly inexplicable.

Or maybe I'll get lucky, and she'll simply wear down and realize how essential I am. It could be a war of attrition.

At any rate, it's too soon for Hugh to know Madeline's deep dark secret. I've kept it for, what, fifteen years now? (Madeline's the one who's good with dates, not me.) I'm hoping to keep it forever. But that's going to depend on her.

It's apparent that she doesn't need me on a logistical level. She's got that more than covered, while I'm feeling the pinch of her absence. I'm in awe, actually. How did we never run out of soap or paper towels or food or, you know, anything in all those years? How was she never late on a bill or late to an occasion? How did she manage to keep me on track without nagging or shaming? She's a fucking marvel.

But that's not the main reason I miss her. I miss the scent of her hair and the sight of that gorgeous face. The way she moves, the soft musicality of her voice, how she takes interest and care of Lola and me...

I've been trying not to think about it and now Hugh wants me to do an inventory? That would be like staring directly into the sun.

I can't do it. I slam the door behind me and go out for a(nother) drink.

THIRTEEN

MADELINE

2/6/2009: I attend a party with my best friend, Sidney. We meet Greg and his friend Steve (who I later find out is his "work friend Steve" as Greg doesn't have friends).

Sidney is initially attracted to Greg but his attention is on me to a degree that I find somewhat unsettling. He is, however, undeniably attractive and persistent. I finally give him my number, slightly reluctantly.

2/14/2009: I go out to dinner with Greg. He's entirely too much, especially when he declares that he fell in love with me at first sight.

2/21/2009: I agreed to a second date largely because I did respect how passionate Greg was about architecture. He talked about wanting to leave his firm because he felt that they were always constricting his vision. He wanted to work without limits.

While I found him grandiose, I also found him compelling. He was so different from me. I had only ever wanted to work for a medical clinic and never for myself.

Since I tend to get anxious when things feel out of control, I don't particularly like to be the boss. It's soothing to work within a defined structure, not having to make the rules. There was a yin/yang to my dialogue with Greg that drew me in.

To a degree. When he went to kiss me, I pulled back. I said I wasn't sure if I saw him that way. He laughed ruefully and said, "I wouldn't know how to see you any other." I was slightly charmed.

2/25/2009: Third date. I was becoming more attracted to him and I decided to test the chemistry with a kiss.

We had sex that night.

2/27/2009: Greg asked me to move in with him. I said absolutely not. But his enthusiasm for me was now appealing rather than off-putting.

Rest of 2009: We spent a lot of time together. Our differences seemed largely complementary. We could disagree without conflict. There were a lot of small details that he didn't care about and in those cases, he yielded to me. On certain big-ticket items, he could be nearly feral, and then I yielded to him. (I can provide examples, if that would be helpful, though the building of the house is the most significant and it's detailed below.)

Sidney had concerns. She used to tell me she thought he was controlling but I didn't see it that way. She said she dodged a bullet—meaning, she'd been attracted to him at first but they never would have worked out because she's too strong and independent. (Maybe you should talk to Sidney, see if she has any anecdotes or stories that might be helpful, just in case?)

He continued to declare his love and engage in extravagant romantic gestures and gifts. There were expensive trips, which led me to believe his salary was much higher than it was. Like many laypeople, I had the misapprehension that the average architect is well-paid. It later turned out he was running up debt and when we became serious in 2010 and he told me the amount, I immediately created a budget for him and a plan to pay it down, which he did follow.

While my feelings never matched his in intensity, I did feel love for him by the end of the year. I told him that around Thanksgiving. He proposed at Christmas during a trip to New York City. We'd been ice skating and were sitting rink-side, drinking hot chocolate. I responded, "Not yet." He was unsurprised, and undeterred.

3/12/2010: We moved into a new apartment together. Sidney furnished it for us. There was a lot of conflict because Greg didn't want money to be an object; I said money's always an object, particularly given my medical school loans and the debt from his lavish spending. (Sidney witnessed some of this conflict—again, maybe talk to her?) There was no intimation of physical violence. Greg raised his voice frequently but never said anything mean. I was much quieter but with more of a propensity toward character assassination. I thought it was foolish that he would spend so much when he would be starting his own business that year (for more on this, please see "Life Event/Work History" document).

I made a compromise that I regret: I said that once his business had taken off, we could dispense with a budget. Unfortunately, he held me to that.

Rest of 2010: Greg and I barely saw each other. He was consumed with networking and trying to build his business. I was supportive emotionally and also financially. For a time, I was the primary breadwinner. But I fully believed in Greg and admired his passion.

1/12/2011: Greg's networking paid off. After a fluke introduction, he made a strong connection with tech billionaire Peter Tramboni. Against all odds, Greg was awarded the commission for the Tramboni Center. Thus began Greg's meteoric rise.

We continued to have little time together but Greg made the most of what we did have, showering me with luxurious gifts and lavish nights out.

11/18/2011: Greg and I eloped. We don't ski but Aspen's a beautiful destination. Neither of us are close to our families (and I wouldn't dare put my parents in the same room together). I've never liked the idea of spending heaps of money on just one day. I'm not very romantic, maybe because I witnessed the slow-motion train wreck of my parents' marriage and divorce.

Also, I couldn't even imagine trying to plan a wedding with Greg; he might want actual reindeer or to arrive on a flying sleigh. I didn't want to spend a year fighting to keep him to a wedding budget.

So it was just the two of us, and it was perfect. I really thought I'd gotten it right.

As soon as we got home, Greg surprised me with my "wedding present."

He brought me to the lot in the Oakland Hills and said he'd already bought it. All the plans had been drawn up and the equipment was already there, ready to start the build. He said he'd gotten a great deal and that if I didn't like it, he could always build and then resell at a significant profit but it was clear that I'd need a bulldozer myself to convince him to do that. He assured me that the house would be completed in under six months because he knew people; he'd cut through all the red tape.

I'd never been a huge fan of the neighborhood. Sure, the views are spellbinding but the drive up from the flats is harrowing and you can't walk anywhere. Only Greg can be a force of nature once he sets his mind and heart on something.

Sidney was working on me, too. She said the house would be phenomenal and an amazing investment. The two of them didn't normally tag team, though later, once she became our interior designer, that would happen frequently.

She had come to believe that while Greg would never be her cup of tea, his love for me was genuine and abundant. If she continued to have reservations, they went unspoken.

Throughout 2012: Construction of the house, with multiple delays and much frustration on Greg's part. I empathized and subtly suggested that he might want to give up and sell to a developer. That way, I'd never have to express my true feelings. But he remained determined.

Meanwhile, his business was stratospheric. He was a true starchitect.

We were trying to get pregnant every time we saw each other.

April 2012: I was pregnant! Happy months followed, with lots of fantasies (his) and planning (mine) though my anxiety about the house mounted. He kept calling it our forever home.

December 2012: The house was finished and we moved in with mere weeks to spare before the baby was due. I tried to focus on the positives—there were many, I was the envy of all my friends—and on my pregnancy.

1/7/13: Lola was born. I was in love.

(But maybe not with Greg anymore??? I'm not entirely sure if I ever had been, or if I'd simply been swept up by his conviction. As you've probably figured out by now, he's a very influential person.)

2013–Now: I thought Greg would work less after becoming a father but he's never been able to turn down a chance to flex his imagination with a billionaire's blank check. Meanwhile, I deal in the day to day.

I built us a social world out of the parents of Lola's friends. My sense is that the husbands looked up to Greg and the wives envied me. I've always found that uncomfortable, and distancing. But being enviable is important to Greg.

I should mention that when Greg is around, he's as over the top in his love for Lola as he's always been in his love for me. (For important milestones in Lola's life and a detailed record of our parenting decisions, see "Lola/Parenting" doc.)

For the longest time, I told myself the problem in our marriage was his absence but then I started to notice how bored I was in his presence. And I think, if he's honest with himself, I bore him, too.

Sometimes I wonder if he ever really saw me. I've always been his dream girl, same as this is his dream house. All surface, no depth. So much glass, built on sand.

FOURTEEN

GREG

"I think it's awesome that you've both chosen to be here," Dr. Vaughn says. "A lot of people wait until it's gotten really ugly between them and then the court mandates it. Showing up voluntarily tells me just how much you each love your daughter and respect one another."

Dr. Vaughn beams at Madeline and then at me. She's fresh-faced with dark hair that flips up at the bottom. I'd guess she's under thirty. From her website, I could tell that she's only been in private practice for a few years, and her "favorite specialty is couples therapy!" (Exclamation point hers.) What she lacks in experience, she makes up for in enthusiasm. She's perfect. Really, it's like I designed her myself: someone who so evidently still believes in love and should have the energy to break through Madeline's walls. I'd have expected Madeline to pick someone more seasoned so this is a great sign. My wife and I are more aligned than I thought.

This office will be a psychological challenge. It's small and windowless, and the furniture is inexpensive, generic mid-century modern, in light-brown faux-wood. There's taupe carpet and nature photography on the walls so amateurish that it might have been taken by Dr. Vaughn herself.

"I'm excited about this," I say, 100 percent truthfully, though I am a little bewildered by Madeline's reasoning. After all, we haven't been disagreeing on anything—I've gone along with her every demand, request, and whim—and Lola's doing great. She loves one-on-one time with me and is all about the vacation vibe of my new neighborhood. By Madeline's report, it's all smooth sailing on her end, too. She said that her lawyer suggested we do this but why didn't Madeline push back against the recommendation, given that she's generally disinclined to waste money? Still, I'm not about to look a gift horse in the mouth. This is my opportunity to search for answers and plead my case for reconciliation, face to face.

"Madeline," Dr. Vaughn says, "you haven't said much. Do you have any questions about the process?"

"Please don't take it personally," Madeline says. "I'm still a little shell-shocked to be here."

Shell-shocked? She initiated this.

"It can be hard to place your trust in a supposed expert," Dr. Vaughn says, which seems entirely non-responsive to Madeline's last comment. "I totally get that. I know I look young but I'm twenty-nine, and I have my doctorate of psychology with a specialty in dynamics."

"Shell-shocked by what?" I ask Madeline, suddenly realizing that not only has she said little but she's barely looked at me since we got here.

Dr. Vaughn continues as if she hasn't heard. "Dynamics are the intricacies of relationships. How we affect and trigger one another. I help people hear each other's hearts and believe in each other's good intentions."

"That sounds great," I say. Then to Madeline, "What do you mean shell-shocked?"

"This is a safe space and I've got plenty of tissues," Dr. Vaughn says. "Divorce brings up many emotions."

"It's not a divorce," I say. "We're only separated."

Madeline looks at Dr. Vaughn meaningfully. "It's a divorce. I need Greg to understand that. Our conversations should just be about Lola now. That's why we're here, in co-parenting counseling. He can't keep asking me to go to couples therapy. We have to uphold appropriate boundaries."

Dr. Vaughn nods. "Boundaries are crucial."

"I stopped asking about couples therapy weeks ago!" Now I'm the one addressing Dr. Vaughn. That's not how I want this to go so I turn back to Madeline. "Do you really think divorce is the best thing for Lola?"

"See?" Madeline asks Dr. Vaughn. "This is what I'm dealing with."

"I've given you everything!" I say, trying to keep my voice even. "Not just in the separation but throughout our marriage."

"I've given you everything, too." Madeline won't look at me. "The elephant in this room, Dr. Vaughn, is that Greg is outwardly cooperative, agreeing with whatever I say, and then his attorney is trying to tear it all apart."

I thought the elephant in the room was the true explanation for this separation/divorce, what Sidney was holding back from me the other day. Or is the elephant the months that Madeline spent planning while she kept me in the dark? "Hugh is just trying to get clarity."

"At this point, it's better for me to talk directly to Greg, but with a witness present," Madeline says. "We really need to get the parenting time sorted out, officially. Greg had agreed to 70/30 and now his lawyer is pushing for 65/35. Or maybe 60/40; he's given my attorney different messages each time they talk. Their conversations are a complete waste of money."

So Madeline didn't come here to talk about our relationship. She came to make her demands with a witness present.

"I miss Lola," I say, tears springing to my eyes. "That's why the percentages keep changing. It's hard to sign away your time with your kid." I see that my pathos has landed with Dr. Vaughn, but Madeline looks unmoved.

"I'm just confused," she answers. "You barely saw Lola during the week when we were together. Thirty percent time is already a stretch. You were late picking her up from school on Wednesday." How does she know that? "I don't see how you'll manage all your clients and do thirty-five or forty percent time with Lola." Seeing me bristle, she softens her tone. "We can put down 70/30 and then if you want more time, all you have to do is ask. We don't need to have everything spelled out precisely in a legal document. We can just talk to each other."

As in, she wants the ability to tell me what's what, without any pesky legal protections for me? I'm suddenly looking through Dr. Vaughn's eyes and realizing how manipulative Madeline can be.

"Lola's doing well," Madeline says, "and I want to keep it that way."

"That might be how it seems but that can't be how it is." I pivot toward Dr. Vaughn. "Isn't it suspicious that Lola seems to be doing so well? Like she's pretending or suppressing or something?"

"This will be part of a larger conversation," Dr. Vaughn says carefully. "A larger assessment." I have the sense that she didn't expect this to be the tenor of the first session.

"Do you have children?" Madeline inquires.

"Would it make a difference to you if I did? Let's unpack that." Dr. Vaughn's cheeks are turning pink.

"Is that a no, then?"

"That's a no," Dr. Vaughn admits, "but I've studied child development extensively, particularly when it comes to divorce."

"This isn't a divorce," I say. "We're in a safe space, right?

Where we can talk openly about what the finality of a divorce would mean for Lola, how it's going to affect the rest of her life? How she'll feel about us and herself and her future relationships?" I've done some choice reading about child development when it comes to divorce, too, and I'm prepared to bring in all the horror stories. Another elephant in the room is that Madeline went through her parents' split and now she's ending her perfectly good marriage with no qualms at all. Coincidence? Or perhaps a midlife crisis? A midlife crisis could explain a lot.

"Greg could really use an individual session," Madeline says. "For emotional support."

So now she's dictating treatment, pawning me off on the therapist?

"What about you?" Dr. Vaughn asks. "Do you need emotional support?"

"It's easier for women, I think," Madeline says. "We know how to open up. I have my best friend, Sidney. Greg's really only had me, and that's not practical anymore. I can't help him get over me."

"I don't want to get over you. I love you." My voice threatens to break. Why won't she just look at me? It's like she can't even see me anymore. "Whatever I've done wrong, just tell me. I'll do anything to fix it. I'll change."

"You're wonderful," she says miserably. "You don't need to change."

"If I'm so wonderful, then why are you leaving me? It must be something. Just tell me. I'm dying here, Maddie."

At least now Madeline is reaching into the proffered tissue box and dabbing her eyes. I'm glad to see I can still have some effect on her.

But then she talks to Dr. Vaughn. "The truth is, Greg's been like this since I first told him how I feel. Can you help him let me go, please?"

Dr. Vaughn is speechless for a long moment. "Well," she

finally says, "that might be one of our treatment goals. But first, we have to get through the assessment. How old is Lola again?" She lifts her pen.

For the next thirty minutes, she asks us questions that go barely deeper than the ones on her initial intake form (and some are actually duplicates from the intake form). Madeline seems more comfortable now, on surer footing, especially when she can reference her knowledge as a pediatrician and apply it to Lola. I want to snap that we're talking about our child, not Patient X, but snapping won't get me anywhere. Besides, Madeline and I are nothing if not cordial. Our whole marriage, we've barely fought. I used to think that was a good thing.

"Thank you for coming in." Dr. Vaughn smiles and gets to her feet. We follow suit. "I'm excited to see what we can do together."

Madeline and I make our silent escape. Once outside, she gestures vaguely down the street. "I'm parked that way."

"I'll walk you."

"No, thanks."

"What, you're mad at me?" Unbelievable. "You asked me to do this, and I'm doing it. I'll always show up for you."

"I wish I could trust that." Then, more quietly, "I wish I could trust you." Sadness washes over her face.

I want to reach for her but her body language advises against it.

"It's just so unnecessary," she says. "All this money going to attorneys and therapists when it should be financing Lola's future. I really thought we'd be able to talk to each other."

"Then talk to me. It's just us. Tell me everything."

She takes a step back, shaking her head. "I can't. Not now."

"Then when?" I ask.

"When your attorney stops fighting mine. When you've signed off on the agreements that you and I made."

I stare at her. Is that an ultimatum?

"I can't trust you if you're saying one thing to my face and another thing to Hugh Warshaw." As she says his name, her distaste is apparent.

"All lawyers are shady," I say. "But maybe some pediatricians are, too." Her eyes narrow. "I'm sorry, I didn't mean that." Well, I didn't mean to say it out loud.

"I'm leaving." She spins on her heel.

"I'll talk to Hugh, okay?" I call after her. When she doesn't turn around, I hate myself for the instantaneous desolation (and desperation) that I feel. "I'm sorry! I'll take care of this!"

Staring at her receding back, it feels like she might really be slipping away for good. But no, that can't happen.

I'm going to save my family, whether she likes it or not.

FIFTEEN

MADELINE

"See you tomorrow!" I say cheerily to the receptionists, sailing out the front door. But once I hit the pavement, the smile vanishes from my face. On Thursdays, I'm done at 3 p.m. Despite the day's brevity, it felt interminable, and I had to force myself to focus on the patients in front of me. I just keep playing back that co-parenting session, trying to sort out the discrepancies. The gnawing question for me is whether Hugh Warshaw is the villain or just the scapegoat, doing Greg's dirty work.

It's terrible to think this way, and to feel this way about Greg. Throughout our marriage, I wasn't sure that he truly saw me yet I never doubted that he was on my side and wanted the best for me. He hasn't always been the most reliable but I've always assumed that's because he gets caught up in whatever's most focal at that moment. I've never thought of him as spitefully capricious, or remotely devious. He can't even plan for next week. Now, though, I'm wondering what I could have missed all these years, what's been camouflaged and normalized. Could my blind spots have been as pronounced as his? Maybe that's why divorces go haywire. People finally take off the love goggles and are shocked by what's been right in front of them the whole time.

Or I'm just being paranoid. Greg said he'd take care of this, he'll talk to Hugh Warshaw, and I have to trust that. Trust but verify. Innocent until proven guilty.

Besides, I'm the one who's been lying. It hurts to remember how pained Greg looked on that street as he implored me to tell him everything. Though he's never had any reason to doubt my fidelity or my character, he might have a sixth sense about Tarek. But there's no way I can confirm. Things would spin even more out of control.

I've never been good with uncertainty and loose ends, with waiting for someone to get back to me. If I want it done right (or done quickly, is more like it), I do it myself. If I had my way, I'd be the one sorting this out with Hugh Warshaw.

That tendency of mine is part of how I've wound up over-loaded and, at times, resentful. I know it's why Lola thinks I'm not nearly as fun as Greg is. I can't play, I'm too busy attending to a million and one details, whereas he can waltz in and enjoy the spoils of my labor.

But it's different now. As Dr. Vaughn said, the dynamics are shifting.

I drive extra slowly up into the hills. Ever since I almost hit those deer, I've been exceedingly careful. That was a wake-up call. I can't let the stress of this process frazzle my nerves and flavor my decision-making. I'm still hoping to be divorced in six months but I can't let urgency overrun my good sense. I can't afford to make mistakes.

But speaking of urgency, I can't believe how much I miss him.

(Not Greg. Never Greg.)

I let myself into the house, kicking off my shoes. I don't have to set them aside carefully in the built-in, ingeniously concealed shoe rack since I'll be leaving to pick Lola up at soccer practice in an hour. I decide that I'll surprise her with dinner out tonight. It's not a competition with Greg; I'm not trying to buy her affection. I just think it would be healthy to cultivate my more spontaneous side.

I always get errands done during this hour but today's tasks feel more onerous than usual. I'm supposed to work on demonstrating my moral character, as if that's even in question. But like Esther says, better to be overprepared than under.

One of Greg's favorite architectural tricks is giving people multiple ways to move through their houses. Our home features external steps, internal steps, and a glass elevator, which makes even the most jaded guest swoon as they descend and ascend. I barely notice the view as I journey down three stories to the basement.

Another Greg trick? That the basement is done up like a wine cellar—an actual cellar, like you'd find at a Napa vineyard —with stone floors and archways and recessed lighting that makes you feel like you're spelunking. Storage is in massive wine barrels that are discreetly labelled (by me), which is why I have an easy time finding what I need.

I lift some accordion folders out and then take them up to my office. Greg thinks it's a travesty that I have my desk facing away from the view but I just work better that way. No distractions.

It's hard to focus. I wish I felt more confident about the next steps, and about Dr. Vaughn. Her age and inexperience had been showing like a bra strap, especially during that first part of the session when Greg had acted so inappropriately. I couldn't have been more clear with him about the distinction between co-parenting counseling and couples therapy but he'd still tried to alchemize one into the other. I would have liked if Dr. Vaughn had been firmer.

I remind myself that it's early days, she probably didn't want to hurt her rapport with Greg, and besides, the rest of the session proceeded as expected. I need to keep an open mind. Dr. Vaughn's done wonders for Sidney's friends who were much more contentious than Greg and I could ever be.

I sift through the first folder. It's cards and letters that Greg and I have exchanged over the years, as well as handmade cards and art projects from Lola for my birthday and Mother's Day. I try to evaluate them objectively and select the ones that best highlight my particular strengths as a loving, supportive wife and mother. At the clinic, I've learned how to compartmentalize, to not get bogged down by emotion. Sentimentality is the enemy of efficiency. So I draw on those same skills now.

I do know that I still need to grieve, and I'll find time for that. But grief's not time-sensitive.

I organize Lola's report cards and document my participation in the PTA. I notice that I don't have nearly as many pictures of Lola and me together as I'd like for my dossier. Many are on Greg's phone. I decide that could be an olive branch of sorts since we had kind of an abrupt ending yesterday, so I fire off a friendly text asking if he could send those photos. I stop short of offering to do the same for him since I have the definite sense that Esther wouldn't want me to provide them so readily. If he asks, I'd never withhold them. But since all signs point to Greg and his attorney playing hardball, I can't be too easy.

Esther said that I should turn over any copies of emails, screenshots of text messages, voicemails, and audio recordings that show Greg engaging in hostility or undermining but fortunately, there's none of that. I need to remember that Greg is an upstanding husband and father; we'll be able to work this out.

Okay, so he has the tendency to be lax in his discipline, he was a Disneyland Dad even while we were together, but that's no cause for alarm. So what if he spoils Lola during his 30 percent time, if I try to spoil her a little more during my 70 percent? We're just cushioning the blow.

And no, Greg's never been a heavy drinker or a womanizer

or a gambler. He's not a liar or a cheater. He doesn't hide money. He doesn't look at pornography (not that I'm aware of, not that I'd care if he did). Our sex life has dwindled significantly over the past few years—all my doing—and he has the right to take care of himself.

But I haven't been having sex with anyone else either. While my behavior is Esther's business, quite literally, my private thoughts and feelings are not. In that one area, I'm keeping my own counsel.

Lately, I've been retreating more into fantasy about what it'll be like when this divorce is final, when I'm free to act in accordance with my desires. Sometimes I have the most inconvenient sexual impulses, almost as uncontrollable as I imagine a hot flash will be one day. Like now, I can't stop imagining him, and there's this heat growing inside me, flames licking at...

Here I go again. I stumble down the hall to the bedroom, tearing at my clothes, opening the nightstand and grabbing the new vibrator I bought the other day. I'm seeing him in my mind's eye so vividly that it's like I can really feel him on me, inside me.

It doesn't take long. I guess you could say I'm a model of efficiency in all things.

I lay there, gasping and gulping for air, and I know I should head back to the office but I just want to stay in this post-coital state a while longer. I feel wanton and liberated, my clothes thrown on the floor, having afternoon orgasms.

Yes, plural. I decide to go again. And again.

Greg thinks he's the only one with a potent imagination but it's not entirely true.

Not that I'm inclined to think about Greg at a time like this.

I tease myself, moving the vibrator slowly around my clit, picturing the man I'm almost certain I love. I writhe and moan, finally shuddering to a stop. Then I start up again. It's nearly compulsive and yet it feels strangely powerful to be so out of control.

Finally, I'm sated. That's when I glance at the clock for a very different kind of "oh shit" moment. I race upstairs and see that there's a message from Lola's soccer coach, saying that Lola was positive it was my day to pick her up but it must be Greg's since I'm never even a minute late. Practice ended over a half hour ago.

I call the coach back, mortified and apologetic. She's sympathetic ("Mix-ups can happen when there's a change in family structure") and she knows that I'm nothing if not reliable. The undercurrent seems to be that Greg is less so. I have to ask, "Did you call him?" She tells me yes, she left a message for him, too. Dammit. "I'm so sorry," I say again, "I'm on my way."

I shouldn't hurry down the hill, I should take the curves with caution, but fuck those deer. I'm on the cusp of a custody battle.

No, I can't think that way. That's not where this is heading. Besides, the coach knows that this is a total one-off, that I'm never irresponsible. Greg's the one who's barely done a pick-up before, not that I'll use that against him.

Unless I have to.

SIXTEEN

GREG

Lola's asleep in her room—not what I think of as her real room, just the one in my apartment. Even though it's not technically my weekend, Lola asked Madeline if she could spend Saturday night with Daddy, and Madeline agreed. So far, Lola seems to be thriving under the new arrangement. Me, though? I'm deteriorating. But I must be doing a good job of hiding it since Lola seems eager to spend extra time with me.

I know Madeline was late to pick Lola up on Thursday. Lola mentioned it but I already knew, having received a message from the coach. I defended Madeline to Lola, saying that she's under a lot of stress. Lola didn't quite roll her eyes but she didn't seem to want to talk about it further.

I like thinking that the lateness could be an indication of what's really going on with Madeline, deep down. She looks put together on the outside and seemed detached for much of our co-parenting session, but underneath, she's unraveling without me.

Now I just need to get her to admit it during the next session. I suspect that Dr. Vaughn will be a willing accomplice. While she initially seemed thrown by just how vulnerable I was willing to be, later on I could see that she really got off on it, which will be a distinct advantage given how loath Madeline is to show any. Madeline was acting so formal, referencing benchmarks and milestones, acting like she and Dr. Vaughn were just two child development experts having a consultation. Maybe Madeline assumes they have a natural bond since they're both professionals but I don't think Dr. Vaughn saw it that way at all. Madeline's most comfortable being dispassionate and analytical while Dr. Vaughn is hungry for emotion. In the next session, I'm more than prepared to feed her.

Tonight, though, I'm having to resist the lure of drinking. I'm not going to let myself do that with Lola here but it's tempting. It's the only thing that lulls me to sleep, and that gets me through the days, too.

Since I'm sober, I should probably start working on that relationship chronology for Hugh. I know it's overdue.

I first met Madeline at a party. She was with her friend Sidney. I was with Steve, my wingman from work. I saw Madeline and almost dropped my drink.

It wasn't just the way she looked, which was gorgeous. It was the way she carried herself. A little reserved but not a prude. She doesn't just give you everything, you have to earn it. That first impression was borne out when we started dating. I was head over heels immediately. I made the mistake of telling her that it was love at first sight and that almost got me deleted from her phone. From her life. She's no-nonsense. But she's not uncompassionate. Far from it. You should hear how she talks about some of the kids she works with, especially the ones from low-income families. She'll fight to the death for those kids.

I'm bad with dates, I don't know what year that was.

I convinced her to keep going out with me and she got less reserved. A WHOLE lot less reserved.

I'm not going to kiss and tell. Let's just say she was a

goddam revelation. In every way. She rocked my world and organized my life. She's the reason I was able to strike out on my own professionally. Not just her belief but her support, how she was willing to take care of everything so that when I was at work, I was completely at work. That's why I want to be fair about the money. She invested in me. She built me up. But let's get real. I'm the one who deals with some of the most demanding and exacting men on the planet. She makes sure that we always have toilet paper and dinner on the table, which is important, and I'm grateful, but it's not exactly equivalent.

I built us a palace. I oversaw every element so that we could cut costs without ever sacrificing quality. I stayed up until 3 a.m. every night doing that. She didn't really appreciate the toll that took and what a sacrifice it was. I was sacrificing for our family. She was just sorry we didn't have a yard. Not that she said that often but I could tell she thought it often. Too many people care more about what they don't have than what they do. Maybe that's what's really going on here, that Madeline's started focusing on the wrong things and just needs to reconnect with her true priorities.

What you need to remember is that I worked a lot but I always worshipped her. And I worshipped Lola, too. I brought the fun; they'll both attest to that. I made sure we went on adventures. I made sure they had luxuries. I told Madeline to never skimp on anything that mattered to her, or on anything for Lola. I've delivered on every promise. But here I am, on my own.

Tell me, how is that fair?

SEVENTEEN

MADELINE

I take another sip of Chardonnay, asking myself, "What's the worst that'll happen?" So Lola will be a pain to wake up tomorrow morning. So she'll be tired throughout the school day. She'll survive, we'll survive. And meanwhile, she's out bonding with her father. She's seeing a lot more of Greg now than she did when he and I were together, that's for sure. I thought that a rebalancing of time and duties would be a good thing; I didn't realize that it could feel like theft.

I let him have my Saturday night—at Lola's request, which, I'll admit, hurt—and then she called on Sunday morning and asked to spend part of the day with him, too. I agreed because I didn't want to force her to be with me when she wants him. But now he's five hours late bringing her back from the renegotiated time. She's missed the nutritious dinner I cooked. I can't believe that this is how he's repaying my flexibility.

The past twenty-four hours have been a struggle. So much time on my hands, fighting the pull to get in touch with my special someone. To confirm if he even is my special someone. It's possible he won't stay interested in pursuing a relationship with me, that he doesn't think I'm worth waiting for.

Earlier, I broke down and texted him: *Divorce is progressing. Hope nothing's changed on your end since nothing's changed on mine.* Meaning, I miss you. Meaning, I might very well love you.

He texted back a thumbs up.

WHAT THE ACTUAL FUCK?

Does that mean that he likes that I still care for him, or is he saying ditto, he feels the same way? I know I told him to be circumspect, given my situation. If things went fully awry, I don't want my texts being subpoenaed. But a thumbs up?

All day, I've been debating whether I can send another text to clarify or if I need to play it cool. We can all agree, cool is generally better. Needy isn't attractive. Just look at Greg.

"Hey, Mom!" Lola pushes the front door open and bounds in, startling me. She's in such high spirits that she doesn't remember to take her shoes off. I point, and she rectifies.

Greg is right behind her. He looks tentative as he comes inside, as well he should. "Hi there. Sorry we're late."

I don't want to absolve him but I also don't want to make a fuss in front of Lola and dampen her mood. So I turn to her with a smile, ignoring him completely. "What were you doing?"

She starts reeling off activities—paddleboarding, shopping, and eating at two different restaurants, one for brunch and one for dinner—and I try to hang onto my smile. Secretly, I'm fuming. Not at Lola; she's just a kid, she doesn't know better. But Greg had to know what he was doing, having her make the calls asking for a time extension, putting me in the position of telling her no, reinforcing those infernal roles: Dad as purveyor of delight, Mom as killjoy.

We'll have to talk with Dr. Vaughn about changing those dynamics and the importance of respecting the schedule. No one should be prevailed upon to give up their time, and we should only be late in the event of an emergency. Lola spying a restaurant that she really, really wants to try does not qualify.

"That sounds like a great weekend," I say. "I'm so glad you had fun." Then to Greg, "It's eight o'clock, and Lola still needs to take her bath and finish her schoolwork. Next time, please make sure she brings her work with her and does it at your place."

"I didn't think of that."

"I didn't either, since I thought she'd be home way earlier." Because that was the fucking agreement. But Greg doesn't seem to think he needs to stick to agreements, does he? "Next time, she'll bring her backpack, just in case." Just in case. My new motto.

"Of course." He hesitates near the front door. Is he thinking that he's going to be invited in for a drink? Or maybe he's just not sure if I'm truly upset or not. I've always been adept at concealment to keep things nice. Stability above all else.

I like that he's not sure what to make of me right now. Uncertainty might be what it'll take to get him and his lawyer in line.

"Have a good rest of your night," I say, with finality. Lola throws herself into his arms for a goodbye hug, and then he's gone.

Now I have the unwelcome job of putting Lola through her paces. She doesn't fight me much, though I notice that when it's time for her to go to bed (more than an hour late), she's not throwing herself into my arms. She hasn't even touched me since coming home, hasn't looked even slightly happy to see me.

As I'm standing in her doorway, about to wish her good night and turn the light out, I just can't contain myself. "It's great that you had fun but it can't stay this way," I say. "Dad needs to actually parent."

"What do you mean?"

"He has to make sure you get your work done. It can't just be me." I instantly regret having said anything. This is an adult conversation; she's the child. I snap the light off hurriedly. "I'm probably just crabby because I missed you a lot, Lo. Love you, see you in the morning."

I know I'm right, that Greg does have to start parenting differently, but I need to say it directly to him in the next co-parenting session.

Once I'm seated beside Greg several days later, I see that he's beaten me to the punch. Dr. Vaughn announces right at the start, "Greg left a voicemail to alert me to some inappropriate behavior we need to discuss." She gives me a studiedly compassionate stare and I realize that she's waiting for me to explain myself.

A surge of adrenaline shoots through me. Greg actually reported me, in advance, to our counselor? For what?

"There has been inappropriate behavior," I say, keeping my voice calm and neutral. "Greg brought Lola home five hours late, on my weekend."

"We can talk about that. But first, did you badmouth Greg to Lola?" Dr. Vaughn says.

"No, of course not. She might have picked up on some annoyance I felt when Greg brought her home late but I would never do that." I make sure to look as trustworthy as possible. I don't want to wind up with a professional witness against me, should things continue to spiral.

But I really can't believe that Lola ratted me out to Greg, and that Greg ratted me out to Dr. Vaughn.

"Maybe Lola misunderstood," Greg allows. How generous of him.

"I was trying to be a good mom and a flexible co-parent," I say. "When Lola asked if she could spend extra time with Greg, I didn't want to deny her that. I didn't want to deny him that. But can we all agree that it's not a good practice, going forward?

Greg and I should tell Lola together that the parenting plan is firm."

"Except it's not," he says. "The lawyers are still working on it. If Lola wants to be with me every weekend—"

"Then all I'd get is the grunt work while you got all the fun?" I demand. I look to Dr. Vaughn. "Does that seem reasonable to you?"

"It's important to consider the child's wishes," Dr. Vaughn begins, and Greg looks pleased while I'm fighting to keep my eyes from bulging, "but wishes aren't the same as her best interest."

Well, that was diplomatic. And useless. "What would you recommend?" I ask her.

"It can be a slippery slope, changing the prearranged dates. I would suggest that you tell Lola that whatever's on the calendar is set."

I feel a note of triumph.

"But if Lola wants to be with me more and we're telling her no, what will the judge think about that?" Greg says.

I stare at him. "You want to take this to court? I thought we were determined to sort this out just between us."

"I'm only asking what a judge is likely to think." His expression is innocent. "What is the best interest of a child, really? How is that determined?"

"It is a somewhat vague standard," Dr. Vaughn says. "It'll vary from case to case and judge to judge." She seems nervous. "So what you really want is to stay out of court as much as you can."

"That's what my attorney said, too," I add. "Once you get in front of a judge, all bets are off." While I don't like that kind of unpredictability, it occurs to me that Greg might. Since he can't defeat me on the merits, since he can't out-organize or out-argue me, he might want to make some sort of emotional appeal to a judge, the same as he's been making emotional appeals to Dr. Vaughn.

"This must be why we each have our own counsel," Greg says. "My attorney sees the situation differently."

"But how are you seeing it?" I try to tamp down my frustration. "I thought we were in this together but now—"

"You're divorcing me, Madeline. It seems like you only want to be in it together when it's convenient for you."

"We're still Lola's parents! We both want what's best for her. And that means staying out of court." I look to Dr. Vaughn. "Wouldn't you agree?" She must. I'm only asking her to reiterate a position she's already taken.

Yet she looks torn before she starts speechifying about negative cycles and triggers and dynamics—always with the dynamics—when all I want is for her to cut to the chase and take a stand for what's right. Greg needs to work with me, not against me.

"I hear you about the dynamics," Greg says. "Sometimes I felt steamrolled in the marriage, and now I'm feeling steamrolled in the divorce."

"What? You've never said that!" I'm stunned.

"You never asked. I've probably always been too worried to say anything negative and get on your bad side. You've never taken constructive criticism very well." He looks sincere but can he be for real? Or is he just trying to get Dr. Vaughn on his side, same as he's managed to do with Lola? It hasn't even been a month and he already seems to have bought Lola's affection.

"I handle constructive criticism fine," I say tightly. "You must be thinking of yourself."

"I love you, Madeline," he says, and again, he seems sincere, but who knows anymore? "All I want is you."

"And if you can't have me, then what?" What's he been saying to Lola—and to Hugh Warshaw—behind my back?

He seems confused. "Then I'll have to learn to live without you. But the idea kills me."

"It's not an idea. It's reality." I look at Dr. Vaughn. "I haven't led him on. I haven't given him any false reassurances. But he only hears what he wants."

"That's not true. I've always listened to you. We do things your way, what, ninety percent of the time?"

"The ten percent are the biggest," I say. "What about the house? You must have sensed what I felt, you knew what I thought was important in a family home, but you were the one steamrolling me."

"Look at this." He's talking to Dr. Vaughn, not me, and now he's scrolling on his phone. He stands up and walks over to her, looming over her like a proud papa showing off baby pictures. "Tell me, who wouldn't want to live like this?"

"Wow," she murmurs appreciatively. "That is stunning."

This is becoming surreal. "I shouldn't have brought up the house," I say. "It's not about that; it's about Lola. What's in her best interest is to have a strong bond with both of her parents, and when you take her on my days, you weaken mine."

"And you think I'm doing that on purpose?" he says. "It was Lola's suggestion!"

"But you're a parent," I counter. "You can say no."

Dr. Vaughn turns to me. "He made a mistake and now that we've clarified, he won't make it again. Tell him you trust him."

I'm taken aback. I wouldn't have thought a therapist would put me on the spot like that. "I always have trusted him," I manage.

Greg can hear that I'm hedging. "All I've ever done is love you."

"Oh, come on, Greg." I can't conceal my exasperation anymore. "What about what your lawyer's doing? Did you even talk to him like you said you would? My attorney hasn't seen any change. The divorce is going to take a year at this rate!"

"So what if it does?" Greg's eyes narrow slightly. "Why are you in such a rush? You have somewhere you need to be?"

That hits a little too close to home.

I feel my breath growing shallow. I haven't had panic attacks since I was a kid, when everything was beyond my control. I cannot have a panic attack in front of Dr. Vaughn. It would completely blow my image.

But maybe it's already been blown. I see the way she's looking at me. Like she doesn't quite trust me. Like Greg is winning.

Does that mean I could actually lose Lola?

No, of course not. All Greg's asking for is 65/35 parenting time. Or maybe 60/40.

Greg's become a loose cannon. But I need to remember that I have weapons, too. There are things I could share with Dr. Vaughn that would change the dynamics in this room for sure.

It's a calming thought.

EIGHTEEN

GREG

"Yeah, I know," I say gruffly as I answer the phone. "I still owe you documents."

I take a peculiar pleasure in these hectoring calls from Hugh Warshaw. I don't have to pretend with him, which is a relief. With work, I'm trying to seem competent; with Lola, I'm aiming for normal; with Madeline, I'm—fuck, I don't even know anymore. Sidney's texted a few times, asking if I'm okay but what am I supposed to say? As she reminded me on the day she served the papers, her first allegiance is to Madeline. But Hugh Warshaw's allegiance has been bought and paid for, and I enjoy the simplicity of our transactional relationship.

"I got you the chronology already," I remind him.

"A chronology has dates. More importantly, it has data. You gave me a diary entry. Redo it."

"I'll get right on that."

"I'm pretty sure your wife isn't dragging her feet." He's got that right. "You want me to keep stalling and delaying, you need to give me something to work with. I'm starting to look like an idiot here."

I take another sip—okay, a swig—of bourbon. I don't know if

it's one of the benefits of working from home and for myself, or if it's the curse of a lack of accountability. It's just after 3 p.m. and I've wrapped for the day, which would stress Lucas out if he knew so I'm not about to tell him. He's the one who's been running interference with clients, explaining that there are some unavoidable delays. Meanwhile, I'm lounging on the Jonathan Adler couch that Sidney had to call in a favor to source in record time, same as she had to do with most of the furniture given how quickly Madeline wanted me out of the house.

Is this speed-divorce about her temperamental drive toward efficiency, or about not being like her parents, whose own custody battle went on for almost half a decade? Or could it be a clue about her true motivation? I've been wracking my brain, thinking why she needs to be single in September.

I lean into the phone so Hugh can hear me good. "Keep stalling; I pay you to look stupid. I need more time. Madeline and I aren't getting anywhere in therapy."

I couldn't believe that shit yesterday. Hearing that Madeline doesn't trust me, as if I'm trying to use Lola or turning her against Madeline—it's insanity. Makes me wonder if there was some reason she *already* didn't trust me, if that's why she's so set on divorce. What does she know? Or what does she think she knows? I wish she'd just come out and tell me but the fact that she won't seems to be another indicator of damaged trust.

Honestly, if I didn't know Madeline better, I'd think she was the shady one with something to hide. But she's always been ethical to a fault. She even objected to certain creative (though legitimate) tax deductions my accountant proposed; she said they went against her morals.

"Just get me the documents," Hugh says. "You're not my only client. I have a reputation to protect."

"Unfortunately for you, you're my lawyer, not Madeline's." I pour a little more bourbon into my glass. "The only area where I'm more together than Madeline is in terms of pictures. She barely takes any. Hates selfies. That's why I had to text her all those photos of her and Lola."

"What do you mean, you had to?"

"She asked for them."

Long pause. "Jesus Christ, Greg. Don't you get it? She's building a case for Mother of the Year. Some judge will eat it up. And she'll use your photos to do it!"

"No, Madeline definitely doesn't want to get in front of a judge." She's made that crystal clear. "She wants to look at pictures of Lola when Lola's not around. When she's with me. Which is going to be more often." I feel a surge of satisfaction. Not because I'm trying to destroy their bond or whatever, but because I want to cement mine. If there's one positive that can come out of all this, it's how close Lola and I are these days. I'd never realized just how devoted she was to me.

"I'm going to need pictures, too," Hugh says. "Of you and the kid. And you've got to smarten up. You want me to make Madeline's lawyer wait, fine, but never make your own lawyer wait."

I promise to get on that pronto, like I always do, but this time, I mean it. He's right, I have to smarten up and stop giving Madeline all the advantages. It's time to bite the bullet and go through the stack of bills that she provided me weeks ago. See, she's not withholding. We're still in this together, still a team, sort of, no matter what she said in therapy.

It's not actually a stack of bills; it's a box. As I start to spread the contents out over the coffee table, I see that it goes back more than three years and that it's organized by date rather than by type, which makes it a much bigger job for me. I think of a movie I once saw that depicted a trick of corporate litigation, burying the opposing counsel in paperwork, forcing the other side's attorneys to sort through an entire truck's worth of documents. Madeline knows me and how little patience I have for minutiae. I'm a big picture guy, not a big box guy.

But Madeline wants this to be fair. Fair, and fast. Fast is the operative word, where she's concerned.

The finances have always been her domain. She refuses to do auto-pay because she wants to catch any mistake. She reviews everything and asks me about anything she thinks might be a discrepancy. But I've never done the same with her.

The bills are telling a story, one that I wish I'd read sooner.

Madeline paid for consultations with multiple attorneys more than six months before she even gave me an inkling that she was unhappy in the marriage. I recognize the name of one of the attorneys: Esther Kahn. That was on the paperwork that I was served.

So it's official. Madeline was thinking about leaving me long before she admitted to it. She never intended to work on our marriage at all. She was stringing me along while she got her ducks in a row. She wanted a head start.

As much as I don't want to believe that, I can't ignore a pattern that's emerging in terms of her spending. A little before she started seeing the attorneys, there was a significant uptick in shopping trips to expensive boutiques. Was Madeline giving herself a makeover, knowing she'd be going back on the open market?

With a rising feeling of dread, I force myself to continue going through the stacks. I notice something that turns my stomach. Nine months ago, Madeline took herself off our shared cell phone plan. Obviously, she must have switched to a new plan, all on her own, without telling me. There are no bills in my stack to reflect that change. So much for transparency, and full disclosure.

Who's Madeline been calling? What doesn't she want me to see?

NINETEEN

MADELINE

I'm out on the deck, pacing. I can't even look at the view; it feels like even that is a betrayal. I hate this fucking house. I hate that fucking man.

I need to be outside. I need air because, inside, I'm broiling. I held it together while I met with Esther to review Greg's legal response, a copy of which is now in my hand. I feel like throwing it over the side, watching it get caught on a breeze and fly away. I want to scream into the wind about what a lowlife cocksucker my husband's turned out to be.

But of course I won't. Because I know he's not, deep down. He's a man scorned who's being led astray by his nefarious attorney. Once I calm down, I'll reread the document and notate it. I'll give Esther what she needs to refute every one of these bald-faced lies.

I dig my nails into my palm and bite my lip hard enough to draw blood. I just can't believe that Hugh Warshaw painted me as someone who's essentially abandoned my family, and that Greg let him.

According to Greg's legal response, I showed little regard for his well-being or for Lola's best interests. I hid my true feelings and intentions for months while consulting with attorneys behind his back and then once I did tell him I wanted a separation, I repeatedly and callously refused to attend even one session of couples therapy. I'm a control freak who dictated every term of the separation, coercing, cajoling, and manipulating. Greg was advised by his counsel to renegotiate, particularly around the parenting plan since Lola has expressed "a distinct preference" for his home over mine. With less time at my house, the child support payments would need to be reduced accordingly. And given the type of poor character and bad faith that I've exhibited thus far in the proceedings, I should be entitled to the minimum in terms of division of assets.

California's a no-fault divorce state but you wouldn't know that from the legal brief. I'm furious, I'm mortified, but you know what? I'm not nearly as shocked as I should be. Esther Kahn wasn't shocked at all.

Greg's the one who's been acting in bad faith. He had the nerve to send me a series of disingenuous texts earlier:

> *Just wanted to give you a heads up about the legal response Hugh filed. It might seem harsh but Hugh said it's actually pretty standard.*

> *It's like an opening bid. A starting point for negotiation.*

> *I'm still hoping you'll reconsider, Mads. I'd go to couples counseling with you anytime.* *Smile emoji* *Wink emoji*

Has he lost his mind, or is he hoping that I have? That wasn't an opening bid. This is terrorism, plain and simple. He's putting me on notice: If I don't take him back, he's prepared to destroy me. I will not negotiate with terrorists.

I go inside the house and to my office where I take a seat in front of my computer. Then I start playing back the recording of my first meeting with Esther Kahn and making notes with trembling fingers. I'm ready to do what she recommended from the start. I'm going to collect the evidence that will prove I'm credible, and he's not.

Fortunately, I never delete emails, text messages, or voicemails anyway. I'll have to go through and curate. Find the ones that show inconsistencies and inaccuracies, that expose him for the liar he's turned out to be.

I'll tell him that we are now communicating exclusively through the co-parenting app. I'll do it nicely, as if I'm just humoring my attorney. That's the thing: To his face, it needs to be entirely civil; business as usual. He can't know I'm collecting evidence because if he does, he'll become more guarded.

As I continue to listen to Esther's organizational suggestions, I start to smile. There's no way Greg can beat me at this game. He doesn't have the skill set. He's not methodical or patient. He's Mr. Big Picture. Mr. Visionary.

I'll make sure to take regular photos and videos of Lola and me playing in the house, neighborhood, and community. The goal is to document active involvement, consistent routines and structure, and a healthy living environment (with pictures of how clean our residence is and how nutritious our meals are, along with grocery receipts). I'll document the way I discipline and how I act as a positive role model.

I've got this.

Never be late for exchanges, pick-ups, or drop-offs, and document every time Greg is. Be careful posting on social media, as it's easily monitored. Keep receipts and invoices of all parenting expenses, along with medical and school records. (I already do all that but what about Greg? What about his lavish spending to induce Lola to spend all her time with him instead of with me? I'll ask Esther what can be done there.) I also need to show my willingness to co-parent and that I'm promoting Greg's involvement.

But that's just the appetizer, according to Esther. It's establishing my credibility. For the main course, I'll have to tarnish his.

Esther has an a la carte menu of how I can do that: showing that he's resistant to co-parenting (that he makes unilateral decisions and withholds information), or that he's failing to meet Lola's   psychological/educational/developmental/medical needs, or that he's emotionally unstable, perhaps with anger issues, ideally having outbursts in Lola's presence or in front of witnesses who can sign affidavits to that effect. Bonus points if he's abusing drugs or alcohol or has a borderline personality or a history of domestic violence. Incidents of child abuse, neglect, or endangerment, maybe?

I can hear in the recording how vehemently I denied all of these to Esther during that meeting, how I assured her that my husband has always been eminently decent and trustworthy. "I'm just not in love with him anymore," I hear myself saying regretfully. "I really wish I was. Everything would be so much easier."

I was so naïve then. Or deluded?

Esther went on to say that Greg was allowed to have a new relationship (which had been music to my ears) but that if there's evidence that the new relationship is the priority and not Lola, that the girlfriend represents a danger, or that Lola has been exposed to the new relationship in a way that's emotionally harmful, I'll need to document, document, document.

I'm also supposed to document any time that Greg has engaged in slander. I wonder if that legal response can be used against Greg in court? That would be sweet irony.

"When it comes to building a case," Esther said, "the key is demonstrating that it's not a one-off. We're not talking about a single error in judgment. It's an ongoing pattern of irresponsible and inappropriate behavior that's doing harm to Lola."

"That's never going to happen," I hear myself saying. I was so sure of myself then. So sure of Greg.

"What I need you to do is start a journal," Esther told me. "It should have regular, dated entries. You make a record of every single day, even if Lola's at Greg's house, even if all it says is, 'Nothing to report.' You write down pick-ups and drop-offs, activities, Lola's meals, her general appetite, mood, health, school issues. You write down any concerning interactions with Greg and notes on his conduct and appearance, as well as any questionable parenting decisions. If he denies you access to Lola, if he violates any court orders—"

"There won't be any court orders," I interrupted. "Just a final divorce decree when this is all over."

"Humor me. Record it all, just in case."

Seriously? I remember thinking at the time. *This is like another job! A totally unnecessary job.*

Now, though, it's essential. Once I get the hang of it, it probably won't even take me that long. I document exhaustively at the clinic already. But Greg has an assistant to handle work details, and at home, he always had me.

Not anymore, he doesn't. He's about to learn what he's up against.

If he gets back in line, then I'd be happy to follow suit. I'm not vindictive by nature, and I'd much prefer we do this clean and above-board. Put our egos in check and keep Lola's best interest front and center. We can still have this divorce wrapped up in six months.

Greg's not some monster. He's always been a family man. Really, he's just gone crazy at the thought of losing Lola and me, and he's under the influence of his disgusting attorney.

Maybe Esther just needs to strike back, hard, and then Greg will come to his senses. When he does, I can forgive.

We're reasonable, loving people who can get back on track. It's not too late. Is it?

TWENTY

GREG

"Thank you for all the documents," Hugh says, managing not to sound sarcastic. Actually, he sounds almost... sympathetic. Which pisses me off.

I stare at the naked lady in the painting behind him. Since it's abstract, it occurs to me that not everyone sees what I do. Maybe it's like a Rorschach test. "You're welcome," I say. "But let's skip the small talk. That's not what I'm paying you for."

What I'm paying for today? Hugh's informed opinion. I'm hoping against hope that the cell phone plan thing isn't what I think, that there's some explanation other than the one that's been pinballing through my head for days now: Madeline was in touch with someone she shouldn't have been, and she was covering her tracks.

I just can't imagine it. Or is it that I don't want to? Madeline feeling passionately about someone else when it's been so long since she seemed passionate about me. Worse, I've been excavating my memories and I'm not sure she ever felt much passion for me. I might have been deluding myself from the start.

I'm afraid I finally have my answer, that the final puzzle piece has just snapped into place. But I'm praying I'm wrong.

"Give me the truth," I say. "What do you think about the cell phone plans?"

"Since it's a no-fault state, we can't use infidelity as grounds for the divorce. But if we need to, we can use this down the line to demonstrate that Madeline is duplicitous and manipulative. What else has she been lying about? Is she even fit to raise your daughter?"

I stare at him, stunned. He's taking it as a given that Madeline's been having an affair. It's as if there's not even the slightest question in his mind. On the one hand, Hugh should know, with his line of work. On the other, he doesn't know Madeline.

It's the first time I've even let myself think in terms of a custody battle.

Since this nightmare began, I've just wanted to come home. But maybe I haven't had a home for a very long time, and Madeline hasn't been who I thought she was for a very long time. If ever.

*

I think of that day often. Who wouldn't? I can see every detail in my mind's eye, right down to that horrifying final image. Someone's dead because of me.

Because of us.

The surprise isn't that I can't stop replaying that day. It's that I can't stop replaying the months leading up to it. Murder became inevitable based on the events that preceded it, as insane as that sounds. It was impossible to turn back since I should have turned back so much sooner, a hundred different times. We both should have.

At the time of the separation, we were two normal people with gas pedals and brake pedals. But at some point, it was pure acceleration, hurtling toward tragedy.

Some nights I can't sleep for trying to pinpoint the exact moment when we stopped being human and became these machines, hell-bent on destruction, all the while convincing ourselves that we were each the good one. That we were righteous.

All I know is, you can't get to hell alone.

COLLATERAL

TWENTY-ONE

MADELINE

"You can't cancel," Esther says. "You have to look cooperative. Remember, you're a model parent, concerned only about Lola's welfare."

"Of course I am." My fingers tighten around the phone reflexively in annoyance. "That's why I didn't cancel."

"But I can understand the temptation," Esther adds. "I get how hard it must be to sit in the same room with him, given this latest betrayal."

Does she really get it? She's obviously witnessed this type of unraveling a thousand times—she practically predicted it during our first meeting—but unless she's experienced the brutality of divorce herself, I don't see how she can truly understand what it feels like. I've wanted to make excuses for Greg throughout, to blame his attorney and his grief. Then he fucked with my money.

"Madeline? Are you still there?" Esther asks.

"Still here. This situation seems pretty cut and dried: He agreed to pay me a certain amount on the first of each month, and then he only deposited half. Can't you make him give me the rest?"

"I can file a motion but only the court can compel him."

"He's in breach of contract!" I can't help it, my voice rises. If I can't express the extent of my frustration to the woman I'm paying $550 an hour, then where can it be expressed? Sidney lets me vent but I can tell that she doesn't want to believe Greg's really this awful and duplicitous, for Lola's sake. I wish I didn't believe it either. "Do you know what I've done for this man? He would have been nothing without me! Sure, he has talent but I'm the one who puffed him up. The one who smoothed his ruffled feathers after every setback. The one who advised him on how to win over Peter Tramboni. Do you know how many disgusting client dinners I've gone to when he needed me to close a deal? If you think Greg's bad, you ought to see the billionaire set. They have tantrums when their soup is five degrees too cold!"

"You don't have an enforceable agreement, unfortunately." Did she hear anything I just said? Empathy is not Esther's forte. But then, I'm not here for therapy. You don't go to the mechanic when you have a toothache.

"I appreciate how level-headed and measured you are in your responses," I say, "but I'm wondering if Hugh Warshaw is taking advantage of that. Maybe we need to get more aggressive. Fight fire with fire." Show that we're not people to be trifled with so that Greg will get back in line and stop this idiocy. Act like the honorable person that I thought he was. Well, I guess that wasn't the first word that came to mind for him but I've always assumed basic integrity. Maybe there just haven't been many times to show his true colors. He's not used to being told no, flat out; I've buffered him from life's irritations and indignities so that he's free to build his absurd mansions in peace. A recent one he designed had a moat.

"And I appreciate the strain you're under," Esther says, "but please leave the strategy to me. Unlike the Hugh Warshaws of the world, I know how to play the long game. Aggression can backfire in the eyes of a judge, and at this point, we're headed to court."

"That's not what I wanted!"

"But it seems to be what Greg wants."

It does, doesn't it? I just want to know why. Why would he do this to me? I can't ask him, though. Esther's made that clear, and I probably can't believe what he says anyway.

Who is this man that I married?

"I'll file a motion for a temporary order of spousal support and child support with the higher amount that you say Greg initially agreed to," Esther says.

"He did agree to it."

"But he didn't sign any paperwork to that effect. It's his word against yours."

"My word is better." It comes out slightly sullen. I've done everything by the book, and I resent finding myself in this position. I know life isn't fair but I've tried to be. Seems like a losing strategy.

"Given where this case is headed, you're going to need to be even more careful about impression management. Behave impeccably in every setting. Be above reproach, in all ways."

"I do, and I am." I'm denying myself the man that my heart —and my other parts—are crying out for, aren't I? Not that she knows that.

"Start thinking of everyone in your, Greg, and especially Lola's life as potential collateral contacts. Those are the people who'd be willing to attest to your character in an affidavit or testify on your behalf at a hearing or trial. They might need to speak to a custody evaluator."

I stare out the window moodily, wanting to glare at all the pedestrians gliding past my car, going on about their business without having to appear impeccable. "Do you think it's going to come to that? A custody evaluation?"

Is she saying that if I'm not careful, I really might lose Lola?

No, Greg might.

"Better to overprepare, just in case," Esther answers. "If I were you, I'd be building my list of collateral contacts now. Passionate supporters are paradoxically the least useful because they can appear too biased. Experts are especially valuable." She pauses. "So be prudent in today's session. Don't even bring up money. This is all about the best interest of the child, remember that."

Greg's the one who's forgotten. This was supposed to be straightforward. That's what we said before the lawyers got involved. Now I wish I'd never brought in the professionals, that we'd done all the paperwork ourselves like he suggested. Where would we be now, if we'd zigged instead of zagged? Can we double back to the beginning or has it already gone too far? "I need to get to my session."

"Yes, you should go. You don't want to be late for anything."

"Can you just hold off on filing the motion for a day or two? I'm not going to say anything in the co-parenting session but afterward, when it's just Greg and me, I'll bring it up delicately."

"I wouldn't, if I were you."

"I just feel like I owe it to our marriage to try, if that makes sense. I owe it to our family." I'll appeal to his sense of decency. It must still be in there somewhere.

"Like I've told judges before: I can't control my clients; I can only advise them. And right now, if you insist on doing this, at least record the conversation."

I do insist. But I'm thinking that maybe the best course is to do it in front of Dr. Vaughn. I won't talk money, not at all; instead, I'll speak from the heart about how a protracted battle will impact Lola, and it'll impact us, too. I don't want antagonism and ugliness; I want an ending that respects the loving marriage that came before. Best-case scenario, it persuades Greg but if it doesn't, then at least it exposes him. Dr. Vaughn will see who I'm really dealing with. I've had the suspicion that she's more on Team Greg. But some vulnerability from me today should move her back to neutral, at a minimum.

During the session, though, I'm finding that I have to fight unusually hard for composure. I've never been violent in my life yet looking at that soft, moony face of his, contrasting it with his behaviors out of session—it's almost too much to bear.

Normally, I'm the ultimate planner but I can't stick to this one. I don't have it in me to mount a vulnerable plea for peace. Instead, I crash-land somewhere slightly more pragmatic, saying, "I know Lola seems okay so far but what she really needs—what all kids need—is security. It would be best for her if we could get all the legalities squared away as soon as possible." I look to Dr. Vaughn for agreement but she appears infuriatingly inert .

"Yes," Greg says, "Lola does need stability." I didn't say stability; I said security! "That's why I let Madeline stay in the house, but I have to be honest, it's been more painful than I ever could have imagined." He launches into a teary-eyed reverie about coming through the front door and seeing me in the kitchen, cooking, while Lola is at the table doing her homework, and about what it's been like for him to exist in exile.

In my peripheral vision, I see that Dr. Vaughn is eating out of his hand, which means that despite my growing fury, I have to feign sympathy.

I want to tell Dr. Vaughn to do her job, to keep him on track. This isn't even the scope of co-parenting. Greg's self-pity has nothing to do with Lola. He's an adult who needs to finally accept this situation and manage his emotions for the good of his child.

"I built that house for our family," he says, looking at me but he must be speaking to Dr. Vaughn because I've heard this a thousand times and I know the truth. That house was for him and he just installed us in it. "One of the things that really hurts is that Madeline loved the idea but not the reality. When I showed her the plans and took her out to the site, she was so excited. She was right there with me, you know?" He's practically wincing in pain at the memory. "But once she was living in it, she had a change of heart."

Oh, he's good. Dr. Vaughn is nodding like she'd follow him anywhere. She gets the subtext, that I'm fickle and arbitrary, that I cast aside beautiful things like houses and family.

"I let her have the house," he says, "even though she doesn't love it. In fact, I think she hates it, and maybe she kept it because she knows I feel the opposite."

"Bullshit!" It explodes out of me. "I'm living in that house for Lola. Because I want to keep things stable for her and she's with me most of the time. That's her home."

"See, that's what I mean. You don't think of it as your home. Or you don't want it to be, anyway." I can see that his sorrow is real, but that only makes it grate more.

"What do you expect, Greg? You ran roughshod over all my objections to that house. In the end, all I could do was ooh and ahh over your plans and over the site. Because what choice did I have?"

"I feel like we might be getting off-topic," Dr. Vaughn says.

"You're the one who runs roughshod over me!" Now Greg's angry, too. I'm glad that he's finally dropped his pose of the wronged, bereft spouse. Dr. Vaughn should get to see this. "For our entire marriage, you've made practically every decision."

"Only the small ones. You get to do big picture, and I do absolutely everything else. Do you know how exhausting that is?"

"You love the control."

I see an opportunity, and turn to Dr. Vaugh. If he's going to work her, then I can, too. I can wield my vulnerability like a knife. "The house is magnificent, that's true. Maybe I did get caught up in Greg's vision initially. He can be captivating. But I did tell him my reservations. That's not a family house, and we always said we'd have children. Children, plural. But we changed our minds—well, I changed my mind—because of how consumed he was with work. I couldn't imagine being up on that hill with two little kids by myself, and yes, he would have been happy to hire a team of nannies but it's not the same. It's not the life I pictured."

"Everything can't be the way you picture it, Madeline!" He's still mad. Good.

I stay fixed on Dr. Vaughn. I vividly recount my terror in driving through the Oakland Hills with tiny Lola in her car seat, how I ached to turn around and check on my newborn but you can't take your eyes off those roads for even a second, not with those switchbacks. As she got older, the house scared me, too. It was nearly impossible to babyproof, so many sharp edges and all those balconies and Greg was against measures that interfered with the aesthetics that he'd labored over so painstakingly. I felt trapped in that castle on a hill. Trapped in a life that had been designed by Greg, around Greg.

The look on Dr. Vaughn's face is heartening. I just might be winning co-parenting counseling. For the first time, I think that she might be on Team Madeline.

TWENTY-TWO

GREG

"So I've been all about me and you've been all about Lola?" I sneer. "Is that what you're selling?"

Madeline looks startled by the vitriol.

For days now, I've been stewing and brewing over her (likely) affair. Even though Hugh thinks it's a foregone conclusion, I've been telling myself that it's still unconfirmed. I came here today planning to make one more (possibly last-ditch) effort to win her over, to force her to confront the cost of tearing our lives apart. All session, I've tried to invoke and resurrect her feelings for me and for our family.

Yet Madeline has seemed curiously and disturbingly unmoved by what I said, even though every bit of it is true. Now she's painting me as some kind of megalomaniacal deadbeat who cares more about houses than the welfare of my own child.

You know what's crazy? Despite that, I'm still hoping that Hugh's got it wrong, that she switched cell phone plans without telling me because it was a good deal. Or if not that, she'll say that she made a mistake but it's over now. Or she is involved with somebody but it's run its course and she's about to end it.

With proper remorse, I can forgive. I've put in years, and there's Lola to consider. If it's my family or my pride, I'll choose family.

But I have to know the truth. I can't take this anymore.

"You've been talking to someone behind my back for months," I say. "Is that all you've been doing?"

The energy in the room shifts instantly. Dr. Vaughn's face closes up as she stares at Madeline. And Madeline is many things, but a good actress is not among them. My heart plummets.

She flails around for a response, as if completely unprepared for this contingency. Was she so arrogant that she didn't imagine she could ever get caught? Or she thinks I'll accept anything she dishes out, that I'm too weak to stand up for myself?

She's sputtering and feinting and trying to distract. "Greg's been subverting the process since the beginning," she tells Dr. Vaughn. "This isn't couples therapy."

"Honesty is the cornerstone of co-parenting," Dr. Vaughn says, her expression steely. Even though she's young, she's clearly not a pushover, and she doesn't like a liar. "Is what Greg said true?"

"My friendships aren't relevant," Madeline says.

"To collaborate effectively, there needs to be trust." Dr. Vaughn is not about to let this go.

"It's just a friendship."

"What kind of friendship requires that you have your own cell phone plan?" I demand.

Madeline's cheeks grow pink. "I started to develop feelings for someone else but I've never acted on them."

"You're divorcing me! That's not an action?" I'm nearly shouting but I don't think anyone could blame me.

"I'm doing it for me, not for him."

"Who is he?" I say.

"I'm not going to share any details because they're not relevant." Her eyes flick over toward Dr. Vaughn as if she's expecting back-up.

"Fuck relevance!" I burst out.

"I know this is hurtful," Dr. Vaughn says, "but I need you to speak to each other respectfully."

"Where did you meet?" I ask Madeline.

"I'm not going to answer these kinds of questions. It won't do either of us any good." Madeline addresses Dr. Vaughn. "I never expected to have feelings for someone else, and when I did, it made me realize some things. Like how shut down I'd been for so long, just going through the motions. Those feelings woke me up. I started to reflect on who I am as a person and how I want to evolve."

I snort derisively. All the therapy speak is just pathetic, a desperate attempt to convince Dr. Vaughn that she's not a liar and a cheater. But I'm the one she should be trying to convince.

"I can't believe how she's rationalizing," I say. "She hasn't even apologized."

Madeline whirls on me. "So this is why you halved my monthly payments. You're willing to screw over your own daughter to punish me? I can't afford the mortgage and the upkeep on that house without you, and you know it."

"I'm not the one on trial here," I say.

"No one's on trial," Dr. Vaughn intervenes meekly.

I'm seething. Even if Madeline is telling the truth about not fucking that guy, she clearly wants to fuck him. She's been holding back because... why? It's obviously not because of her love for me. Maybe it's so she can keep thinking of herself as a good person.

Meanwhile I've been out earning three-quarters of our household income, having to kiss the asses of the most entitled, most insufferable sons of bitches you could ever meet. I came from nothing. I've never had a handout, or been given a hand up. I've done it all on my own, and yes, Madeline has supported me emotionally and practically, she created a wonderful stable home, blah blah, but the fact is, she played me. She's been running around behind my back and building a relationship with someone else. Even if she's telling the truth and it hasn't been physical yet, it's still categorically a betrayal, especially when I've made her whole life possible. A pediatrician in the Bay Area? That's barely middle class.

I could destroy her. I'm not going to, but I could.

TWENTY-THREE

MADELINE

After the co-parenting session, Greg's the lucky one. He gets to pick Lola up at school and take her to his place for the night. I'm left on my own, filled with restless energy and impotent rage.

I spend hours scrubbing the house. For the time being, I still have cleaners but I'm going to have to reduce their hours. I need to think what other expenses I can cut since Greg's decided to stiff me. It's ridiculous how much maintenance this house requires (a herd of grass-grazing goats delivered every month to keep the slope tidy, and window washers dangling off the cliff in safety harnesses, to name just two).

When this started, we opened separate bank accounts and divided our savings straight down the middle but a lot of our assets aren't liquid. The funds are tied up in this house and in investments that Esther says neither of us can touch until everything's decided. Meanwhile, our credit cards are joint, and the sizable debt (mostly amassed by Greg) legally belongs to both of us. I'm solely responsible for my hefty student loans from medical school since that's from before Greg and I met.

It won't take many months of Greg's withholding for me to

run out of money. So this is his next act of terrorism: threatening to bleed me dry while he's sitting pretty.

The rent on his apartment is much less than the mortgage, with no additional maintenance fees. He makes way more than me, obviously, and I've never had access to the bank account for his firm. Now I'm wondering what he might have held back all these years, if there could be a secret account somewhere. That had never crossed my mind when we were together but it's hard to imagine that the dishonesty he's shown developed overnight. Maybe he's been lying to me for years.

I could ask Esther about hiring a forensic accountant, if it comes to that.

Has it already come to that?

I hate the idea of eating into my half of the savings to pay yet another professional, but I have to protect myself. I've worked too hard to build this family and to create financial security for Lola. I always thought that Greg wanted that for her, too, since it's something neither he nor I had when we were growing up.

I'm angry, yes, but I'm also frightened. Greg seems determined to force me into painful and difficult decisions. If he keeps halving my support payments and I'm out of money, how do I pay the mortgage? Can I call his bluff by threatening to sell the house? Can he stop me from selling it while forcing me to live here? Could I also be forced to increase my hours and take out a second mortgage? What if I just stop paying each month? Will I go into bankruptcy? Will the house go into foreclosure? Where will Lola and I live?

And how much will it cost me in legal fees to have Esther answer all these questions?

I scrape at the shower grout with a tiny brush. It's a five-million-dollar house and we still get pink mold in a week if we're not careful. That seems symbolic of something.

Maybe I'm lingering on the money concerns because

they're actually less scary than thinking of what could happen with Lola. As Esther said, I need to line up my collateral contacts because I'm in for a fight. And it's time to admit it: Dr. Vaughn is a class A bitch. She's not even thirty with no wedding ring, and yet she feels qualified to sit in judgment of me? I'm pretty sure she didn't believe me even though I was telling the God's honest truth about not sleeping with anyone but Greg. Not that I was even sleeping with Greg over the past months. But we're in a no-fault state. I could give hand jobs to the entire defensive line of the San Francisco 49ers and I'd still be an amazing mother. Greg, on the other hand, has practically been an absentee father but I'm fairly certain Dr. Vaughn has the hots for him.

It's too late to switch to another co-parenting therapist. Starting over would mean going through the history again, and who knows if I'd wind up ahead? I just don't want to do it anymore, with anyone. I can't stand the idea of sitting in a room with Greg week after week with his disingenuous sniveling. What he did today was inarguably underhanded. He could have talked to me anytime but he obviously wanted the element of surprise, to blindside and humiliate me when I'm just trying to build my credibility.

I should tell Esther what he knows, or what he thinks he knows. I *will* tell Esther, sometime. Tomorrow, maybe. Or next week.

The thing is, Greg's done me a favor. Now that he knows about Tarek, there's no reason for me to hold back. Maybe I should start seeing Tarek. Platonically, that is. In public places in distant suburbs where no one we know would be caught dead, where no one would see us, including Greg or Esther. I've been denying myself for months and look where it's gotten me: a tenuous if not perilous relationship with Greg; an escalating legal situation; the precipice of financial ruin. It might be high time to switch it up.

Tarek and I met when he spent two months as a visiting nurse at my clinic. Prior to that, he'd been living abroad and working for Doctors Without Borders. He'd been raised in Los Angeles, one of four children born to wealthy Egyptian *émigrés*. His siblings are all employed in the lucrative family business but Tarek had decided to go his own way. While his parents would have been supportive of him becoming a doctor, he'd chosen to become a nurse. He likes how hands-on it is, and that he has more of a chance to connect meaningfully to each patient. Money means little to him.

I was impressed from our very first meeting and my admiration only grew when I saw him interacting with the patients. He was soft-spoken yet decisive, his confidence more reassuring than any words. People relax in his presence, including me. This might sound strange but until I spent time with Tarek, I didn't realize the impact that Greg has on my nervous system. He's often so amped up that it's like a shot of adrenaline, unwelcome after a long day at work and domestic responsibilities.

That's not to say that Tarek is dull. Far from it. He has incredible stories from his travels, and he truly believes that every experience and every person has something to teach him. That means he's also the best listener I've ever met. I feel both fascinated and fascinating when I'm around him, whereas around Greg, my role is much more limited. I'm adored, but we both know I'm not the interesting one.

To be clear, I didn't go looking for another man; I wasn't even aware of just how dissatisfied I was with my marriage until Tarek awakened all these feelings in me. They weren't only feelings toward him. They're feelings about my purpose in the world. While I know I can't volunteer with Doctors Without Borders with Lola being this young, it's something I'd like to do when she's older. I want to have more impact, and I want to be impacted. Tarek's convinced me that encounters can change you in ways you never foresaw, sending you on a whole new trajectory.

Tarek and I started taking coffee breaks together. Then we were going to lunch. Then we were texting each other at night. I couldn't wait to go to work each day and see him. I didn't admit to myself that my entire life trajectory was being altered, but that's what was happening. I couldn't see Greg the same way anymore. His creative endeavors are largely selfish, and in the vast majority of cases, he designs for men who care about profit, not people. Their philanthropic work is just a whitewash. There was picketing at the Tramboni Center's ribbon-cutting ceremony because of Peter Tramboni's exploitative style of capitalism. His actions have contributed to the suffering of millions, if not billions of people.

But Greg couldn't care less about global inequities. None of that's remotely real to him. He just wants to erect beautiful buildings, entire futuristic realms, and maybe I never would have thought there was anything wrong with that if I hadn't met Tarek. If I hadn't fallen in love with him.

The craziest part isn't my feelings for him. How could I have avoided falling for someone so handsome and brilliant and worldly and principled? No, the craziest part is that he fell back.

We confessed to our mutual crush over text. There were so many texts by that point that I decided to get a separate cell phone. I guess the frequency of our contact, the intensity of the attraction, and the secrecy means it was technically an emotional affair. But neither Tarek nor I are the types to have a physical one.

He's helped me realize that I want to live much more simply than Greg ever would. My gut told me this wasn't my forever home; my time here is temporary. I've thought about offering Greg the option to buy me out but I know that he can't afford it. As much as he earns, he spends a ton, too. So at some point, once Lola has completely adjusted to the divorce, we'll sell this house. Then we can both start over. I'll be with Tarek, and Greg will find someone who wants to live as he does. In the long run, we'll both be better off.

I love the idea of Tarek becoming Lola's stepfather. He'd bring such a different perspective. He doesn't think wealth is about what you own; it's about what you can pay forward and how you can connect with other people. Meanwhile, Greg is materialistic and never acknowledges his privilege as a classically handsome white man. To hear him tell it, he's entirely self-made. Because of Greg, Lola's never even been on a camping trip, let alone done adventure travel. She and I both have so much to learn from Tarek.

Until Greg's recent conduct, I always thought so highly of him as a husband and a father; I just thought we'd ceased to be a match. Talking to Tarek made me see how little Greg and I have in common anymore, and how bored I've become by our conversations. I'd normalized my discontent. But the truth is, I was tired of being Greg's personal assistant at home while being revered in company. I don't want to hear about the blueprints and construction of a new mega-estate in Silicon Valley or San Francisco or Marin ever again.

Tarek genuinely, deeply cares about people, which is why he chose his vocation. Until very recently, I thought that Greg at the very least genuinely and deeply cared about me and about Lola. But with how dishonorably and callously he's behaving, it makes me wonder if these are new colors or true colors.

Since I started the separation process, he's been pretending that he respects my feelings and decisions but he's actually tried to undermine and devalue them at every turn. He doesn't care what I want. What he wants is to have a sweet little wifey stand on a pedestal and manage his whole life for him.

That's not for me, not anymore. I want a full partnership, and with Tarek, I can have that.

Greg probably thought that by confronting me about Tarek, he'd seize control of the situation. He expects me to cower and retreat. But I've allowed his wishes to supersede mine for long enough. Since he knows about Tarek, I have nothing left to hide. Greg's little gambit just backfired, big time.

I grab my phone and text Tarek: *The wait is over*.

TWENTY-FOUR

GREG

"I thought it might be better to meet in person," Lucas says. "Could I come in?"

"This is extremely unprofessional," I huff, barring the door. Really, Lucas has always been the consummate professional, and he's right to be concerned about my limited output. But I'm his boss and mentor, he's always looked up to me, so there's no way I can let him into my apartment.

The bourbon is sitting right out on the table, uncapped, with a half-full highball glass beside it. The place looks as ravaged as I do. The cleaners come tomorrow, before Lola arrives. It might sound dramatic but she's all I'm living for these days. Work feels irrelevant, to borrow Madeline's word. It was enraging, the way she kept downplaying the significance of the other man, even though he's obviously the real reason she ended our marriage.

Tried to end our marriage. It's not done yet.

"I'm sorry," Lucas says. As usual, he's perfectly coiffed, shaven, and bespoke (I have no idea how he affords those clothes on the amount I'm paying him). He graduated summa from Harvard but he practically begged for the assistant job, saying he'd give anything to be my protégé and learn from my genius. "The Tramboni Center is perfection," he'd said, his eyes shining, and I'd hired him on the spot. He hasn't disappointed.

I have. "I'm the one who's sorry," I say. "I know it hasn't been easy for you these past weeks, dealing with me and with all the clients."

"It hasn't," he responds, with his trademark earnestness. "But it must be way worse for you."

His simple compassion has me on the verge of tears. That's what's been missing from all my interactions with Madeline. She doesn't give a shit if I live or die anymore, now that she has what's-his-face.

Esther Kahn has filed a motion for temporary child support and spousal support that's downright vindictive, using high-handed language to in essence call me a liar and a manipulator. It says that the respondent (i.e. me) is intentionally and unreasonably prolonging litigation so she's asking that I be responsible for her fees. Meanwhile, my own billable hours have dwindled to almost nothing ever since I found out about Madeline's betrayal. She should be the one paying me.

"I've got drafter's block," I say. "I'm out of ideas."

"Have you looked over old plans for inspiration?"

I shake my head. "That's not how I work. I can't give Peter Tramboni some pastiche for his private island. That house needs to be a masterpiece."

"Could you skip that for the time being? Go to the next project and then circle back."

"That's not how I work," I repeat.

"Maybe it's how you need to work for now?" Lucas suggests delicately. "And I'd be more than happy to try my hand at some designs in my off-hours. If you decide any of it's usable, then you pay me."

"You mean I'd pass off your designs as my own?"

"You'd just be incorporating some of my ideas as a jump-start. A way to spur your creativity. I've been studying at your side for almost two years now. I'd appreciate the opportunity to demonstrate all I've learned. It would be an honor to collaborate." Sometimes he speaks like a nineteenth-century butler. I don't know if he comes from a lot of money (he doesn't volunteer personal details) or if that kind of obsequiousness is bred into them at Harvard.

But I had promised him a chance to be an associate at some point and instead, he's a glorified project manager, without the glory. "Let me think about it."

He smiles. "Is there anything I can do while I'm here? As you probably know by now, I'm good at cleaning up messes."

Is he actually suggesting that he cleans my apartment? I guess I haven't obstructed his view of the interior well enough. I flush. "Thank you, but I'll be fine."

It's mortifying to be seen in this state, especially by Lucas. As he's said on more than one occasion, I'm his idol. Working remotely was supposed to preserve that image. Usually, we only meet in person at clients' homes and future building sites. To borrow another Madeline word, it's all about boundaries. While I know he means well, showing up here was definitely a breach.

"I appreciate your concern and your dedication," I say, "but don't do this again."

"My apologies." Though I notice he doesn't seem at all chastened. "Please consider my offer. This could be great for us both. A true win-win."

Once I've shut the door behind him, I collapse onto my couch. It's stiff and uncomfortable, like so much expensive furniture is. I should have just bought everything from IKEA, but Sidney had been so insistent and I wanted to keep Madeline's best friend close. I thought I might need her someday.

She's been texting me, doing welfare checks. I text back enough to maintain the connection, such as it is, to let her know that I'm not completely breaking down but I'm not well either. I guess you could say I'm stringing her along. She asked if she could hang out with Lola and me this weekend. I said I'd think about it but I'm leaning toward no. Sidney means well (she probably just wants to make sure Lola's okay) but I imagine she'd report back whatever she sees to Madeline. After all, she told me flat-out that Madeline's the priority. How did she put it? Madeline gets custody of her in the divorce.

Hugh says I shouldn't worry about the motion that Madeline's lawyer filed. It's not an emergency and hasn't even been calendared by the court yet. With how overloaded the system is, it won't be considered for at least six weeks.

The money isn't my big worry. Maybe it should be since I have a definite cash flow problem but that's not why I halved Madeline's payment this month. I'd followed Hugh's recommendation in a fit of pique, wanting to punish her. Now I'm regretting it.

That motion and the co-parenting session both serve to highlight the dangerous game I'm playing. I could be damaging my credibility with the court and my relationship with Madeline. I should just give her the rest of the money. In other words, admit defeat. Stop dragging my feet and delaying the inevitable. She doesn't want me anymore; she wants him, whoever he is.

But the thought of rolling over, just letting him have her... Maybe the problem isn't that I've been too hard on her but rather, the inverse. I vacated that house—my house—way too easily.

It was the story of our marriage and now it'll be the story of our divorce. I've been railroaded all along. With that soft, measured tone of hers, that way she has of seeming like the most reasonable person alive, she convinced me at every turn that what's right for her is what's right, period. That house was the one time I dug in my heels, and she's never forgiven me for it.

Despite everything, the fact remains that I love her. That I want her. That I'm lost without her.

Whoever that other guy is, he can't possibly feel for her what I do. He hasn't built his life around her; they don't have a family.

Without knowing anything about him, I don't see how I can compete. And until I can compete, I need to make sure that I do no further harm. Sitting tight has never been my style but it's time for a change in tactics.

First, I'll need to cancel the next co-parenting session. Then I start looking for private investigators. And from there, who knows? Depends what I find out. But one thing's for sure: Nobody fucks with my family.

TWENTY-FIVE

MADELINE

"I really do love it here," Sidney says with a contented sigh, gazing out from the balcony at the view that first I stopped seeing and now I actively resent. The sprawl of the houses below, and the indifferent bay. I'm like a princess imprisoned in a tower.

"It's beautiful," I say mechanically. I tear a hunk off my bagel and pop it in my mouth for an aggressive chew. Bagels and mimosas, the laziest (and cheapest) entertaining ever, the province of best friendship.

"Are you mad at me?"

"No!" But she is picking up a certain undercurrent. She just hasn't seemed appropriately outraged by Greg's behavior in co-parenting counseling (thankfully he cancelled this week's session, which I noted in my daily record). Sidney is sympathetic to me but she's not unsympathetic to him.

I get it, she's walking a fine line. She wants everything to be civil between Greg and me since that's what's best for Lola, and Sidney takes her role as Lola's godmother very seriously. Which I appreciate. But is a little outrage really too much to ask, at this juncture?

"You're not mad at me," Sidney says, "but you are mad."

"Of course. Greg blindsided me about Tarek in front of Dr. Vaughn, and he's trying to bankrupt me. What's next? He's like a viper waiting to strike."

"You're hardly going to wind up destitute. Just consider the equity in this house. And to play devil's advocate for a second, how would you have preferred that he handle the Tarek thing? I mean, he wasn't going to ask you during a drop-off or a pick-up with Lola there, and you don't really talk any other time. Did you want him to text you through the app?"

"He could have texted me through the app and asked to meet up." Is she being deliberately dense? "He wanted me to look like a cheater in front of Dr. Vaughn, and he succeeded. I could tell by the way she looked at me."

"Isn't being non-judgmental in her job description?"

"She might not be amazing at her job." I've tried not to badmouth Dr. Vaughn to Sidney because I don't want her to feel guilty for having steered me wrong. But oh boy, was she wrong. "I didn't want to face it either, but the clues are really adding up. In light of Greg's behavior, I can't help questioning a lot of what really went on in our marriage."

Sidney sets down her bagel, and the expression that flits across her face—it's as if she's lost her appetite. It seems a touch dramatic. I mean, it's not her husband we're talking about. We're never talking about her husband because they have the perfect marriage. Because he's hardly ever around. She's basically a work widow, except for all those sexy, exotic trips they take around the world.

Which means she can't possibly understand what I'm going through.

"How's everything with Jared?" I ask.

"Really good. He's in Belgium right now. He asked if I could join him for a few days but I'm too slammed with a design project. We'll do Prague together next month."

I wonder what Sidney would say about the kind of travel that Tarek enjoys. With her and Jared, it's five star all the way. Jared is in finance and makes ungodly amounts of money. Tarek would say that Jared is a prime example of a broken system. Double dates might be awkward. Fortunately, with Jared's travel schedule, double dates were rare even when I was with Greg.

Part of me wants to bring Greg up again because his antics and the resulting stress they've caused are never far from my mind. But even though Sidney has been there since the beginning, since the very night Greg and I met, she might not be the best confidante. While early on, she had her concerns about him and the relationship, she's since decided to latch onto the narrative of the golden couple. She wants to stay in denial just like Greg, and she's been upfront with me about the fact that she's continuing to check up on him. I don't like imagining their conversations. An irrational part of me would like my best friend to be firmly on my side. To see only my side.

So I've decided not to tell her that I'm back in touch with Tarek. If Dr. Vaughn couldn't contain her judgment despite years of training, then Sidney probably won't be able to either. Not that she'd ever express it outright but it would be there between us, festering. And what if it happened to slip out when Sidney talks to Greg?

No, Sidney can't know, and neither can Esther. I'm keeping it just between Tarek and me, our delicious little secret.

On the face of things, it's been entirely innocent. I mean, it doesn't get much less romantic than a Starbucks in Benicia. But Tarek made that setting feel nearly magical. I'd established the ground rules ahead of time—no touching of any kind, not even a hug hello or goodbye—and we both followed them. In some ways, it made the sexual tension, the anticipation, even more acute. Our connection is still there. If anything, it's grown stronger.

I told him how well Lola is doing, and that the one who hasn't adjusted is Greg. Tarek provided all the validation and commiseration I could have hoped for. He understands that I never wanted to hurt Greg, that I've taken pains to avoid that. It meant everything to be affirmed by someone as principled and decent as Tarek.

"Loving someone is never wrong," he said. "It's about the path you take to be together. I'm proud of our path so far."

I wanted so badly to reach for his hand, and I could tell he felt the same. "I'm proud, too. But I hope it won't take much longer. I mean, I'm separated. Greg knows you exist. We can't be far off."

Tarek smiled. "No, we can't."

When I think of my future with Tarek, I feel so much optimism and buoyancy. I wish I could share that with Sidney but it's too fraught. She's my number one collateral contact, a character witness who's known me for the past twenty years and witnessed my unwavering devotion to my daughter for the past ten.

She's also continuing to witness Greg. I know she wants to see the good in him but, sooner or later, she's going to have to admit the truth. For now, she's my woman on the inside, my eyes and ears. I trust her to tell me if she sees anything concerning between Greg and Lola. First, I'll document, and later, she might need to testify.

It's beyond uncomfortable, having an ulterior motive when it comes to my relationship with Sidney. I don't like using my best friend but what choice do I have? Greg's forced my hand.

TWENTY-SIX

GREG

"I'm glad you finally called me back." Sidney's tone is playful but it's hard for me to read her expression, given that I'm squinting into the sun. This is the kind of bright, warm day that has everyone around us exulting. The restaurant has its own outdoor bocce ball courts and a group of competitors are trash talking loudly and cracking themselves up with their witticisms. It's noxious.

Lola likes it, though. Sidney and I are taking a break from bocce and Lola's off rolling balls by herself, occasionally glancing over so that we can applaud her best shots.

"I haven't been calling anyone," I say. I run my hand through my hair. I missed my most recent cut and I feel border-line unkempt. But that might be more internal than external. I just can't seem to keep track of anything these days, probably because I don't care about anything these days. Other than Madeline and Lola, that is. At least one of them still cares about me, and she's right over there, jumping up and down.

"Have you thought about calling Madeline?" Sidney moves to take a sip of her beer, and I try not to gaze at it longingly as it makes its ascent to her mouth. I'm staying sober and keeping my wits about me, both for Lola and for this conversation. I don't want what I say to remain confidential; I'm hoping it'll get back to Madeline.

"Did she tell you that she wants that?" I raise an eyebrow both skeptically and hopefully.

She shakes her head. "It's probably a bad idea. Sometimes I just think that if you and Madeline spent time together like normal people, you'd remember that you are. Normal, I mean. That you don't have to be friends but you're not enemies."

"I'd love that. But she's insisting that all our communication goes through the co-parenting app. She gave her attorney viewing privileges." My frustration rises. "I just want the chance to show Madeline I'm still the man she married."

As Sidney nods in empathy, a strand of her long auburn-dyed hair attaches itself to her lipstick. She's always highly made up, not like Madeline, who's a natural beauty. "Madeline's shutting down. She was really hurt that you didn't speak to her privately about Tarek, that you brought him up in front of Dr. Vaughn."

"Tarek?" I say, like I'm having trouble placing the name, like I don't think he's behind everything. Meanwhile, the private detective I hired is currently conducting a background check.

"Daddy! Aunt Sidney!" Lola waves her arms frantically. "Look!" We look, and whoop. She does a bow and then goes to pick up all the balls so she can play again.

The smile dies on my lips as I turn back to Sidney. "So this guy, this Tarek—what's really going on with him and Madeline?"

"It's true, what she told you. She and Tarek haven't slept together." Is a "yet" hanging in the air? "She's tried to be honest about everything. She didn't end your marriage because of someone else, she ended it because—"

"*Tried* to be honest?" I can't stop myself from cutting her off.

"She has been honest."

"Did Madeline send you here to vouch for her?" And to spy on me and Lola?

"No. Absolutely not. She knows I'm here, though. I'm sure she wants me to take care of you since she knows she can't anymore. Deep down, she still cares about you, Greg. Very much."

"She loves me, she's just not in love with me," I mutter. "Noted."

"Are you still trying to get her back? Because I hate to be the bearer of bad news but that ship has sailed."

I don't care what Sidney says, or what Madeline says. If Tarek hadn't been in the picture, Madeline would have at least been willing to do couples therapy. Instead of trying to be honest, she would have tried to save our marriage. This isn't about self-discovery or exploration or whatever Madeline was claiming to Dr. Vaughn.

"I'm not trying to get her back," I lie. That's the message I want Sidney to transmit. Let Madeline think I've given up, that my ship has sailed. She's felt firmly in control this whole time, knowing that I'm the pursuer and she's the object of my desire. This could change the dynamics completely.

That, and me finding out who Tarek really is. Then I can destroy his burgeoning romance with my wife, and she'll start thinking straight again.

"Good." Sidney appears relieved. "Everything will go much smoother if you can accept the way things really are. Then the two of you can stop fighting and start talking again. You'll be able to iron this out in no time." She does a brilliant smile just as the nachos arrive. She turns it on the server. "Thanks so much!" She grabs a chip. "This place has the best guacamole."

I put some food on my plate just for something to do but I

know that my stomach will revolt at the first bite. "I really appreciate your optimism." Then I shout, "Lola! Nachos!"

"Yay!" she calls back. "Be there in a minute!"

Sidney smiles fondly at her, and then at me. "Who wouldn't be optimistic after seeing you and Madeline together all these years, and seeing you with Lola? You're both great parents, in your own ways."

That's music to my ears. Hugh's been warning me that Madeline and I are now in a competition to woo the people in our lives who've observed us, especially with Lola. I would have thought that in the case of Sidney, I'm a distant second to Madeline. But it seems like I might have a chance.

According to Hugh, the challenge for me is that everyone knows Madeline so much better. She's always been in closer contact with teachers, coaches, and the parents of Lola's friends. She does all the arranging, and apparently that's pretty important when we could be heading to court. It makes her look involved and makes me look detached.

On the flip side, no one will have much negative to say about me either. Madeline can occasionally rub people the wrong way by seeming too perfect; on rare occasions, she can be condescending. The wives in the couples that we used to spend time with made occasional joking comments to that effect. If this progresses to a full-on battle, I'll make sure to reach back out to them and see if they might be willing to talk to Hugh.

Sidney would be a much bigger get, though. If Madeline's oldest friend is willing to testify on my behalf, that would have to be pretty compelling to a judge.

The thing is, Madeline was the perfect wife for me, more or less, until Tarek came along. Which is why I can't rule out any strategies at this point. I have to put my family back together. For me, for Lola, and for Madeline (even if she can't see that right now).

I'm still hoping she'll come to her senses before this reaches the court. But if I need to use what I know—including her forgetting to pick up our kid, including Tarek, including everything that came long before him and even before me—then that's what I'll do.

Winning Madeline back is the best-case scenario. But I will not lose Lola.

TWENTY-SEVEN

MADELINE

I send Greg a text through the app saying that I'll need to cancel the next co-parenting session. I don't give a reason. After all, he didn't when he cancelled last week. I'm grateful to him for opening that door; I wouldn't have dared to be first for fear of seeming uncooperative.

I reach out to Dr. Vaughn separately, leaving her a voicemail that says how very much I appreciate her work and that I look forward to seeing her soon. "I'm just focusing on my self-care right now," I say. "I'm still recovering from how aggressive Greg was the last time I was in your office. I want to get back to a place of trust and safety with him. It's not going to be easy but I'm determined to do it, for Lola's sake. Thank you so much for all your help."

We should talk, just the two of us, Greg texts, outside of the app. *Let's meet up.*

Has he lost his mind, or is he just playing dumb? Or could he be playing some game I can't fathom? I text him back, via the app: *It's not a good idea for us to meet up on our own.*

Again, he texts normally: *If we're going to unfuck this situation, it'll be on our own.*

I need you to use the app.

So Esther can read over our shoulders? We don't need adult supervision. The lawyers are just making everything worse.

His is making everything worse, that's for sure.

Back on the app, I issue a warning: *Please use this app exclusively. I won't respond to messages sent by any other means.*

Seriously, Madeline? Well, at least he's following directions. That was in the app.

Please watch your tone, Greg. Taking the high road can be a little bit fun. *To reiterate, I won't be meeting you privately. Negotiations about the settlement will be done through our attorneys. Communication about Lola must occur through this app. More extensive conversations about her will happen in the next co-parenting session.*

There's a long pause. I wonder if he's deciding whether to defy me or not. He stays on the app: *Is this really how you want it, Mads?*

I feel a jab of sadness. Is he feeling that, too? *It's how it needs to be.*

It's like we're headed for some kind of showdown. His tone is inscrutable. I don't know if that was an expression of regret or a threat. But if I asked, I wouldn't believe his answer.

If I had my way, we would have wrapped this up weeks ago, I remind him.

He doesn't respond, not even to say goodbye. Maybe that's what does it, what convinces me that it was a threat, what pushes me over the edge. I text Bliss's mother, Morgan. Bliss and Lola have been best friends for years, and I used to be close-ish with Morgan; we were coffee friends and couple friends. Since the separation, Morgan's distanced herself, like they all have. She's never overtly rude or even chilly; she's just always in a rush, was always just about to text me back but then, you know, life!

I ran into her yesterday when I picked Lola up at soccer. Lola and Bliss accosted us both, begging for a sleepover. Morgan said, "I'll host, what with, you know, everything on your end." She told me to text her some dates, and I'd been planning to tell her my weekend nights with Lola. Now, instead, I text her with Greg's.

She responds quickly and I imagine that's not out of respect for me but that Bliss must be nagging her. During the exchange, I make sure to hint that co-parenting with Greg has been a challenge—*you know how he is with work, how he loses track of time, he's just so passionate,* etc.—to reinforce the impression that I'm the responsible one and Greg's flighty. I need that to be top of mind for Morgan since she's one of the names on my collateral contact list for Esther. I also suspect that she'll disseminate it to some of the other female names from that list.

On the co-parenting app, I message Greg, leading with an apology and a commitment to protecting his time with Lola going forward. *That's the date Morgan gave me. Otherwise, Bliss isn't available for another month, and you know how much Lola wants this sleepover.*

Maybe Bliss can sleep over at my place.

Morgan specifically said she wanted to host. That part, at least, is true.

Fine. But this better not happen again. See, there it is. The threat. I hadn't imagined it earlier, which makes me feel thoroughly vindicated in taking this action (though I'm not about to mention any of this pettiness to Tarek). While it's become necessary, I'm not proud of it.

It won't happen again, I write. *Not if I can help it.*

TWENTY-EIGHT

GREG

Antonio Fognini (pronounced Foe-Nee-Nee) has a fancy name and an accent that even the straightest man in America would admit is a thing of beauty. But he's all business. He didn't bat an eyelash at my disaster area of an apartment, and he waves aside all bellyaching, editorializing, and rationalizing.

I haven't told Hugh about Antonio. Hugh's all about what we can use against Madeline when we get to court, and that's not what this background check is about. I need to know who Tarek Nabil really is, what kind of man is likely to be around my daughter.

I already know the most important fact—that he's a home-wrecker—but obviously, that doesn't bother Madeline any. There must be something from Tarek's past that Madeline isn't aware of, something I can use to sever their connection.

"So what's the dirt?" I ask Antonio.

"Unfortunately," Antonio says, "this man Nabil is very clean."

"Then you must not have dug deep enough. I've got plenty of money, and I'll pay whatever I have to."

Antonio raises a hand. "Please. Save your money. I'm not

traveling to some of the countries where this man has lived, voluntarily. He's a saint."

"Jesus Christ!" I rake my hand through my too-long hair. I need to remember to call my stylist for a house call, but everything's fallen through the cracks. I wiped my ass with a coffee filter this morning. I need Madeline. "You can't be serious."

His face is somber. "I went to L.A. and learned everything about this man's childhood through early adulthood. People were only too eager to talk about him and sing his praises. His preschool teachers remember him. His professors at UC Irvine remember him. His supervisors at Doctors Without Borders—"

"He's a doctor?"

"A nurse. He was a visiting nurse at your wife's clinic last year, which is how they met. Everyone at the clinic—"

"Sings his praises. I get it." I stare at him in frustration. "It's got to be a trick. No one's that perfect."

"Most people are not that perfect," Antonio allows. "But a few are."

"You really think that Madeline's fucking around on me with a saintly unicorn?" Unbelievable.

Antonio spreads his hands wide, palms upturned.

"Dig deeper. I mean, everyone thinks I'm perfect. They think Madeline's perfect. It's all a lie."

"So you think that if I did a background check on you, it would come back clean?" He raises an eyebrow. "No one would have a negative thing to say?"

"Well, Madeline would, now." And possibly a few of my clients but those guys are assholes. Sidney likes me better than she ever has. Then there's Lola. Lola loves me to the moon and back, like the kids' book says.

"This man, Nabil, turned down a family business that is worth millions. All his siblings make hundreds of thousands a year, doing very little from what I can tell, and Nabil refuses to participate. He wants to do good in the world instead. He's delivered vaccines and medicines to the sick. He's willingly worked with Ebola patients." Antonio is staring at me sternly. "Are you hearing me?"

"I'm hearing you." But I'm not drawing the same conclusion. I mean, working with Ebola patients might just mean he has a savior complex.

"This man Nabil is—"

"You're talking like you're his biggest fan! He's not Mother-fucking-Teresa!" I glare. "Your man Nabil is doing some crazy voodoo magic on everyone he meets. He's like a cult leader or something." Which is a little bit reassuring, actually. Madeline's under a spell that can be broken. "He must have brainwashed Madeine because cheating—even if it's only an emotional affair—is not in her DNA. This isn't her."

Antonio nods mildly.

"What, you don't believe me?"

"Do you want me to do a background check on Madeline? There could be things you don't know about her that could offer an explanation. Things you didn't know about your own marriage. It's hard to see it while you're living it."

"You're asking if I want to commission a background check on my marriage?" I ask incredulously.

He does a small shrug. "It's not a bad idea, since you're headed to court. I'm sometimes hired by attorneys to do background checks on their clients, to make sure there aren't any surprises."

If Hugh Warshaw's got some PI tailing me without my consent, he's fired.

"So you don't want to do any more research into Tarek," I sum up. "Instead, you're proposing that I pay you for a background check on Madeline, on me, and on our marriage?"

"It's not a bad idea, as I said, but I don't make propositions."

"I don't see how any of that will get my wife back." It could make it so that I don't want her back, though. But I do want my old life back, pronto.

He stands up. "It might provide answers as to how you got here. That can help with grief, and moving on."

I'm not interested in those kinds of answers. This is just a blip. A hiatus. An interruption in the regularly scheduled programming.

Speaking of which, Madeline's cutting into my parenting time for next weekend since she scheduled that sleepover with Bliss. I made it clear that I'm not putting up with that again. I need more time with Lola, not less.

Antonio sees himself out. Frustrated, I pour myself a drink. I hadn't even considered that the background check might be a dead end but, in a way, this makes sense. How could I have competed with a saint/cult leader? This wasn't my fault or Madeline's. My enemy is Tarek.

His infiltration took place over months. There were times when I noticed she seemed distant or easily irritated and I asked if there was anything she needed to talk about. She always said no, and for the next few days, she'd be extra nice. I trusted her completely. Never even suspected.

I can't make those kinds of mistakes anymore. What's that saying: Hope for the best, prepare for the worst?

Madeline's closer to Bliss's mom, Morgan, but I've always gotten along well with the dad, Sandy. I scroll through my phone, searching for his contact information. That's been one of my problems, that Madeline's got everything at her fingertips. Early in the separation, I could have just asked her for the contacts but that time is long past.

There he is, like a beacon in the darkness. Sandy gave me his number because he's a senior developer who hates his company and would love to make a change but tech is a young man's game and he's north of forty-five (he had Bliss late). The man sure can ramble. Anyway, the point is, he's always wanted to have a personal connection to Peter Tramboni.

I can't exactly make an introduction—Peter doesn't deal with HR matters and couldn't give a shit less about senior developers and, besides, I've been avoiding him for days—but I can at least bait a hook for Sandy. Hint at a little quid pro quo where he helps me out with an affidavit or whatever Hugh needs and I try to further his career prospects. And while we're in communication, I could mention how much I'm hurting, drop the tidbit that there's likely another man involved in my divorce. Once Sandy tells Morgan and she tells the other moms, they won't be lining up to rave about Madeline's parenting skills anymore.

Since I can't tarnish Tarek in Madeline's eyes, I might be forced to tarnish Madeline in everyone else's. It's only fair.

TWENTY-NINE

MADELINE

"Dr. Stanton?"

I look up, realizing that it's probably not the first time Pru's said my name. She's at my office door wearing Snoopy scrubs, which makes my recent thoughts feel even more unseemly. "Sorry," I say, with a rueful smile. "I was somewhere else for a minute there."

All day, I've found myself getting lost in soft-focus reveries —okay, soft-focus porn—about last night with Tarek. After three meetings where we kept our hands to ourselves, we hadn't been able to hold back any longer. It felt like I was in a self-driving car that was on autopilot. It didn't feel volitional. It felt preordained. Necessary.

I took precautions, of course. Lola was with Greg, and Tarek lives in a shitty Oakland neighborhood where no one I know would ever go. The seediness worked for me. It was a huge turn-on, the fact that Tarek was born into wealth but has rejected its trappings. He's the anti-Greg.

I can have orgasms with Greg if I work hard enough. But with Tarek, they're effortless, cascading one after the other. I've never felt this way with anyone in my entire life. I didn't think I was capable of a passion that turned my body to mush at night, and my brain to mush all the next day. I'm glad that my patients have been straightforward cases, with no advanced thinking required.

My other secret? That I kind of love having a secret.

I'm going to remain the soul of discretion. I'll only see Tarek when Lola's away and it'll always be at his place, never at the house. I won't even tell Sidney. While I know she'd never out me to Greg on purpose, I don't want her to be in the position of seeing him while possessing that knowledge. She's never had a poker face.

What it comes down to is that I can't trust Greg at all. Our most recent co-parenting session was cagey bullshit. Esther said that as stressed as I am about finances these days, I can't mention it in session. I don't want to run the risk of Dr. Vaughn thinking I care more about money than about my child. And Hugh Warshaw must have finally given Greg a lecture on impression management. The two of us were both campaigning for the title of Most Cooperative Parent as awarded by Dr. Vaughn while we discussed soccer games and scheduling. He didn't complain about the sleepover being on his night but he made sure to mention it. For my part, I made sure to apologize and reiterate my commitment to his bond with Lola. It was hard not to gag.

Sidney told me that Greg's not trying to win me back anymore, and it showed. On the one hand, that's a relief; on the other, it might mean he has nothing left to lose. If he's stopped using co-parenting counseling to get back into my good graces, then he must be using it to get into Dr. Vaughn's. He's preparing for battle, lining up his collateral contacts, same as me.

THIRTY

GREG

"So none of the issues have been decided?" The family law facilitator has the very cool name of Zane, and there's nothing else cool about him. He's maybe in his thirties with thinning, wispy hair, and a high, reedy voice. He's officious, peering frequently at the paperwork in front of him with tortoiseshell glasses that keep sliding down his nose. He might be trying to avoid eye contact. I don't blame him. The tension in the room is thick.

"That's correct," Esther Kahn confirms. She seems like another version of Madeline: expensively dressed, composed, soft-spoken but steely. Women of indeterminate age scare me a little.

Hugh said there's no need to fear the mandatory status conference. It's just a way for the judge to get an update on our situation and that information will then be used for scheduling court dates. In some cases, Hugh said, issues can be resolved during the conference; in our case, that's not going to happen. We're standing firm so that Madeline realizes that she'd rather reconcile than fight. Despite everything, I know she still loves me. Tarek's temporarily clouded her judgment, that's all.

Madeline, Esther, Hugh, and I were ordered to meet at the family law facilitator's office. The conference room has wood-paneled walls and a cheap lacquer eight-person table. I'm across from Madeline; Hugh's across from Esther; and Zane is on the end. I keep trying to meet Madeline's eyes but she's not having it.

"You haven't agreed on spousal support, child support, or a parenting plan?" Zane asks. Even if I hadn't been told ahead of time that he's not the judge, that he wields no actual power and is more of a bureaucrat, it would be obvious from his demeanor.

"That's correct," Hugh says. His voice comes out too loud, and I wince. Compared to Esther and Madeline, he seems gauche. If we ever get to court, I worry about the optics of him versus Esther, her polish next to his rough edges. "The plaintiff has been coercive toward the respondent since she first spoke with him about separating. That trend has continued throughout these proceedings."

"Could you be more specific, please?" Esther says.

"The plaintiff knew my client was desperate to curry her favor and would have signed anything. She pressed that advantage to the hilt. The supposed 'agreement' was all to her benefit."

"We're not here to adjudicate—" Zane begins.

"Respondent and his attorney have attempted to paint my client in a false and unflattering light throughout these proceedings," Esther says, "and apparently, that 'trend' will continue here today." You can intuit the derisive air quotes around the word "trend" though her voice never changes. She's going to run circles around him in front of a judge, I can feel it.

I glance at Madeline. She can feel it, too. Nothing in her face or posture has shifted, yet I know that she knows.

"My client has wanted a fair, amicable, and expeditious settlement since the beginning," Esther says. "My attempts to reach that settlement have been thwarted at every turn."

Hugh snorts. He looks at me like we're in it together, which unfortunately we are. "So I've been thwarting her? That's what she calls fighting for my client's best interest?"

"My understanding is that the plaintiff is living in the marital home," Zane says. "Is that correct?"

"Correct," Esther says.

"So that issue has been settled?"

"Yes," Esther says. Hugh makes a noise that could mean "not so fast," and Esther's head swivels toward him. "If there's a problem on that front, this is the first I'm hearing of it."

"We're reserving the right to renegotiate," Hugh says.

Now Madeline is staring at me. I look down.

"This is the first I'm hearing of this, too," Madeline says.

"Your client wants my client to move out so that he can move in?" Esther asks Hugh. "Or he wants her to move out so that he can sell it?"

"We're reserving the right to renegotiate," Hugh repeats. Madeline suddenly looks upbeat, as if selling the house would be the answer to her prayers.

Esther addresses Zane. "This is why my recent motion requested relief in the form of damages. It seems that Mr. Warshaw's client doesn't have any preferences of his own. Instead, he prefers to have my client state hers so that he can block them. It's about retribution."

"Please," Zane says. "Let's avoid any inflammatory rhetoric. What I'd like to establish is whether the two parties are close on any of the issues."

"I would love that," Esther answers. "Because I can't tell precisely where respondent stands on any issue, only that it's in opposition to plaintiff. He's failed to produce paperwork for much of our negotiation and Mr. Warshaw has insisted on speaking in generalities."

"But you've got all the paperwork now, don't you?" Hugh rejoins. "It's your client who hasn't budged."

"We haven't received any financials from the respondent's accountant. All we have are the spreadsheets made by my client, who refuses to accept less than she's entitled to by law. To be clear, she hasn't asked for a penny more." Esther looks to Zane. "The original agreement that she presented to the respondent before they ever consulted with attorneys was based on the California state formula. There was nothing irregular in it. It should have been signed off on weeks ago."

"Before she ever consulted with an attorney?" It just bursts out of me, unbidden. I stare at Madeline. "You consulted with Esther and three other attorneys months ago! Before you consulted with me. Before you even told me you were unhappy."

Madeline's face is expressionless. Shameless.

"You don't have anything to say to me?" My voice is a plaintive howl.

"This isn't the forum," Esther says. "Respondent is continuing his pattern of harassing, inappropriate behavior, using the co-parenting sessions for confrontations about non-parenting matters, sending texts outside of the approved app, demanding to meet up."

"I never demanded to meet up!" I only suggested it, based on Sidney's recommendation.

"Mr. Warshaw, please instruct your client not to address mine," Esther says.

"My client has only been trying to get proper answers from your client," Hugh says. "Your client's been dicking him around—"

"Oh, is that a legal term?" Esther asks.

"It's not the only dicking—" Hugh begins.

"Enough," Madeline says. I see a flicker of something in her face. Fear. She doesn't want Hugh talking about her affair. Is it possible that Esther Kahn doesn't know about it?

I decide to do her a favor. I'll save her one last time and

maybe then she'll see that Tarek can't possibly love her the way I do. He would never put up with a tenth of this shit.

"It is enough," I tell Hugh.

He says to Zane, "Let's wrap this up. You can let the court know we're not close on any issues, and we're coming their way. There's going to be a trial."

Now Madeline is looking at me with contained fury. I can't believe it after what I just did for her.

"What?" I snap. She shakes her head, refusing to engage. "You think it's my fault we're going to trial?"

"Cool it," Hugh says to me, under his breath, but of course they can all hear. Everyone knows that Madeline's always cool and I'm hot and that used to be what worked about us. She loved my passion because she had so little of her own. She needed my fire.

"You're the one who destroyed our family!" I tell her. "I've done nothing but cooperate! I moved out of my house because you asked me to! All this is your fucking fault!" I look at Zane. "Write that down and tell it to the judge!"

Madeline is back to ignoring me, as if I'm a toddler having a tantrum. Zane's uncomfortable, even Hugh seems slightly embarrassed but Esther, I can tell, is pleased.

I want to storm out of the room but that would only delight Esther. So instead, I sit and force myself to endure, to white-knuckle it just like I've been doing ever since Madeline told me our marriage was over.

Zane says that we'll be entering the discovery phase in preparation for trial. He explains to Madeline and me, "Discovery is when both sides will be able to examine evidence that the other considers pertinent to the case." He shuffles through his papers and begins reading. "California Code of Civil Procedure Section 2017.010 allows for discovery of anything, not protected by privilege, that is relevant to the subject matter involved in the pending action or to the determination of any motion made in that action, if the matter either is itself admissible in evidence or appears reasonably calculated to lead to the discovery of admissible evidence." I'd spaced out but he insists on making eye contact with Madeline and me in turn. "As in, nothing's really off-limits. So bear that in mind."

I cast a quick glance at Madeline, who's gazing at him like a woman with nothing to hide. She's always been so good at the Bambi routine, hasn't she?

I don't have much to fear—what you see is what you get, more or less—but she should be getting very worried right about now.

Or maybe she thinks that what she did to her father during her parents' divorce proceedings will never come out. She doesn't know that he told me one drunken night, in tears. He's never recovered from the betrayal. He begged me not to say anything to her, and I promised I wouldn't. I was true to my word, because I'm honorable like that.

California might be a no-fault state but I'm sure our judge would be very interested to know that Madeline once perjured herself in court. Goes to credibility, doesn't it?

I guess somehow I never thought so. I believed that what she'd done when she was sixteen had been purely situational. I was convinced that Madeline's the most upstanding person I knew. Hell, when I was running through possible reasons why she really wanted to end our marriage, they were all about my own failings. It never occurred to me that she could be coveting another man. Not my Madeline.

I'm such an idiot.

But Madeline's a liar and if I need to, I can prove it.

THIRTY-ONE

MADELINE

There is one lone folder on Esther's desk. It underscores the pristine nature of the space while also lending an air of foreboding to this conversation. Esther's not smiling.

"I just paid the mortgage," I say. "Out of my checking account. I'm getting worried about how soon I'll have to tap into my savings."

"We've been over this." She sounds impatient. Maybe even slightly annoyed? "You and Greg each said you'd be responsible for two credit cards each but if he doesn't want to play by the rules and honor the agreements, then you don't have to either. Your cards are joint, with high limits. Charge absolutely everything, including the mortgage payments. Then you only pay the minimums."

"I'm uncomfortable about what that would do to my credit score—"

Now she is visibly annoyed. She doesn't like being second-guessed. "I told you, once we win—if we win—we'll be able to get every penny back from Greg, plus penalties and interest. We'll make him pay."

I stare at her, my heart seizing with anxiety. "What do you

mean, if we win? I thought you were confident after seeing how he acted during the status conference."

She'd told me before the conference that it was unlikely that we'd settle, and that with Hugh Warshaw, it was bound to get ugly. I acquitted myself admirably under the circumstances, I think, in contrast to Greg. I'm not sure why I've been urgently summoned here to Esther's office just a few days later.

"Who's Tarek Nabil?" I can't help it, I flinch. "Mr. Warshaw and I had a conversation earlier today." Her tone is clipped, and somehow her use of "Mr." when it's just the two of us feels like a jab.

I've never said Tarek's name to Greg, and Sidney doesn't even know his full name (or that he and I have started sleeping together), so how did anything get back to Hugh Warshaw, and now Esther? I can't keep the stunned expression from my face.

"That's how I felt," Esther says.

"Tarek is a friend, that's all. We used to work together." This is as close to pissed as Esther gets so it's not the time for me to come clean. "Tarek's not relevant. How does Greg even know about him?"

"Maybe he's got a source inside your camp." I never thought of myself as having a camp. "Maybe he hired a private investigator. I thought I made it clear from the beginning that there should be no secrets between you and me."

"Tarek's not the reason that I asked Greg to move out. Absolutely nothing went on between us while Greg and I were still together." All technically true. I've watched enough legal TV shows and movies to know that you don't want to put your attorney in the position to lie. Keeping the facts properly curated is best for everyone.

Esther nods, somewhat placated. "I'm not surprised that Greg is the type who needs to think it's about another man. That protects his ego and gives him a villain. I'll tell you what I saw in that conference room: a narcissist who can't imagine or accept the idea that you want your own life. He can't stomach the possibility of you being happy with anyone other than him. He'll do anything he can to prevent that."

My stomach drops. I think—I hope—that she's wrong.

"Consider whether he fits the profile. An inflated sense of self-importance, an unwavering need for admiration, and an inability to empathize with others. Oh, also an inability to accept blame; everyone else needs to be wrong. A liar who can justify anything because it's for the greater good. *His* good."

I can't meet her eyes. Before the separation, I wouldn't have thought any of that described Greg. "No," I say weakly. "That's not Greg." It can't be. Things have gotten out of hand and we've both been engaging in some nasty behavior but no matter what, he's Lola's father. I'd never want to take her away from him entirely. If what Esther's saying is true, though...

"Not all narcissists are overt," she continues. "Sometimes they know how to hide in plain sight. You can tell that Greg thinks he's the victim in all this. What went on during that conference looked an awful lot like a narcissistic collapse."

"What's that?" I ask, afraid to hear the answer.

"It's when a narcissist's fantasies of himself are shattered by the reality that you exist as a separate person with boundaries. When he realizes he's all alone as the result of his own actions, he can't handle it. He detonates. And he wants to take everyone else down with him."

*

If someone had asked me a year, a month, a week, a day, or even hours before, "Would you kill someone?", I would have said, "No, of course not." I wouldn't have been lying either. Despite everything, it would have still seemed unfathomable until mere minutes before.

What people don't realize is that a split-second decision—a crime of passion—is all about the lead-up. It's about giving yourself permission to go a little further and a little further all the time. It's about the rationalizations and justifications and vilifications that have taken root in the fertile soil of your soul.

Would I ever kill again?

I want to say, "No, of course not," but how can I be sure?

DISCOVERY

THIRTY-TWO

GREG

"Lola is not okay," I tell Madeline and Dr. Vaughn.

I hope they aren't going to do their shtick where they act like two experts and I'm the novice. I'm just as much of a professional parent as Madeline is. I'm starting to think that she's always wanted me to feel inadequate. That way, she'd have the upper hand. She'd get the final say.

But not anymore. I've come into my own.

I knew that Lola was handling things too well. Extra shopping trips, restaurants, and paddleboards could only distract her for so long. I told Madeline that this day would come.

I hate watching Lola struggle. I never wanted her to pay the price for Madeline's selfishness. But I do feel some sense of vindication. See, Madeline? Everything can't work out to your exact specifications.

Ever since I witnessed how coldly vicious Madeline could be during that status conference, I've been drinking myself to sleep and drinking myself to wake. Lucas is doing an impressive job holding down the fort. His renderings have been excellent (if only because they're derivative of my own) and when I've shared them, the clients have been pleased. But I wouldn't dare pull that with Peter Tramboni. It's a combustible situation: I'm incapable of inspiration and he won't accept anything less than a masterpiece. Plus, he hates to wait. I can't fend him off much longer, so I temporarily dull that knowledge with alcohol.

Only I can't drink away that self-satisfied prick Tarek. I know what he looks like because Antonio gave me photos from the stakeout he conducted. I couldn't find anything online because Tarek is too pristine for an online footprint, too godly for social media. He's handsome, of course, as all Madeline's men have been, but that's where his resemblance to me ends. His hair, eyes, and skin are all dark, and his hair is long and glossy. He dresses in these sort of tunics in wicking fabrics like he might take an impromptu trek in the wilderness at any moment. While I have to work out for my physique (I haven't been so I'm losing muscle mass at an alarming rate and am fast on my way to a whiskey gut), Tarek is sinewy and fit in a way that looks effortless. He probably never has to exercise since he burns all his calories off through smug beneficence.

He can't be good. He's certainly not pure. I don't care how many orphans he's saved in Botswana, that doesn't mean he should get to pursue a married woman with impunity.

I want Madeline to look at him the way she was looking at me—looking through me—during that status conference. But how? So far, Antonio's been useless. I'm not giving up, though. Lola needs me to put our family back together. Her recent behavior attests to that.

"What do you mean, Lola's not okay?" Madeline's left eyebrow shoots up, a sign she's suspicious of me when she should be worried about our daughter.

"So you haven't noticed the changes?" I ask. Some pro she is.

"What kind of changes?" Dr. Vaughn's pen lowers over her notepad. She's been waiting weeks now for something worth writing down. I've never thought before what it must be like for her to work with us, how aggravating we must be.

How aggravating Madeline is. After all, she's the one who initiated counseling, and then thwarted it at every turn.

"Lola hasn't changed," Madeline says. "She's still doing well."

Enraging as her dismissal is, I can't let her rile me up the way she did at the status conference. "I'm not surprised that Madeline's missed the symptoms," I say mildly. "Lola told me how preoccupied her mom's been."

Madeline flushes, looking guilty as hell. "That's not true!"

See who's riled up now. "Are you calling our daughter a liar?"

She reddens further, probably recognizing her limited options: Either she calls Lola a liar, or she calls me a liar. Dr. Vaughn is unlikely to appreciate either. "I don't know why Lola said that," Madeline finally says. "But I'll talk about it with her later."

"I'm not sure that's the best idea," Dr. Vaughn says. "We don't want Lola to be put on the spot, or to feel like everything she tells one parent goes back to the other."

Ha! So Dr. Vaughn is questioning Madeline's judgment. Not that I brought this up to score points; I actually want us to work together and help Lola. Something's wrong, and Madeline's oblivious because all her attention is on Tarek.

"Aren't Greg and I supposed to be a united front?" Madeline asks Dr. Vaughn, sounding the teensiest bit annoyed at having her parental authority questioned.

"Lola is allowed to have feelings about one parent that she chooses to share with the other," Dr. Vaughn says.

"And when she chooses to share feelings," Madeline's tone is careful, "what is the other parent supposed to do?"

"You can validate her experiences while also expressing your confidence in the other parent's good intentions," Dr.

Vaughn answers. "Remind Lola that you each have her best interests in mind."

Madeline's face is so neutral that I take it for dubiousness. She doesn't believe I have Lola's best interests in mind, even though I'm the one who's been observant enough to see what she's going through.

"That's exactly what I did," I say. It's true, more or less.

"I'm wondering what preceded that comment from Lola," Madeline says. "She just volunteered out of the clear-blue sky that I've been preoccupied?"

"Yes, while I was tucking her in. Like I do every night she's with me."

"Apropos of nothing?" Madeline's got that left eyebrow cocked again. "You didn't elicit it in any way?" She glances at Dr. Vaughn. "I agree with you, Lola shouldn't be in the middle of this. Putting her there is a form of abuse."

"Hold up." I stare at her in amazement. "Are you accusing me of abusing Lola?"

"I never said that."

"No, you just heavily implied it."

Dr. Vaughn clicks her pen impatiently. "What kind of changes, Greg?"

"Lola's showing less interest in her schoolwork. She wants to do anything else. She might finally get through it but it takes a really long time and she doesn't enjoy it."

"When she's with me," Madeline says, "she does her schoolwork without arguing or procrastinating. It's about keeping to a certain schedule and conveying consistent expectations."

I'm nearly choking on her condescension. Dr. Vaughn is scribbling, saying nothing.

"This is nothing new," Madeline says. "I mean, Lola does really like certain subjects but there are others she just has to get through. School isn't always fun, and sometimes kids have to do things they don't want to do."

"I know that," I say. "But I'm talking about assignments and subjects that she should enjoy, like writing poetry."

"She likes prose more than poetry."

I turn to Dr. Vaughn in frustration. "I wanted to bring this up now before it becomes a bigger problem. Aren't we supposed to be alerting each other to any behavioral changes at home or at school? Isn't that what co-parenting counseling is for?"

"You are, and it is," Dr. Vaughn affirms.

"He only thinks this is a change because he's been so uninvolved for so long," Madeline says.

"That's not fair." I push it out through gritted teeth.

"He's never liked to do the hard stuff." Madeline's talking to Dr. Vaughn like I'm not even in the room. "He's pushing for more parenting time but what he really wants is to be the Disneyland Dad on the weekends. So why not stick to our original arrangement?"

"I'm not a Disneyland Dad." Sure, I prefer fun times with my kid to forcing her to do homework. Doesn't every parent?

"I wasn't going to bring this up but Lola's missed a few assignments on Greg's watch," Madeline says. I detect a gleam in her eyes; I've created the perfect opening for her to malign me without looking petty. "Like all children, Lola thrives in an environment with structure, discipline, and clear expectations."

"Let me guess. That's the environment you think you provide?" She's just so unbelievably transparent. I cast a quick glance at Dr. Vaughn. She has to be clocking this, right?

Dr. Vaughn is nodding. At Madeline.

"That's what I do provide," Madeline says. "I've spent years establishing effective habits and routines. I understand that it's all new to Greg."

"It's not all new." I push down my rising fury. "Have you really just erased me from our family life?"

"Come on, Greg." Madeline sounds gentle, like she hates to be the bearer of bad news. "We both know structure and discipline isn't your forte. You always had me at home for that, and Lucas at work. You're about ideas; I'm about follow-through."

"Let's be careful about generalizations—" Dr. Vaughn begins.

"You see this?" I ask her. "She's trying out arguments for court."

"I'm being honest." So now she cares about honesty?

"She's trying to make me look like... like..." I sputter.

"We both have to be honest about our strengths and weaknesses," Madeline says. "I've always been more academically minded while Greg wanted Lola to find her passion. He thinks it doesn't matter if she gets Bs if she's having fun playing soccer and hanging out with her friends. But we've chosen to raise her in the Bay Area, which is highly competitive, and I don't think it's acceptable for us to model laxity around responsibilities like homework."

Is "laxity" even a word? "Lola's always been self-motivated. The fact that she isn't currently is a symptom."

Madeline lets out a soft noise that is distinctly snort-like. She says to Dr. Vaughn, "What looks like self-motivation to him is what I call parenting. It's a careful system of rewards and natural consequences."

Dr. Vaughn is actually writing this down.

"Lola's changed," I say, "and I'm the only one who's noticed it because Madeline's been preoccupied."

"Untrue," she pronounces, but I spy just the tiniest crack in her veneer of calm.

Tarek. Fucking Tarek.

As in, she's fucking Tarek. I can see it, clear as day, and I'm going to prove it. Show who the liar is. Who the poor role model is.

But once she's out from under his spell, once she's turned back into the loving woman I married, I'm still open to rebuilding. That's the kind of loving man I am.

"Lola's symptoms are a natural result of the stress of the divorce," I say. "It was only a matter of time before they showed up."

"I think the only person having trouble with the divorce at this point is you," Madeline says.

I plow on, undeterred. "Having one home is superior to two. Yes, Madeline and I have different strengths and weaknesses. That's why we're a great team. Lola's always benefitted from the contrast."

"Do you see what I'm dealing with here?" Madeline asks Dr. Vaughn.

"I'm just saying that I'd still forgive you, despite everything. For Lola."

"What a generous offer." Madeline glares at me. "All this time, you've been portraying me as manipulative and controlling but you're the one who's made this process as difficult as possible so that I'd have no choice but to get back together with you. That's why you chose a bottom feeder like Hugh Warshaw to represent you instead of an attorney from my list."

"A list you personally selected so that I'd wind up with someone meek and pliant. You wanted this done in six months flat so you could be with Tarek." I decide to take a shot in the dark. "You've already been with Tarek. I can smell him on you."

Madeline blanches, and I see that I've scored a direct hit. But the ricochet is so painful that I wish I'd missed.

THIRTY-THREE

MADELINE

There's no way Greg can know that I've been sleeping with Tarek, not for sure. He has to be bluffing.

Except what did Esther say when we last met? That Greg might have hired a private investigator already, which would explain how he (and Hugh Warshaw) knew Tarek's last name.

I thought I was so smart. I've been so careful. Not careful enough, obviously.

For once in my life, I'd decided that I needed to take some risks. Playing it safe hasn't gotten me anywhere in this divorce, and Tarek's now the only thing keeping me afloat.

I knew he and I had a connection but I never expected it to manifest like this. We haven't "made love" once. It's far more raw, visceral, and pulse-pounding than that. It's like exorcising a demon, in the very best way. I've never acted like this before, like a woman possessed, not even in adolescence when my friends were masturbating with shower heads and hairbrushes (anything with a handle was pretty much fair game) and I was focused on studying. Back then, I was determined to be a good girl getting good grades because that would be the quickest path out. I didn't dream of opulence or even affluence; I just wanted to get to a place that was free of dirt, both literal and figurative. My parents' divorce hadn't improved either of their housekeeping. Instead, I had to go between two filthy apartments in the same nasty neighborhood, with two separate caregivers whose emotional range was from depressed to enraged. Divorce also failed to stop the shouting and the backbiting. What they each seemed to want more than happiness for themselves? Misery for the other. By that measure, they were both successes.

History can't possibly repeat itself. My station in life is vastly different. I have resources my parents could never have dreamed of. What happened to me will never happen to my child.

Greg doesn't know what he's talking about. Lola's fine. He's probably just inventing some bullshit to elevate himself in Dr. Vaughn's eyes, playing the role of concerned parent.

Could he possibly smell Tarek on me, though? I took a detour to Tarek's apartment before coming here and of course I showered but could a man as territorial as Greg simply know?

All my life, I've followed the rules. But for the past week, I've been sneaking over to Tarek's every chance I got, sometimes even creating chances. I cancelled patients so that I could have extended lunch hours or cut out of the office a little early for some late afternoon delight before picking up Lola. I just wanted something entirely my own, a bit of respite from all the stress I'm under. Is that really so wrong?

"We're here to talk about Lola," I say, keeping my voice perfectly steady. "And if Lola is experiencing symptoms—which is news to me—then it's only because Greg is dragging this out, clinging to his fantasy of reconciliation, still pretending we were some perfect match. What Lola needs is to abandon hope and adjust to the reality that her parents are divorcing. How can she do that if her father won't?" I look at him without a shred of love. "Accept reality, Greg. Stop wasting our time and money."

He looks to Dr. Vaughn. Of course he does. He's determined to manipulate at least one woman here today. "Madeline has always been an amazing wife. But she's become someone else. Tarek's turned her into someone else."

I hate hearing Tarek's name from Greg's lips. "I'm more myself than I've ever been. Greg has always seen what he wants to see. He thinks that since he's struggling, Lola must be, too. He can't tell where he ends and Lola—or I—begin."

He shakes his head. "That's not it."

"He needs this to be about another man," I tell Dr. Vaughn, "because he can't face that it's actually about him. It's about dynamics, Dr. Vaughn, just like you've always said. I've outgrown our dynamic but his ego won't let me go."

"You really think this is about my ego?" He seems genuinely flabbergasted. "You've humiliated me for months! You're sleeping with someone else and here I am, still willing to give you another chance—"

"I don't want another chance! I want out! And for your information, I did not have an affair while we were together. Even though I very much wanted to." Now he's refusing to look at me but he needs to finally hear this. The truth will set both of us free. "I'm in love with someone else, okay? Is that what you need to hear to move on with your life? Because I'm more than ready to move on with mine."

The mic has dropped. We're all speechless, including Dr. Vaughn.

"This isn't working," Greg says, in a broken voice just above a whisper. "It hurts too much, and we're not getting anywhere."

Good. I wanted him to be the one to say it. To call this thing off, like the uncooperative parent that he is. "He's right," I say. "This is only making things worse."

"She doesn't even want to talk about Lola," he says.

"I only want to talk about Lola!" I counter. "But I won't let him use her to advance his agenda. This is no longer a safe space."

"No, it isn't," he seconds.

At least we can agree on one thing. We can't bear to be in the same room anymore.

THIRTY-FOUR

GREG

Inside the sanctity of my car, I bash the steering wheel one two three times. I know pedestrians must be staring in at me. I can't care.

But I can't very well sit here losing my shit indefinitely, can I?

I pick up my phone and dial, knowing it's the wrong thing but that nothing's right. I'm not surprised to go straight to voicemail.

"I shouldn't be calling you," I say. "I just don't have anyone else. Madeline kept the friends in the divorce, like women always do, and she's probably got the coach and the teachers and Dr. Vaughn on her side. Soon enough, she'll be telling you what a liar I am, that I just made up things about Lola in our session, but I swear to you, I'm not making it up. Lola's in trouble, and Madeline doesn't want to see it. She's blind from..." I'm about to say "love goggles" or "sex goggles" but then I stop myself. Insulting Madeline to her best friend would not be a good look right now.

"Maybe you see it, though? Maybe Lola's told you what she's feeling?" I pause. "I know you love Lola and that the two of you have heart-to-hearts. Lola and I really need you, you know?" My voice breaks, just like it did during the session. Madeline had been completely inured, but Sidney is her own person, not Madeline's puppet. "Things are going from bad to worse between Madeline and me, and I'm scared for Lola. I don't want to lose my family but I'm starting to think there's nothing I can do.

"I know you've told me that before, that I should just give up and move on, and Madeline's been saying it this whole time. But what about Lola? That's the real question. What about Lola?" It comes out loud enough that passersby turn to gawk at me.

I lower my voice. "I'm the only one who can protect her, Sid. That's what it means to be a parent. You'll stop at nothing."

THIRTY-FIVE

MADELINE

As I stride toward my car, I'm already dialing Esther's number. It feels like a weight has been lifted. The gloves can truly come off. You can't save a man from himself.

While I wish it could have been different—quick, clean, and respectful has been my preference all along—I've always appreciated clarity of purpose. Greg's my adversary now, plain and simple.

"Hi, Esther," I say. "I just had my last co-parenting session. As you know, I've been wanting out for a while now but I couldn't be the one to say it because of the optics. Fortunately, Greg was the one who called it." I describe what happened. Really, it was just the right note to end on, Greg suggesting termination after another of his hissy fits and a failed attempt to gaslight me.

How dare he use Lola like that, inventing a symptom? Or maybe he actually induced the symptom himself like Munchausen's syndrome by proxy. On some subconscious level, Lola knows her dad wants her to be messed up about the divorce and she's complying. That would explain why the "symptom" only exists in his home and not mine. He probably thought he was telling the truth. Most dangerous is if he doesn't even know when he's conniving anymore.

It's taken me a while to fully recognize Dr. Vaughn's ineptitude. I'd trusted Sidney's recommendation, and I generally give fellow professionals the benefit of the doubt. For a while, I just assumed that's how therapy works, that things get worse before they get better, like the pain of cleaning out a wound so that it'll heal properly. Now I'm thinking it was just poor treatment and that Dr. Vaughn might be part of the reason Greg and I spiraled so quickly. But we would have gotten here anyway, given Greg's delusions and manipulations. Dr. Vaughn just sped it up.

But where does her allegiance lie?

Throughout the counseling, my gut has told me that she's favorably predisposed toward Greg. Today, though, she was doing an awful lot of nodding in my direction, and she took plenty of notes after all those sessions with a stalled pen.

If I'm lucky, Dr. Vaughn's finally seen through Greg. But I can't depend on luck.

"Are you able to reach out to Dr. Vaughn as part of the discovery process?" I ask Esther's voicemail. "If you get the sense that she's going to be partial to me, then great. But if it looks like she's going the other way, you'll need to shred her. Humiliate her. Demonstrate her utter incompetence. Or maybe you can just hint at destroying her reputation? I'm happy to provide the session recordings if it would help and leave the particulars to you."

I sign off just as I arrive at my car. I call Sidney, and it's not until I've launched into the story that I realize the call is not only for support; it's also a loyalty test.

We haven't really spent time together since our bagel brunch, haven't been texting nearly as much. We can each feel that something subtle has changed in our relationship but neither of us is prepared to name it. She's taken Lola out a couple of times, giving me breaks that I've claimed are for my mental health (true) and so I can have extra time to take care of divorce details (false). I've been spending every freed-up minute with Tarek. Sidney doesn't know that I've started sleeping with him and I suspect she doesn't want to know since she hasn't asked about him at all. (Even now, she's not asking if Greg's accusation about Tarek is true, and I don't volunteer.) Perhaps that's part of the distance between us, that I'm not able to share something this precious to me, this sustaining. I can't imagine where I'd be without Tarek.

I'm also grateful for Sidney's presence in Lola's life. It's a relief that Lola has one more loving adult that she (and I) can trust implicitly.

I've never impinged on that relationship, have never asked Sidney to break Lola's confidence unless it's basically a psychological emergency. But I have to admit, right now, it's tempting.

"Wow," Sidney says, when I've completed my recitation. "That sounds intense."

"It was. I never thought he'd stoop that low. He really must be a narcissist, like Esther said." Silence. "What, you don't think so? You spent years saying how self-involved he was."

"I did think that, once upon a time. But I don't anymore. It seems like he's been so heartbroken over you that he's acting out."

"A narcissist can have a broken heart." I start to lay out the facts based on articles and blogs I've been reading. For years, Greg had me doing his emotional labor as well as practical.

He often got his way through indirect means, acting like he was incapable of doing mundane tasks as well as I did them. The onus was on me to do nearly all the legwork (all the scutwork) for things I never even wanted. On the rare occasions that I complained, he suggested that I was doing too much, making veiled references to me having control issues. That was rich, given that he was happy to do too little and I was always covering for him, making him look good.

The tell-tale sign of his narcissism? That he mistakes looking good for being a good person, and he needs everyone he interacts with to see him in that light. Look what he just tried to do with Dr. Vaughn.

Oh, and throughout our relationship, he was all about the big gestures, the kind that I was supposed to tell my friends about or that he could mention during the nights with the other couples. In other words, he knows how to put on a show to mask the emptiness inside and the dearth of true feeling. He's probably not even capable of empathy because that would mean seeing me as a full person distinct from him, with needs that are separate from his. He wanted to engage in extravagant gestures of love without ever stopping to think whether that's how I wanted to be loved. (Spoiler alert: It wasn't!) I've had to listen to him telling a hundred people that he built a house for me when, really, it was all for him. It's a monument to his narcissism.

But that's just the marriage. If you need more proof, look at the divorce.

I'm not going to let him get away with it, though. I'm building my case, carefully and methodically. Slow and steady will win this race. His every lateness and cancellation is being documented. Lola's soccer coach knows to text me whenever Greg demonstrates his irresponsibility—i.e. his selfishness, the way he feels that it's okay to make others wait, how he puts himself above everyone else, including Lola.

The most compelling evidence will be his own words, like the self-aggrandizing love letters he's written me over the years. Then there are the more recent pleas for me not to leave him, the texts where he's begged me to take me back, and finally the veiled threats when I said I was moving forward with the divorce.

"The judge will be able to read between the lines," I tell Sidney. "He'll see who—and what—Greg really is."

Another long pause. "I'm not sure the name-calling will

help you, or Lola." I'm catching a whiff of disapproval in her tone.

How can Sidney reduce what I just said to name-calling? I laid out an entire case for her! The chasm between us may have widened to a gulf.

When I don't answer, she says, "I'm sorry the counseling didn't work out better. I feel awful because I was the one who suggested Dr. Vaughn."

"You couldn't know. Your friends had a totally opposite experience." It comes out in a monotone.

"Yeah, they started out at each other's throats and ended up amicable. Which could still happen for you and Greg," she adds hastily. "You just need to keep Lola front and center, you know? She's what matters."

"Obviously."

"You're really not concerned about what Greg's observed?"

"You mean the fact that a child didn't want to do homework?" I need to end this call, pronto, before I snap.

"And about you seeming preoccupied."

So Sidney thinks that Greg was telling the truth? I'd brushed that off as an exaggeration, a manifestation, or another figment of his overactive imagination. "Has Lola said anything to you about me being preoccupied?"

"Please don't ask me that. I'm trying to stay out of the middle. I want to be a good friend to you, and to Greg, and a good aunt to Lola." Since when does she even consider Greg a friend, let alone a good one?

Now might not be the time to pump Sidney for more information about what she's seen at Greg's apartment or what Lola's told her about his parenting—basically anything I can use against him—but that time is coming. Greg's made sure of it.

THIRTY-SIX

GREG

"Something bad happened, didn't it?" Lola asks, her voice small in the darkness. "Between you and Mom." When the three of us were all together in the house, I often used to miss tuck-ins but now I treasure them. It seems like Lola can be the most honest when she can't be seen.

"That's grown-up stuff," I say, smoothing out the covers around her in the way she likes.

"That's what Mom says." Lola's voice is so full of sudden derision that I'm taken aback.

I probably shouldn't be, though. It's hardly the first time I've picked up negativity toward Madeline. Just an hour ago, Madeline called to say good night to Lola but I couldn't convince her to come to the phone. When I told that to Madeline, her tone became tight and suspicious as she said, "Lola's my child, too. You can't keep her from me." I answered, honestly, "I'm not trying to get in the way of your relationship. I'm just respecting her decision." Madeline huffed and basically hung up on me. I imagine there will be some texts in the co-parenting app to document this for Esther Kahn's posterity.

"Mom was in the worst mood last night," Lola says, "but

when I tried to talk to her, she said everything's fine. She's such a liar."

Even though I've been thinking along those same lines myself lately, I don't want Lola talking like that, or feeling like that. It's no good for her. "She just believes that there are things that kids aren't ready to know."

"But I already know. You guys hate each other."

"No," I say, with genuine force. "I love your mom. If it were up to me, we'd still be together."

Shit. I told Madeline that I wouldn't blame her for the divorce, that I'd stick to the party line and say things like, "We've grown apart." Madeline had convinced me that it was better for Lola that way. But is it, really, with a kid as smart as Lola?

"I knew that, too." She sounds almost triumphant. "Mom doesn't care that you're gone, and you're, like, this total wreck."

I thought I'd been hiding my anguish from Lola but of course she picked it up. She's no ordinary ten-year-old.

"I wish I didn't have to see her all the time."

"I wish you could spend more time here, too." I should have kept the house and pushed for 50/50 custody from the start. But I didn't know then that I wouldn't be up for working my normal hours, and more than that, I'd assumed Madeline's parental superiority, just like she wanted me to. But look at me now. Lola prefers me, even in this state, to Madeline. It's like I said in session: Lola basically told me that Madeline's mind is always elsewhere.

I can't tell Lola about Tarek, but she deserves to know the truth about me.

"I've been fighting really hard to put our family back together," I say. "You know that Mom and I have been in counseling? Well, we quit. I realized I need to stop hoping for a miracle."

"Yeah, Mom's done with you." Lola sounds so matter-of-fact that it breaks my heart one more time.

"I guess I haven't wanted to believe that."

"Because of how much you love her, and how much you love me."

"Exactly." I know it's time to come clean. I'm a terrible actor, and Lola's been able to see how distraught I am this whole time. Continuing to follow Madeline's directive of concealment would only breed distrust. Lola would see me as a liar the same way she sees Madeline.

While Madeline can't force me to stick to her playbook, if she knew about this conversation, things would only get more incendiary. Esther Kahn would take it entirely out of context.

"Do me a favor, Lo?" I say. "Don't tell your mom what we talked about tonight."

"I don't tell her anything." There it is again, that contempt. How did it develop so quickly? Just a few months ago, I thought we were a happy family.

THIRTY-SEVEN
MADELINE

Greg has hit a new low. He's either pretending Lola doesn't want to come to the phone or subtly encouraging her not to come to the phone. I don't give a shit whether he believes his lies or not; I just need to make sure that Lola doesn't. I need access to my child at all times.

Which is why I break my own rule. For the past year, she's been asking for a phone (Bliss and her other friends all have them) but I haven't felt like it's good for her developmentally for reasons that are well-documented in the pediatric literature. In weighing out the risk factors, it's more damaging for Lola to have Greg acting as a gatekeeper. Lola needs consistent contact with the one parent who puts her best interests at the forefront. So when I get her the latest iPhone, it's not because I'm trying to buy her love and affection. It's because she needs me.

I know that Greg and I are supposed to be making significant parenting decisions together. But given that he's always been fine with a phone and I've been the holdout, I decide to go ahead and act unilaterally. If he protests, it only cements what a hypocrite he is.

When I surprise Lola with her iPhone (complete with the

$500 monogrammed case that Bliss has), instead of acting over-joyed like she does for all of Greg's lavish gifts, Lola gives me a subdued thanks. It's a marked contrast with how she glows every time he comes to pick her up, even when he's empty-handed. I don't know what's going on between those two these days. It's almost like they're conspiring against me.

Though Lola's never been the most forthcoming, my bond with her has always been solid. She knows she can rely on me, that I won't let her down or leave her in the lurch, and in return, she's given me respect more than cuddles. I've always been okay with that. It's about raising the best human I can, not receiving ego strokes.

But now I'm in campaign mode. Periodically throughout the day, I'm sending her texts to register my affection and when we are together, I'm taking pains to demonstrate that she has my full and undivided attention.

Greg is pissed about the phone though he won't say it directly. Based on his app messages, he thinks I'm trying to one-up him. But I've ceded ground for our entire marriage, letting him play Santa all year long. I'm just leveling the playing field, finally. I have to protect my relationship with Lola because he's actively undermining it.

But it turns out that he wasn't entirely wrong in our final session with Dr. Vaughn. Lola got her first F ever, and when I asked her about it, she made it clear that she could not care less. Yesterday, she had an anger outburst during class. Right now, Greg and I have to meet with her teacher to discuss the situation.

He looks like utter shit. I register this without a hint of pity (though I'm a little dismayed by my own callousness). My suspicion is that he's sleeping too little and drinking too much. He isn't keeping up with his physical maintenance and his hair's starting to flop forward like he's some skater boy. I've noticed a small but growing paunch. His shirt is expensive and well-cut but could have used a quick ironing or a dry clean.

Mrs. Lewis (we parents call her that, same as the students) is a neatly dressed African-American woman in her sixties, on the verge of retirement. She is the very definition of old school. She probably hasn't had a fuck to give in fifteen years.

She puts on her reading glasses, consults the paper in front of her, and launches into the charges against Lola. "Three missed homework assignments," she announces. I'd thought it was two? Greg must have screwed up again. In response to my unasked question, she clarifies, "She didn't turn in her essay this morning." Wait, Lola was with me last night. Greg is too dazed to even give me a glance. Could he be drunk right now? "Sometimes she doesn't complete her work in class either. During a group project last week, she was belligerent with her classmates. Yesterday, as you already know, she had an anger outburst where she used several obscenities. I sent her to the principal where she talked at length about your divorce." Mrs. Lewis looks up. "There is a custody battle going on, am I right about that?"

"I don't think of it that way," I say. "I've definitely never said that in front of Lola. But Greg and I are having trouble coming to an agreement on certain key issues and we'll likely be going before a judge."

"Well, kids know how to simplify." Mrs. Lewis takes off her glasses. "I've been teaching since the Mesozoic age, and, obviously, I have compassion for children in crisis. But even when I first started out, when bullying wasn't yet a buzzword, I had no tolerance for it."

"Who's bullying Lola?" Greg asks. Seriously? If he's not drunk, just this dim, that could be even more concerning. Drunk wears off.

Mrs. Lewis slows down her next words to make sure he can grasp her meaning. "I have a strong intuition that Lola has started bullying our newest student. Has Lola mentioned her? She recently moved from Kentucky and it's been a real culture shock."

"No, she hasn't mentioned her," I say quietly.

"Not to me either." Greg sounds defiant, as if the fact that he hasn't heard about this girl means that Lola couldn't have been bullying her when, really, the reverse is more likely true. Lola wouldn't want us to know about her latest extracurricular activity.

"What do you think Lola's done?" I ask.

"I'm not exactly sure," Mrs. Lewis says, "which is why I haven't been able to take any disciplinary measures. It's an energy that I'm picking up, as if Lola's accosting this other student, but when I've made inquiries, the other student isn't talking. My sense is that Lola may have threatened her in some way."

"Threatened her with what?" Greg seems incredulous.

"Lola has a lot of social cache at this school. She's very popular, and influential. My concern is that her behavior will not only continue but spread. This other student's already gone through a rough transition; I don't want her traumatized further."

"And I don't want my daughter being wrongfully accused," Greg says, not seeming to realize how combative he seems. Almost like he's a bully himself.

Mrs. Lewis is not cowed. "Let me be clear. I'm not only speaking to you out of concern for the other child. I'm deeply concerned about Lola. Right now, this is out of character for her. I don't want it to become her character. That's why you as parents need to intervene."

"Of course," I say, shaken. "I'll talk to Lola as soon as we're done here. She's coming home with me." I'm already running over potential natural consequences—and unnatural ones—in my head. This is beyond unacceptable. It has to stop immediately.

"It might not be about what you say. It's about what you do. What she's witnessing." Mrs. Lewis shifts in her chair, taking in both Greg and me. "Lola may be picking up on aggression between you two and mirroring it."

I'm horrified, and mortified. For us, and for Lola. But Greg is unabashed. "First, you accuse Lola with no proof," he says, "and now you're accusing us?"

"I have full compassion for your situation, and for Lola's," Mrs. Lewis says. "I know you love your daughter very much, and I also know how brutal divorce can be. Good people can wind up behaving in ways that are—well, not so good. I'm asking you to do some self-reflection and to really put yourself in Lola's shoes. Think about what she might be seeing and feeling. Does she have a therapist?"

"No, not yet," I say.

"A bad therapist can do more harm than good," Greg says.

"A good one can do wonders, though," Mrs. Lewis responds gently.

"Maybe Greg and I should talk to Lola together," I say. "Make it clear that we're all on the same team. We're on Team Lola." I turn to him. "Let's go to the house—"

"The house I built," he tells Mrs. Lewis, "that she insisted on keeping."

See? Mortifying. "I didn't insist; we agreed." I cast a quick glance at Mrs. Lewis. "I'm sorry, you don't need to hear our dirty laundry. Please know that we're taking this very seriously—"

"You didn't take it very seriously in our co-parenting session," Greg interrupts again. "When I told you that Lola was having problems and you said I was making it up. When I told you that Lola said you were—"

"This isn't relevant," I cut him off. Right now, I'm the parent who's making a positive impression on Mrs. Lewis and I can't afford for that to change. She's a very important collateral contact. If Greg keeps acting like this, she could become my star witness. "Greg and I will figure out together how to address this with Lola."

"You mean you'll write another script for me?" Greg asks. Before I can answer, he's turning to Mrs. Lewis. "I know my daughter. Your suspicions are flat-out wrong. No matter what's happening at home—in either home—she'd never push around the new kid. It's laughable."

I can't believe he just called Mrs. Lewis laughable. It's like he doesn't even realize he'll need her down the line. I knew he was a poor planner but this? He's making it almost too easy for me.

"What Mrs. Lewis is saying is that Lola isn't herself right now," I tell him. "Which is why we need to help her."

"I know my daughter," Greg repeats ominously. He stands up. "Thank you for your time, Mrs. Lewis. I'll definitely talk with Lola about the homework, the distractibility in class, and improving her frustration tolerance. You won't be seeing any more anger outbursts."

He's pointedly left out the bullying. Mrs. Lewis nods, her expression benign. She probably doesn't have the energy for unwinnable battles anymore. When did he become this recalcitrant? Could it be the divorce that's done this to him?

No, he's just showing his true colors. All these years, he's gotten what he wanted and now that I'm not just rolling over, he's lost all camouflage. The mandatory mediation next week is going to be a real delight.

Greg leaves the room, and I remain seated. "I'm sorry," I say. "About how Lola's been acting, and about—that." I gesture toward the door through which Greg just disappeared. "I really thought the divorce was going to be quick and amicable. We made a pact at the outset. We were always going to put Lola first."

Mrs. Lewis nods slowly. "I understand. I have an ex-husband, too."

"I just didn't expect..." Tears pierce my eyes. "I don't know how I didn't see this in him. I mean, way back when."

"Well, if you'd seen it way back when, you wouldn't have Lola. And despite her recent behavior, she's a wonderful girl. She just doesn't know what to do with all her hurt and anger."

"I'll find her a therapist." I stand up. "Thank you so much for calling us in, and for caring. Lola's very lucky to have you."

Mrs. Lewis smiles, but I can't help noticing that she doesn't say it back. It stings, but I get it. At the moment, Lola doesn't seem too lucky on the parent front.

I go to the main office where Lola's supposed to be waiting. In response to my quizzical expression, I'm told that she just left with her dad. I race out to the parking lot, looking around for that stupid tricked-out Tesla of his. What is he trying to pull?

They're already gone. I check my phone. He's messaged me on the co-parenting app to say that he'll meet me at the house.

Is he offering to have a joint conversation with Lola after all? There's no way I'd go for that now. I have no idea what he'd say. What's he saying right now to Lola, in private?

Just drop her off, I message back.

I force myself to drive calmly, going extra slow around all the curves, because I need time to get into the right frame of mind. This can't be a confrontation or Lola will get defensive. Obviously, she has to stop what she's doing and get herself back under control, but I'm more than willing to own my part. If I've been a bad role model, I can do better. I will do better.

The problem is, Greg only seems to be getting worse.

The Tesla is in the carport, and Greg and Lola are sitting side by side on the sofa, snuggled up. Cuddling! After what he just heard?

Neither of them look at me. Greg does one more squeeze and then gets to his feet. "Call me later, all right?" he tells her. She nods fervently. "Love you the most." It's something he's always said, and I once took it to mean that he loves her more than anything else in the world, but now it sounds different. Like he's saying that he loves her more than I do.

I try not to glare at him since absorbing our negativity has apparently been so damaging to Lola. "Thanks for driving her," I say.

"You're welcome." His pleasantness back is exaggerated to the point of mockery.

Once he's gone, I sit opposite Lola. I want to sit closer so the talk has a more intimate feel but it's like there's a force field around her. She's avoided eye contact since I arrived.

"I know what you're going to say," she tells me. "Dad's on my side."

"You don't know what I'm going to say." I'm projecting all the patience and compassion I can possibly muster. But fuck Greg. "I'm on your side, too. You're not acting like yourself because you're so hurt and angry. I want to help you with that." It's not the smoothest delivery but then, I haven't had a chance to rehearse. I'm having to improv. Also, again, fuck Greg.

"Dad told me you just believed everything Mrs. Lewis said without even asking me."

"I haven't had a chance to ask you yet. What's going on, Lola?"

She shakes her head, eyes still downcast but suddenly brimming with tears. "I don't want to tell you."

"I'm not going to get mad. I just want to understand."

"It's too much work, trying to talk to you. With Dad, it's just way easier."

"Why is that?" I try to sound inquisitive, though it hurts that she so clearly prefers Greg to me.

She shrugs. "It just is."

"Well, what's he doing that I'm not? Or what does he not do that I do?" I'm stumbling over my words. "I can take feedback. I can change."

"He's just a different person, that's all." She looks visibly uncomfortable, like she's participating in the world's most awkward focus group.

I realize how strange this whole situation is, that she's been bullying the new girl and I'm the one asking her how I can be better. "Since splitting up, your father and I haven't been the greatest role models. We all need to take a hard look at how we've been behaving."

"So what's my consequence?" she asks.

"I guess what I just said is the natural consequence. Having to take a hard look in the mirror and decide who you want to be. It won't be fun, but I think if you do that, you'll make different choices. We all will."

I'm thinking that came out pretty well, until she stands up and walks downstairs without another word. Actually, she flounces, her phone firmly in hand.

THIRTY-EIGHT

GREG

Motherfuckers. They're all motherfuckers.

I'm driving home via the 880 highway after the mediation. First, they mandated the status conference, now the mediation. I'm sick of being ordered to sit in a room and soak up Madeline's disdain.

I probably shouldn't be behind the wheel when I don't know that I'd mind being plowed into, or plowing into someone else.

I won't do it. I wouldn't do it. That's what separates us from the animals: self-control, the ability to desire without action.

Madeline and Tarek are animals, that's all there is to it.

This highway is a bitch, too. There's a stretch of stop-and-start, and then I'll start flying again, and then I'll have to pull up suddenly for another inexplicably slow patch. Nothing can be counted on. Nothing stays the same.

When will I get it through my head once and for all that Madeline doesn't give a shit about me? Her detachment is aggressive. Her apathy is violent. If she could, I'm pretty sure she'd sever every single connection to me, and that includes Lola.

But optimistic idiot that I am, I went into yet another bland conference room with yet another "expert," ready to make my last stand. I've said it before but this time I mean it: This was my final vulnerable appeal to my wife whom I've loved selflessly, ceaselessly, and apparently senselessly for over fifteen years. With no lawyers and no judge, only a mediator who was all in beige and easily ignored, I told Madeline that if it were just about me, I'd give up and move on. Madeline is phenomenal but she is not the last woman on the planet. Only it's not about me, or about her. It's about Lola, whose recent issues are going to get worse unless her family comes back together. Lola is the canary in our coal mine.

Madeline's facial expressions went from irritation to embarrassment (for me? for her?) and finally, to boredom. But still, I shouldered on, hoping that somewhere in that carousel would be love—if not for me, then for Lola.

There was none.

"I think I've made my position clear," Madeline said. She looked at the mediator. "Could we please add something to our agenda? I want to talk about getting Lola an individual therapist to help her adjust to the divorce. One thing Greg said is true. There have been school issues. Lola's teacher has made us aware of a bullying problem, which I find highly troubling."

One thing I said was true?

Mrs. Lewis is like Madeline, the kind of woman who's way too sure of her observations, opinions, and conclusions. Lola told me that she didn't bully that other girl; they just don't like each other. The antipathy is mutual. Some personalities aren't a match. So what, every time you don't like someone and you're honest about that, it's bullying? All these people running around crying about how they feel unsafe, the way Madeline did during that last co-parenting session, and you're just supposed to back off because otherwise you're a bully for trying to express yourself? When all you want is to be heard.

After another stinging rejection by Madeline, I was in no mood to talk semantics. Every time I looked at her, I saw red. The mediator must have realized it because she suggested moving us to two different rooms, with her as the go-between. Basically, she'd talk to us each separately and then run back to the other to attempt to broker an agreement.

She went to talk to Madeline first, and as the minutes ticked by, I just kept imagining the spin that Madeline was putting on everything, the picture she was painting. Or worse, maybe she really was just talking about "the relevant issues." All she cares about is divvying as quickly as possible. Then she can walk hand-in-hand into the sunset with Tarek.

It was a hackneyed image but it still sent me into a rage so complete that I had no choice but to get out of there. By now, the mediator must have returned to find an empty room.

Lucas calls when the traffic has once again become a crawl. "Hello," I bark.

"How was the mediation?" he asks.

"Terrible. What can I do for you?"

"I'm sorry to hear that. I guess we can just talk tomorrow." But his tone is dubious, like he's not sure if it can wait.

"What is it?" My car lurches forward and I come within inches of the Chevy Tahoe in front of me. Normally, Teslas aren't known for lurching but, at the moment, it's slightly satisfying.

"Well, you said that we could rework our compensation agreement this week, given that my duties have increased substantially. But tomorrow's fine for that." Seriously, Lucas? "The other thing—and I hesitate to mention this but it is more time sensitive—is that Peter Tramboni isn't going to be brushed off anymore. He doesn't want to talk to an underling."

"Are those actual quotes?"

"Yes."

I'm in no shape to talk to Peter. I haven't been for weeks, which is why he's been talking to my underling.

Then I hear it before I feel it, the crunch of metal on metal. It's my fender on the Tahoe's bumper. I hadn't even realized that my foot had depressed the accelerator. Or had it just let off the brake?

"FUCK!" I shout at the top of my lungs. "FUCK!!!!!" And damn if it doesn't feel good.

THIRTY-NINE

MADELINE

As I wind up into my neighborhood—the neighborhood that, let's face it, never would have been mine if it weren't for Greg's coercion—I am FUMING. I know that steam can't literally come out of a person's ears but my entire body feels like it's on fire.

Greg did it again. He fucking did it again.

Going into the mediation today, I'd held onto the very faintest hope that if it was just him, me, and a mediator, no attorneys, he would finally see reason and we could get this thing done. I was prepared to be more than reasonable, to make concessions that perhaps Esther would have advised against, but an imperfect deal is better than an interminably delayed deal. Every day that goes by costs us time, money, energy, and emotion. It keeps us tethered to each other and, as Mrs. Lewis said, it's contorting us. Or did she say distorting? Whatever. It's true. This might be exposing Greg's true nature but this isn't mine. I wish I didn't have to be so cold and withdrawn, but he feeds off my compassion and uses it to fuel his denial.

I went in there ready to yield where I could but Greg wouldn't allow us to get within spitting distance of an actual issue. Instead, I had to endure yet another burst of his emotional incontinence, supposedly in Lola's name. "Lola needs both her parents, full-time," he said. "She doesn't need some guy with a man bun wearing Patagonia."

I stared at him. To attack Tarek's appearance in such a childish (though somewhat accurate) way, he has to have been spying on me. For how long? My mind races with what else he could have seen, what else he might know.

Yet I refused to show anger or fear. I would not be baited. So eventually Greg went silent. He glowered with rage, Vesuvius about to erupt. The mediator wisely installed the two of us in separate rooms.

The mediation is mandatory, requiring good faith participation. Once I was alone with the mediator, I told her, "He does that all the time. Would you consider that acting in good faith?" She demurred but the answer's obvious. I asked if she'd be reporting his outrageous conduct back to the judge because, in essence, it's non-compliance. She said no, that since he had shown up, the process would remain confidential. It would either succeed or fail but nothing that went on would be admissible in court. Too bad, since it demonstrates a pattern. This was a retread of the co-parenting counseling where Greg tried to manipulate the process, the professional, and me.

I shouldn't have been surprised when the mediator came back to my room just a few minutes later and said that Greg had left. Of course he had, since he hadn't gotten his way.

Still, I felt like screaming—I still do—and when I take a corner just a tiny bit too fast, a horn blares. My middle finger almost goes up, involuntarily. Uncharacteristically.

I'm not myself, anywhere. It's gotten to a point where it's almost impossible for me not to respond to Greg's antics, much as I want to take the high road. At work, I find that I'm easily aggravated, having to talk myself down multiple times a day. I'm not able to think as clearly as I usually do and I worry that, at some point, my clinical judgment might be compromised.

Even sex with Tarek has ceased to be a cure-all. And sometimes when he and I talk, I find him just a little bit sanctimonious. I can't blame him, though. He hasn't been through anything remotely like this. His longest romantic relationship was under two years and he's never been married or had kids. He can't grasp the depth of the betrayal, or what's truly at stake.

Greg is screwing with my relationship with Lola, there's no question. I've been documenting extensively, especially how he handled (or rather, failed to handle) the bullying situation. It's no accident that he ran to the office and picked up Lola, wanting to drive her to my house so that he'd get to her first. He planted the idea that he'd defended Lola to Mrs. Lewis while I'd immediately accepted Mrs. Lewis's version. It's not untrue but it's without nuance and it was entirely inappropriate to share it with Lola. He'd thrown me under the bus so that she'd think he was the only one on her side. Parenting isn't supposed to be a popularity contest but tell that to Greg, who's winning handily.

Maybe he really doesn't know the meaning of proper boundaries but ignorance of the law is no excuse. The court needs to be apprised of his poor judgment, ASAP.

In the days since, Lola's been short with me. Her tone is harsh and dismissive. When I ask her why, she'll give an answer that's disproportionate to the level of animosity and hostility ("I hate how you dress," or "I hate the way you won't let me have as much sugar as the other kids"). She praises Greg at every opportunity. In her eyes, I'm all bad and he's all good, which is just the kind of black-and-white thinking that narcissists employ.

It's obvious that Lola doesn't want to be with me. How much weight will the court give to her preference? I know how much weight was given to mine, when I was a kid. I vividly recall the day of the final judgment, when my mom was awarded full custody. My father's never forgiven me. I've never forgiven either of my parents.

That couldn't happen to Lola and me.

Could it?

At least she seems to have straightened up at school. I've been checking in with Mrs. Lewis daily and there've been no additional incidents. Maybe that means that Greg and I are doing something right. I wouldn't call it co-parenting, though, since all we do is trade logistics via app.

Esther says it's no surprise that things have degraded to this point when Hugh Warshaw's on the scene. It's also no surprise that Greg and Hugh Warshaw gravitated toward each other. Narcissists of a feather flock together.

But Hugh wasn't there today. No, today was all Greg.

Now I know that he's been watching me, or having me watched. For how long? What I do know is that I can't live in fear of his surveillance. This has to stop. I'm not going to let Greg hijack my life.

Esther needs to go at him harder. Do her worst. End this as quickly as she can because I don't know that I'll be able to take much more.

Just a few more turns and I'll be home. I wish I wasn't; I wish I lived anywhere else, really, but I can't vacate, not without an agreement in place. If only Greg had been willing to come to the table today, to finally act in good faith, we could have found common ground. Now I'm not yielding on anything.

Another angry horn. Another man—of course it is—is driving a massive SUV and gesturing furiously. He's still moving toward me. As in, of course he expects that I'll be the one to pull over or back up, and sure, I've always been careful to avoid potentially deadly "whose dick is bigger" contests, but this time, the bigger dick is me.

I'm still moving, too, albeit slowly, like a predator. Like a boss. He gets it, pulling over into a driveway at the last second, rolling down his window to shout, "You crazy bitch!" I continue on, with a beatific smile and my middle finger stuck up in the air. I feel better than I have all day.

Until I get home and pull into the carport. That's when I start shaking, realizing what just happened. What almost happened. How far I might have gone.

FORTY

GREG

I pour two whiskeys: one for me, one for Sidney. (I've already had three but who's counting.) I shouldn't have called her. She's Madeline's best friend, not mine, except that, sadly, she is. She's all I've got.

We're sitting at my redwood dining room table, the one she picked out. It's too good for me.

"No, it's not," she says, and I realize that I must have said it aloud.

"Jesus, I'm pathetic. I'm sorry you have to deal with me."

"I know there's more to you than this moment. Besides, you wouldn't be this torn up if you weren't capable of enormous love."

"That's true," I say. I knew she was the right person to call. The only other option would have been Lucas, and I'm not ready to sacrifice any last shred of respect he still feels for me.

I haven't called Peter back yet. Tomorrow, maybe.

"She was just totally unreachable during the mediation," I tell Sidney. "It's like she's become inhuman."

Sidney spins her highball glass while I lift mine to my lips.

She doesn't seem to know what to say but I notice she's not rushing to defend Madeline either.

"I worry what this is going to do to Lola. I know she didn't bully that kid but she's showing other signs of, you know, distress."

"It's been really hard for her. I think she blames Madeline for all the pain you're in."

"Well, yeah." I mean, Madeline is the cause.

"I just don't want Lola to feel like she has to choose between the two of you." Sidney finally takes a sip.

"I've never told her she has to choose me." She just wants to.

"It's a terrible situation, that's all. I'm sure Madeline's struggling, too, in her own way."

"You mean you don't know if she is?"

"She's not as open with me as she used to be. I guess maybe because..." Sidney trails off.

"Because she has Tarek," I finish. Sidney doesn't disagree. "He's changed her. Don't you think so?"

"She is different but I don't know if I'd put it like that. She says she's coming into her own."

I'm not touching that one. "She acts like I've been stifling her all these years when she's been controlling me."

Sidney doesn't answer, but I can see the truth in her face. She just doesn't want to be disloyal to Madeline.

"She's fucking him. But you knew that, right?" Antonio and I spoke an hour ago. He sent me the proof along with his invoice.

I'm surprised by Sidney's face. Is it possible that Madeline hadn't even told her oldest, dearest friend about her affair?

"She's changed," I repeat, determined to drive it home. This time, Sidney finally nods, albeit reluctantly.

I'd been on the fence, but now I see. I'll need to go for the nuclear option. Madeline's left me no choice.

*

We'd become rivals and full-on adversaries, if not outright
enemies. But we each thought of ourselves as Lola's protector.
We didn't see her as a pawn. No, she was our reason for being, or
at least, our reason for going as far as we each eventually would.
That's what we had to tell ourselves: Save Lola, at all costs. From
her other terrible, selfish parent.

It became increasingly difficult to remember that we had
ever been lovers. That we had ever been partners. And yet, somehow, it would come full circle. We were about to be handcuffed,
for life.

I know, it sounds improbable, if not impossible. But what's
that saying? Isn't it murder that makes the strangest bedfellows?

CONTEMPT

FORTY-ONE

MADELINE

I could have told Esther over the phone but I'm being billed the same amount for her time so might as well do it in person where I can glean her true reaction. Also, it'd be easier to mitigate the damage if she could see my face and remember that I've had good intentions since the beginning.

That's what I thought, anyway. Now that I'm sitting across the desk in her antiseptic office, I'm starting to quake. She's a very formidable woman and I've always loved that when it's directed at Greg, on my behalf. I know she won't like what she's about to hear, that I've been lying by omission. She's warned me several times to never, ever lie to her. It compromises us both. And Esther Kahn hates to be compromised.

"The mediation hasn't changed anything," she says. "We already knew this thing was going the distance. Buckle up, we're headed to court."

"Right," I say, licking my lips.

She notices. She notices everything. "What's going on, Madeline?" Her eyes narrow almost imperceptibly, though her tone is as crisp and cool as ever.

Ridiculous as it sounds, I don't want to disappoint her. Greg and I stopped being a team, and Esther and I became one. I trust her implicitly in a way that I can't even currently trust Sidney, who still sees Greg (and still manages to see the good in him). That means she's not fully my ally. But Esther is.

I have to tell her, though. Since Greg knows about Tarek's hair and how he dresses, he may very well know about my clandestine trips to Tarek's apartment. It could be only a matter of time before I'm outed by Hugh Warshaw, and I can't let Esther be blindsided for the second time.

"My relationship with my friend Tarek has become sexual," I say.

"It's 'become sexual'?" Esther parrots, almost mockingly. "Oh, Madeline. I didn't take you for someone who'd hide behind the passive voice."

"What do you mean?"

"I thought you're the kind of woman who owns her actions. To her attorney, at least." She stares at me a few extra beats to make her displeasure known. Then she turns brusque. "Well, that'll need to stop immediately."

"I can't."

"Of course you can. You're embroiled in a custody battle."

"I'm not doing anything wrong. I wasn't involved with Tarek until after the separation. I'm not being unfaithful to Greg."

She shakes her head. Now she's disappointed by my denseness. "This is about perception. It's about contrasting your character with Greg's. It's about the fact that, at the moment, Greg's making this easy for us. He's the one who storms out of status conferences and mediations. He's drunk and disorderly in front of Lola's teacher. I should be able to destroy him on the stand, no problem."

"Good. Then we've got everything we need."

"But it might not matter if you're acting like a wanton woman." I laugh at the notion. She doesn't. "Judges are mostly male, and mostly retrograde. Even when they're consciously progressive, their subconscious is another story. They're way more likely to judge you than Greg. He's just a lovelorn guy who's been trying to win you back and can't always control his emotions. Meanwhile, you're off spreading your legs and neglecting your child."

I'm not laughing anymore either. "That is absolute bullshit."

"Lola said you're preoccupied."

"No, Greg reported that she said that, and he's hardly a reliable source." Now I'm the one staring her down. "I've done my homework. I know the court is barred from considering certain factors in making custody decisions. Those include race, religion, and the sexual relations of a parent."

"Wake up. Hugh Warshaw won't present this to the judge as if it's about your sex life; he'll argue that it's about the impact of your sex life on Lola. That you're the one causing all her symptoms."

"That's a lie."

"No, that's an argument that it's perfectly legal for him to make, and it could be quite persuasive. Were you sleeping with Tarek before that last co-parenting session? Meaning, were you sleeping with him when Lola told Greg you'd become preoccupied?"

"Lola would never have said 'preoccupied.'"

"Maybe she said distracted. Maybe she said you haven't been paying attention lately. Hugh is going to coach Greg exhaustively on this, and trust me, Greg will not flub this line. My point remains: When did she say it? What's the timeline?"

"I was already sleeping with Tarek," I admit quietly. "But you can get Greg on cross-examination, right? Because you and I both know that if she did say that, it's because he put it in her head."

"That's a serious allegation. Do you have any proof?"

"It's obvious." I remind her of how he swooped in and took

Lola from the school office when it was my night. I should have been the one to introduce the topics from the meeting with Mrs. Lewis but, instead, he got to frame the discussion, to my disadvantage.

"That could be a useful anecdote," Esther says. "But we don't have any specific knowledge about him planting that comment. If we levy a charge like that, we'd better back it up. Otherwise, we could find ourselves in contempt."

"It's about a pattern of behavior. That's what you told me. That's why I document exhaustively."

"As you should. In most ways, you're a model client. But that doesn't change the fact that your sexual relationship with Tarek could jeopardize your case." She leans in. "Keep on like this, and you could see your parenting time significantly reduced. You might even lose custody altogether."

My eyes widen. "I'd never lose Lola." She's being melodramatic. Isn't she?

"Is this guy worth the risk? Is any guy worth it? Ask yourself that. Because Hugh and Greg will try to show that you're choosing a man over your own child."

"It's not like that." But my heart is racing. If I can't even convince my own attorney, then what's going to happen in court? "I haven't been preoccupied. He can't prove that I have."

"It's enough that Lola said it."

"She didn't say it!" I try to tamp down my rising frustration. My panic.

"What if she tells the judge that she did?"

"No!" My voice is quavering, but emphatic. "Lola's not going to be on the stand. That's out of the question." I was sixteen when I took the stand in my parents' divorce, and it was one of the worst experiences of my life. Neither of them could afford lawyers so they were both representing themselves, and I had to look from one to the other and... No. There's no way I'd let that happen to Lola.

"You might not have a choice. The judge could insist on speaking to her. But it's unlikely that it would be in open court. She'd probably talk to the judge in his chambers privately. Ask yourself, though: What would she say?"

It's a chilling question, given how Lola seems to feel about me lately and how she feels about Greg.

"No judge will admit he—and it's probably going to be a he —is considering race, religion, or your sex life but do you really think that it won't factor in, on some level? A lot of judges get into the business because they're judgmental. Greg and his attorney will make it their mission to drag you through the mud and prove that your promiscuity is negatively impacting Lola."

"I'm not promiscuous."

"Like I've told you from the beginning, it's all about percep-tion. Stop seeing this guy, even as a friend, until your divorce has been inked. Don't give Greg anything to work with, and I promise you'll get everything you want."

FORTY-TWO

GREG

"Mom's home," Lola says, her disappointment evident.

"This isn't a social visit. We'll just get Blob and get out." Madeline's is the only car in the carport. Did Antonio get it wrong? Is it possible Tarek's not actually here?

When I finally called Antonio back, it wasn't to take his recommendation for additional background checks; what I needed was surveillance. I had to know what I was up against, if Madeline was, in fact, fucking the sherpa. Antonio's delivered the goods, letting me know about Madeline's assignations at Tarek's shithole apartment. I've been waiting for this opportunity to catch Tarek in the house. In my house. No, in Lola's house. What kind of mother is Madeline anyway?

"Okay, let's do this." Lola and I step out of the rental Tesla. I'd made sure it's identical to mine, which is currently at the body shop, because I can't afford for Madeline to see me in another type of car and start asking questions. Hugh Warshaw told me that I'd better hide all evidence of the accident because it could make me look irresponsible. As Lola and I head for the door, I tell her, "You don't have to knock. You live here."

Lola doesn't seem even slightly suspicious and, as she

reaches for the knob, my heart seizes up. She's so young. This is going to age her, instantly.

She needs to know who her mom really is, though, doesn't she? Madeline fooled me for years into thinking she was a good, loving person. If Lola understands the truth, she can protect herself accordingly. Madeline is a cold, cold fish. She's not to be trusted. How many chances have I given her, in co-parenting sessions and conferences and mediation? How much rejection and abandonment and utter disregard can one man take before he has to strike back?

Even though I'm right about this and about Madeline, I still find myself wanting to tell Lola, *Stop, let's turn around, you can sleep without Blob for one night, or we'll stop by the store and I'll buy you a new Blob.*

But I've come too far. There's no going back.

We step inside and it's completely silent. That could just mean they're downstairs in the bedroom. I designed the house to have incredible soundproofing. With the open floor plan, I can do a quick scan and there's no evidence that Tarek's here—no wine glasses on the kitchen counter, for example, or male shoes by the door. She wouldn't let him walk through the house with shoes on. So he's not here. I'm both disappointed and relieved.

"I'll get Blob," Lola says. She slips her shoes off.

I do the same. "I'll come with you."

She gives me a strange look but she doesn't protest. She's such a good girl. That's how I know she'd never bully anyone. She just happens to be honest, which is a quality that I intend to fully nurture. One of my main jobs will be keeping her from turning into her mother.

When we get to the bottom of the stairs, I can hear them, faintly. Which means that they must be incredibly loud, enough to jump the sound barrier. They sound like a couple of monkeys in heat. It's disgusting.

And it's coming from my bedroom.

Bile rushes into my mouth, and I really think I might have to throw up. Lola wasn't listening for it and now she's headed down the hallway toward her room. What do I do? Do I call her back, call her attention to it? Or should I just let her go on, unaware?

I'm leaning toward preserving her innocence when she turns and sees the expression on my face. She comes back on her own. "What is it?" she says. I don't answer, but she freezes, finally hearing it. She's had sex education classes and Madeline's talked to her about the birds and the bees but maybe she won't connect the audio to the act?

I don't want her to understand. I want her to get Blob and we'll get the hell out, with her ignorance intact. I should never have brought her here.

The noises cease. Madeline and Tarek must have sensed our presence.

Lola studies my face, her eyes wide. I realize that she's worried about me. She thinks that I've stumbled into this accidentally.

My sweet girl. Tears fill my eyes. "It's okay," I say. "Let's get Blob and leave."

"No." She's suddenly filled with anger, and determination. She marches down the hall to Madeline's room, knocking sharply on the door. "Mom, it's me! What were you doing?"

"I was just taking a nap." Through the door, Madeline's voice is frantic. While she's an excellent liar by omission, she's terrible at commission.

"Lola forgot Blob," I say. Or rather, I secretly removed him from Lola's bag during pick-up. "We'll get him and go."

"Mom! What are you doing? Who's in there?"

Madeline is silent. To my shock, I actually feel bad for her.

I shouldn't have done this. I shouldn't have put us all in this position. "I'm sorry," I tell Madeline. "We'll get out of your hair."

Lola whirls on me. "Stop giving in to her," she hisses. Then to Madeline, "I know what you were doing. I heard you."

"I'm an adult in the privacy of my own home," Madeline says.

She almost had me for a second there. But now my anger is back. Her own home? Really?

"Fuck you, Mom," Lola says. I smile to myself, just a little, because that's exactly what I was thinking.

After a long pause, Madeline says, "I get that you're upset, Lola, but you can't talk to me like that. You don't have all the facts."

"No, I don't. Because you're always keeping secrets. Daddy tells me the truth. That's why I want to live with him all the time."

"You don't mean that." Madeline's fighting to keep her voice level. "Give me a minute to come talk to you, face to face. I can explain."

"No," Lola says. "We're leaving." She takes my hand and we head for the stairs. I'm not sure who's leading who.

At the top, I ask her if she's sure she doesn't want Blob.

"I don't need him anymore," she says. "Let's go, Dad."

Dad? I'm Daddy.

She suddenly sounds so grown-up, So in charge, just like Madeline.

What have I done?

FORTY-THREE

MADELINE

"Did that really just happen?" I'm in shock and nearly hyperventilating as I crash to the floor, still naked. "What am I supposed to do? Should I go after her?"

Tarek comes and sits beside me. He's naked, too. He shakes his head. "Take some time to gather your thoughts."

"But right now, she's with Greg. Who knows what he could be telling her?" I feel a note of fury. "He set me up."

"It didn't sound like it. He seemed thrown."

"That was just his good guy act. That's what he wanted Lola to think."

I was planning to heed Esther's advice and give Tarek up, just for a while, just until the court case is over, or until I've gotten some intel that so thoroughly demolishes Greg's credibility that he'll have to cry uncle. He'd have to finally come to the negotiating table and make a deal.

But first, Tarek and I were going to have one last extended romp. It was supposed to be incredible enough to sate us for a while. I was being careful, too. I'd watched Greg drive away with Lola and only after he'd been gone nearly an hour and after I'd visually scanned the hills of my neighborhood thor-

oughly to make sure no one seemed to be watching my house
did I text Tarek the all-clear.

Tarek had shown up in a taxi (he says it's more ethical than
Lyft or, heaven forbid, Uber) and we ran downstairs, him still in
all his clothes and even his shoes, I didn't want to pause for even
a second, and then I plunged into an ecstatic oblivion that
would turn out to be short-lived.

Okay, there had been a vengeful element to doing it here.
On some level, I wanted to defy Greg and defile his dream
house. But mostly, Greg had nothing to do with it. I wanted to
experience Tarek in a place that was full of light and air instead
of his hovel. We're not seedy; we're beautiful.

Tarek was supposed to stay for the whole weekend and it
was going to be epic, enough to make up for all the time we're
not able to have for a while. It was to be an assurance. This is
worth waiting for.

But Greg had other plans.

Whoever he had spying on me had cleverly concealed their
position. And that person couldn't have done it just once
because this was the first and only time Tarek's been to the
house. Greg must have paid for hours of stakeouts in order to
catch me in the act. So Lola could catch me.

Before this moment, I hadn't realized that Greg is constitu-
tionally incapable of being a decent father. He's willing to sacrifice his own child to punish me. Narcissist is far too weak a
word.

Poor Lola, to be in the clutches of a man like that.

"I have to go after them." I get to my feet and start throwing
clothes on. "I have to tell her what her father's done. Then she'll
see him for who he is."

"Whoa," Tarek says. "Do you really think that's the right
approach?"

"She's talking about living with him all the time. What if
she went and told a judge that?"

"You haven't even been in front of a judge yet. Let's just slow down and think this through. You don't want to make the wrong move. What if Greg didn't set you up and this was an honest mistake?"

Impossible. "I've been trying so hard to make the right move. I've been thoughtful and deliberate. But Greg plays by his own rules. Lola wants more openness? Well, she's going to get it."

"This is your child you're talking about."

"I'm just going to tell her the truth."

Tarek's expression is disapproving, bordering on horrified. "This is her father. A man that she loves very much."

"He's trying to get her to stop loving me. That's why he brought her here." I'm fully dressed now, though I'm hardly ready. Nothing in life can prepare you for a moment like this.

"You need to rise above. Set a better example."

He doesn't get it. This is a fight for survival. It's Greg or me. "I am not Michelle Obama. When Greg goes low, I can't go high."

"Instead, you're going lower?"

"No one could possibly go lower than Greg just did." I hold Tarek's gaze. "Don't you understand what just happened? He's deliberately sabotaging my relationship with Lola. He wants her to hate me."

Tarek drops his eyes. Finally, he says, "No. I can't begin to understand."

That's why I love him. Because he can admit what he doesn't know. Because he's a legitimately kind and caring human being.

I throw myself into his arms and cry. Just for a few minutes, since there's work to do. I'm not sure anymore when and how to tell Lola, but I need to call Sidney and tell her what Greg's done. Either Sidney has to cut him off completely so that he's entirely isolated, so that he truly has no one, or she needs to sign on as my spy, getting me what I need to defeat Greg once and for all. There can be no more neutrality in light of what he did. Not just to me, but to Lola. Sidney will have to understand that.

It's dawning on me that as long as Lola and I find a way to work through this, it might not actually be the worst thing. In fact, Greg might have done me a favor.

Now that my relationship with Tarek is going to be used against me anyway, there's no point in taking a break. I'll go the other way. Lola should get to know Tarek. The court should, too. Esther will be able to demonstrate that I'm not some slut; I'm a woman in love with a man of the highest moral fiber and unparalleled character.

Tarek is a huge upgrade from Greg. He's the replacement father that Lola deserves. In the long run, she (and I) will come out way ahead.

FORTY-FOUR

GREG

I almost wish Lola was mad at me, or that I'd been found out. This must be what it's like when you commit a crime but never get caught. You're flayed alive by your own conscience.

Since I engineered it so that Lola discovered the relationship between Madeline and Tarek, she's been looking at me with sympathy and devotion. She's made it clear that she's 100 percent for me and against Madeline. She doesn't want to live with Madeline at all, in fact, and she'd be happy to tell a judge that. But I know the truth: I'm in no shape to take care of Lola full-time.

If I confessed what I've done, any relief would only be temporary. The court would think I'm a monster and instantly award Madeline full custody. Lola would end up feeling she has no good parents. Now she thinks she has one. I have tried to mitigate the damage, telling Lola that there's more than one side to any story and she should listen to her mother's. "Mom loves you," I said. "There's not a doubt in my mind."

Unfortunately, my defense of Madeline backfired. Lola's face hardened and she said, "Dad, you have to stop drinking her Kool-Aid." What are they learning in fourth grade? "You can't always do it her way. It's not fair. You have to be stronger than that."

I never realized that Lola saw me as weak, and it makes me question everything. I mean, I know Madeline's been manipulating me since she asked me to leave, but now I'm thinking it was going on far longer than that. Which is part of why I would never admit to Madeline what I did, that it wasn't an accident that Lola and I walked in on her and Tarek.

She must know, though. She hasn't broached the subject but all our communications have been curt and via app. It's logistics only. I can never apologize or admit fault in any way because Esther Kahn would file a legal brief by morning. But I do feel terrible, like I've turned Lola against Madeline, which has been her fear for a while now and I always said it would never happen. My intention—my hope—had been that once Madeline got caught, she'd come to her senses. She'd come back to her family. I hadn't really thought through all the ways it could play out.

I have to remember that Madeline's largely brought this on herself. No one forced her to fuck Tarek in our bed. Rewind further, and no one forced her to start talking to her crush in secret, on her special cell phone. No one forced her to betray me.

Still, I never suspected how much it would hurt to hurt someone I love, intentionally and with malice aforethought. It's revealed something dark and ugly inside me. If Madeline and I had stayed together, could I have gone my whole life without it ever surfacing, or was it only a matter of time?

I'm painfully aware that I haven't just lost Madeline; I've lost her stabilizing effect. I may have lost her good opinion of me forever, and that makes it harder to see the good in myself. But I can't see much in her either these days. Maybe we really were a perfect match: two lousy humans who raised their game in each other's presence, or at least masked each other's flaws.

I'm a cliché, drinking to escape. Hugh wants updates and additional information and I've been ignoring his calls and emails. He's a slimy son of a bitch, and being his teammate, his partner in crime, sickens me.

I've given Lucas a massive raise and I'm signing off on every draft he submits because, for the first time since I became an architect, I don't care about my livelihood or my reputation. I texted Peter to ask for one more week, then I'll knock his socks off, and all he wrote back was *ok*. The brevity was not reassuring. I'd have preferred if he'd elongated the exchange or even reamed me out. Now he's actually expecting me to deliver, and I have no idea how I'm going to pull that off.

Sidney's worried about Lola, and by extension, she's worried about me. She can see I'm wracked with guilt and shame over having taken Lola to the house without calling first, thereby accidentally discovering Madeline. She's told me that it's not my fault; how could I have known Tarek would be there?

Weirdly, her absolution helps, even if she doesn't know my actual crime. She's all but confirmed that Madeline thinks (correctly) that I did it on purpose.

When I asked if Madeline hates me, Sidney said, "No, not deep down." But we're trying not to talk about Madeline, for the most part.

I know Sidney feels her own guilt about being with me. She hasn't said directly that Madeline forbade her but I can read between the lines. Our time together is never romantic, though it is clandestine. We're both keeping it a secret from Madeline. But then, Madeline didn't tell Sidney that she was fucking Tarek, so maybe they're even. Their friendship ledger balances out.

I have the impression that Sidney thinks Madeline and I have both gone nuts, or as she put it, "Your moral compasses are both a little off these days." It's gratifying to hear that, to get confirmation that, in her own way, Madeline has become as degenerate as I am.

Last night, Sidney accidentally let it slip that Madeline's been documenting every one of my supposed misdeeds since this process began. When I seemed upset, so did she. "I thought you knew," she said. "I mean, that's just Maddie. She's always prepared."

I felt like pouring myself a bourbon but Sidney made me promise not to drink in her presence. I agreed, since I should have more sober hours of the day. Sidney and Lola have become my sobriety gatekeepers.

"It's normal to protect yourself in a custody battle," Sidney said, clearly wishing she could backtrack. She hadn't meant to out Madeline.

"We weren't supposed to be in a custody battle," I said. "She was supposed to trust me, and I used to think I could trust her."

Sidney looked distraught. "You have to pump the brakes, Greg. For Lola's sake."

"Tell that to Madeline."

"I have."

See? Madeline is the one who keeps pushing down on the accelerator. She's the one driving this car. Whatever happens next will be her fault, not mine.

FORTY-FIVE

MADELINE

Rather than act as a spy, Sidney's opted to cut Greg out of her life. Since her commitment to Lola's well-being is unwavering, Sidney and Lola are still spending a good amount of time together. I appreciate that, given that things between Sidney and me feel a bit tenuous. It's nothing major. Nothing irreparable, I should say. Sidney was just hurt that I hadn't confided in her about sleeping with Tarek until I absolutely had to—i.e. because Lola had caught me red-handed and I knew that she'd likely turn to Aunt Sidney to process the discovery.

I explained that I'd kept the secret from everyone, including my attorney. Sidney had found that an unsatisfying defense: "I'm your best friend. I should know more than the lawyer who's been steering you toward Armageddon."

I was surprised to learn that Sidney had such a negative impression of Esther. "Who told you that? Greg?" Sidney shook her head slightly, not quite a denial but the suggestion of a denial. I was surprised again. I've never known Sidney to be cagy. "It's good that you won't be around Greg anymore. I feel like he's poisoning your mind."

"I'm a grown-ass woman," Sidney retorted, even though she

knows how much I hate that expression. "I make up my own mind. I happen to have my own concerns about some of the decisions you've been making lately."

"He started this."

"You're the one who filed for divorce."

"Because I deserve to be happy!" I stared at her, flabbergasted. "I have a right to end my marriage without my former husband declaring war."

"He thinks you're the one who declared it."

"Well, he's wrong. He's been wrong about a lot of things." I studied Sidney. "You do think that he was wrong to bring Lola over when Tarek was here?"

"He probably didn't know Tarek was here. Lola can't sleep without Blob."

This was going exactly nowhere. Sidney refuses to believe that Greg's behaving maliciously despite all the evidence. She doesn't think that he's had someone tailing me even though he made that comment about Tarek's man bun, and she won't acknowledge the providential timing of his visit to get Blob.

We've had to agree to disagree. But at least she did agree not to see him anymore.

I'm still grateful for Sidney's involvement in Lola's life. Lola needs the emotional support of a responsible adult to counteract Greg's influence and, right now, Lola's freezing me out entirely. I've tried on a number of occasions to tell my side of the story—that Tarek wasn't the reason for the divorce, that he was just a friend until after Dad and I split, etc.—but one time, Lola walked right out of the room and another time, she actually put her hands over her ears, and the third time, she screamed, "STOP TALKING TO ME!" It was shocking since we're not a family of screamers, we're a family of stuffers. But maybe this is progress. We're becoming our authentic selves.

I'm not sure that much of my perspective has gotten through so I've asked if Sidney could inject it wherever possible.

Sidney said that it's a delicate operation, given how angry Lola is, but she'll do her best. Sidney knows that Lola needs to have positive relationships with both her parents, even if Greg believes the opposite.

I have the next phase of my plan worked out, though I haven't told Sidney yet. I suspect she wouldn't approve. She thinks I should retreat. Take space from Tarek, same as she's taking space from Greg, but those situations are not at all analogous. Besides, retreat would be playing right into Greg and Hugh Warshaw's hands.

I'm biding my time. I know that Lola will sing another tune once she spends time with Tarek and sees what an amazing person he is. To know him is to love him, truly. I mean, I tried to resist and it was impossible.

I'll give it a week or so, let Sidney soften Lola up for me, and then I'm back on offense.

FORTY-SIX

GREG

Peter Tramboni is in a furor.

His face looms on my computer screen, his massive wiry black eyebrows waggling in a way that would be comic if it wasn't so terrifying. He'd actually summoned me to his office in Silicon Valley but I'd be damned if I was going to spend an hour and a half in traffic each way to hear what a fuck-up I am. I already know.

Besides, my one rule, no matter how bad things get? I will never drive drunk. I will, however, drink bourbon for breakfast.

"Let me get this straight." The eyebrows seem to be glowering at me, all on their own. They're in stark contrast to his bald, shiny pate. "You have nothing to show me. Nada."

"That's correct," I say. "But—"

"Because of our history, I didn't insist on a 3D model. I'm an engineer. I know how to read a blueprint. Hell, I can read a sketch on a napkin. But here you sit, giving me *nothing?*"

"I don't want to waste your time with a design that's anything less than truly inspired."

"You've already wasted my time."

"I'm very sorry about that." I muster contrition but I know

better than to debase myself. With guys like Tramboni, you occasionally have to grovel but you need to retain some semblance of dignity. Otherwise, they'll lose every ounce of respect for you. "With the stress of my divorce, I've been in a bit of a creative wasteland lately. An inspiration desert. But as Lucas told you, I've been doing some travel to get reinvigorated. Once I have the vision, it'll take me no time at all to execute. Your project is the absolute top of my list. Top of mind."

"The top of your list, eh?" Peter is practically leering. "Then how come Clayton Jenks got his designs last week?"

Shit. I'd forgotten that Clayton and Peter are friends or, rather, frenemies. I'd barely looked at Lucas's designs for Clayton before approving them. Then I managed to eke out a presentation to Clayton that was far from my best but he hadn't seemed to know the difference. That, in itself, had been a sobering realization. Maybe what people love isn't my work; it's the hype surrounding it. They see what they want to see. Peter anointed me so maybe they're seeing what he sees.

"What I did for Clayton was great," I say, "but for you, it has to be superlative."

Peter lets out a grunt.

"I know you don't accept excuses and you don't accept substandard work. That's why I'm not going to give you either today."

"What you're supposed to give me is a set of plans. You were already more than a month overdue when you begged me for another week. Now you want another extension? Is that what you're asking for?"

"It's what I need."

He shakes his head, disgust writ large across his features. "Who do you think you are?" I don't say anything. "No, really, who?"

"I'm an architect."

"No. You're my lackey. Like some comedian used to say

about his children: I brought you into this world and I can take you out."

Anger bubbles up inside me, but I hold my tongue. Sticks and stones, right?

"You're fired."

"You can't fire me. You've already flown me to the island. I've walked the property, I've smelled the air. All of that is going to inspire the most beautiful—"

"Zip it. You're unreliable, and you're out."

I stare into the screen. "You can't," I say, roiling at the unfairness of it. At the betrayal. "Not after all we've been through together. All we've built together."

He stares at me, his face like granite.

"How do I make this right?" I ask desperately. "Just tell me what to do." But even as it comes out of my mouth, I know it's a grievous error. You don't try to lick the boots of a man like Peter Tramboni as a way out of trouble. You periodically lick his boots to stay in his good graces. "We have so much history."

"You already said that. Maybe if you'd gotten your ass to my office, we could have had a different conversation."

I thought that the Tramboni Center and four houses meant something to him, and by extension, I meant something. But I don't mean anything to anyone. "You bring in a new architect now, it'll cost you. There will be huge delays. It'll be a disaster."

"You're the disaster."

"And you're the hack. You don't build anything new. You just steal and repackage other people's technology. You haven't disrupted anything, and everyone knows it."

He smirks. "That's your best insult monologue? Guess you really don't have a creative bone in your body."

He disconnects the call and I'm left staring at my own reflection, expanded and center stage, full of impotent rage. He probably flew a back-up architect to the island weeks ago, and now that young stud is about to get the opportunity of a lifetime. A new starchitect will be born.

I don't know how long I sit there just staring at myself with something like amazement. How did I get this fucked this fast?

Then a new video call comes in: Lucas.

I go ahead and take it, only I turn off my video. I'd prefer to be incognito right now. If only I could actually disappear.

Lucas looks highly worried. "I just got a text from Peter saying he's terminating the contract," he says. "Do we have any legal recourse, do you think?"

"As in, you want to try suing Peter Tramboni?" I bark out a laugh. "His legal team would bury us. I can't afford another attorney." I can barely afford Hugh. I'm already dipping into savings, and I don't have as much of a cushion as you'd expect, given the kind of commissions I've had these past years. I really don't know where all the money's gone. But the forensic accountant that Madeline's hired will no doubt figure that out.

"How did your talk with him go? I mean, I know he's not working with us anymore but did you still end on good terms?"

"I would not say that, no."

"Could you call him back and smooth things over?"

I shake my head. "My number is already blocked by now."

"But you could at least try, right?" Lucas has gone from worried straight to panicked. "We've got referrals from his friends in the pipeline—"

"Peter doesn't have friends."

"You know what I mean. If they pull out, you're going to have a pretty big cash flow problem."

I notice that his pronouns just changed from "we" to "you." I already have a cash flow problem since he took advantage of my weakened state to shake me down for a 50 percent raise. "We'll manage," I say shortly.

"Maybe you could call them all proactively? Do some damage control?"

"Sounds delightful. I'll be sure to put that on my To Do list: Give billionaires an unwanted rim job. Check."

"Why's your camera off, Greg?" he asks quietly.

"Because sometimes a man wants a little privacy," I snarl. "Shouldn't I be the one asking the questions and making the suggestions, seeing as you're my lackey?" When I see Lucas's face fall, when I see that he feels incapable of snapping back, I lose my mojo. "I'm sorry. It's just—it's the divorce. I never thought Madeline could be this brutal. I really thought she loved me." To my mortification, a sob rises up in my throat.

"I've seen you together," Lucas says. "I really think she loves you, too."

I get a rush of shame. Lucas is a good man and he's depending on me. "I'm going to get it together, okay? Sure, Peter put me on the map and he's sent a lot of referrals my way over the years, but my work speaks for itself. I'm a star in my own right."

"You are." Lucas's eyes are shining. Oh, to be that young and impressionable. That ready to believe.

I feel so old. So washed up. But I need to buck up and keep his morale high. I'm a leader, sort of. Lucas and Lola are both watching me for direction and I can't let them down.

"You know what I've been thinking?" Lucas asks. "That this might be the time for you to step away, just for a little while. Maybe you could go to an island yourself? Or a meditation retreat?"

"I don't meditate," I say.

"You could learn. It would be a reset, or a detox. You'd come back refreshed and more like yourself."

It's reassuring that Lucas doesn't think this current incarnation is me. "I'm in the middle of a custody battle, Lucas. I can't go anywhere."

The one bright light these days is my relationship with Lola.

We're closer than we've ever been. If I wander off, I'd cede that territory to Madeline.

It's not like I want Lola to hate Madeline; I just want her to love me more. Deep down, doesn't every parent want that?

I can't control what Lola thinks and feels. Sure, I opened the door that day when I probably shouldn't have; I gave Lola access to adult information that she should never have possessed about Madeline and Tarek. But the fact that Lola won't talk to Madeline in the aftermath speaks volumes about the kind of parent that Madeline is. She's always been more comfortable organizing activities and keeping to a schedule than she is expressing emotions. I'm just now realizing that Madeline's always been a cold fish, but Lola's been onto her for years.

I never wanted this. I would have done anything to save my family. But in the end, we all dig our own graves.

FORTY-SEVEN

MADELINE

When I see Tarek approaching from across the restaurant, I can't help but break out into a smile. The cavalry is here.

Lola's prolific silences are no longer saturated with hostility, though our time together consists of me firing off questions and getting monosyllabic replies in return. But I can't imagine she'd behave that way around company, and Tarek happens to be amazing with kids. I know since we first met at a pediatric clinic where he won over children (and their parents) in every exam room he entered. It was effortless, too. Tarek's incapable of trying too hard. Over time, I hope that'll rub off on me. Unlike with Greg, marriage to Tarek would change me for the better.

Not that Tarek and I have talked marriage yet. But given how intensely I feel for him, it's the natural fantasy. No, the natural progression.

Lola is following my eyes, her own narrowed. She's piecing together that Tarek must be the mystery man from behind the door, and she doesn't like what she sees. What bothers her most, I wonder? Is it my happiness?

Once Lola falls in love with him—and she will—then she'll

soften toward me again. She'll want to spend time at my house, since Tarek is so obviously superior to Greg in every way. I'm sure Greg and Hugh Warshaw will want to make me look bad in court for having a relationship with Tarek but it's going to backfire. Tarek will make an incredible impression on the judge. He'll be my secret weapon.

Esther might not be on board with this plan but that's only because I haven't told her. And because she hasn't met him yet. I wanted to start with Lola.

Tarek stops at our table, confirming her suspicion/fear/antagonism. I made sure to choose a loud restaurant that provides lots of buffering noise in case this gets... well, I don't know exactly, with Lola scowling like that. We're in uncharted territory and my chest is tightening with fear. For the first time, I let myself think this might not have been the absolute best idea. Initially Tarek had objected, mostly to the timing, but I'd been so convinced (and convincing) that in the end, he'd said, "Well, you're her mother."

"Lola, this is Tarek," I say. "He's the man I've been seeing."

Lola stares down at the table stonily. She reminds me of Greg these days: always seething, on the cusp of eruption. Have I mentioned that's not the man I married? And this isn't the daughter I've raised.

"Hi, Lola," Tarek says, his voice gentle and friendly yet non-demanding. There's a smile in it, which is convenient since she's not looking at his face. "Lovely to meet you."

"Have a seat," I say. "We haven't ordered yet. I'm getting the chicken souvlaki platter, and Lola is probably getting spanakopita, like usual. Is that what you're having?"

Lola shakes her head, and I can't tell if that's a no on the spanakopita or a refusal to interact with me.

"Lola, I know this is hard for you," I say. She's glaring down at the table. "You don't like picturing me with anyone except

Dad, which is understandable. But I'm not doing anything wrong by—"

"By having sex with someone else when you're married to Dad?" she says at a volume that pierces through the din.

I don't glance at the nearby tables, not wanting to give her the satisfaction, but I do flush. "This isn't about sex." What does Lola even know about sex? I bought her books and tried to talk with her about the correct anatomical terms, the mechanics, and the importance of consent, and she'd evinced no curiosity. She doesn't even have boy friends, let alone boyfriends.

"Your mother and I are just spending a little time together," Tarek says. "That's all."

I shoot him a quick reproving glance. We'd agreed that he would follow my lead.

Lola looks up at him out of the corner of her eye appraisingly. He doesn't flinch or move or even smile. He just shows he's up to the scrutiny, that he's unafraid, and I notice that she's less certain now of her instantaneous hatred of him. It's like catnip for kids (kidnip?), this not trying too hard thing. And while I'm in awe of his superpower, I'm a little bit jealous, too. I could never pull it off. But then, it's a whole lot easier when you don't have to care too much, when you can just go home to your own apartment at the end of the night.

Now Lola's looking at me. "You're just spending time together, like no big deal?"

I'm a little stymied. I can tell what Lola wants to hear but it would be a lie, not to mention an insult to my relationship. But maybe downplaying is the best strategy, until Lola thaws?

She looks exasperated. "This is why I like talking to Dad and not you." Now she's petulant, sitting back in her chair, arms across her chest.

I knew Greg had poisoned her mind against me, making her think I'm calculating and conniving and he's the straight shooter. The good guy.

What I don't understand is how she can believe him so easily, despite all that I've done for her. I've been her primary caregiver all these years and yet she just turned on me. She hasn't given me the benefit of the doubt or even a chance to explain myself. She's just assumed the worst, taking her father's word as gospel.

"You're right," I say, an edge to my voice. "I'm not like Dad. Your father tells you a lot of inappropriate things. I know you don't like this, but there are things that someone your age isn't ready to understand. If you were talking to a five-year-old, would you talk about sex? Of course not, because they wouldn't know what to do with that information."

"I'm not a five-year-old." Now her eyes are roving the restaurant. She's acting bored with me. Bored and casually disgusted. I'd be embarrassed if I didn't know just how non-judgmental Tarek is. Well, I'm still a little embarrassed. But mostly I'm mad.

"What your mother means is, sometimes it takes time to understand complicated situations," Tarek says. "It's not about age. There are things that I'm still trying to understand, and I'm thirty-eight."

"So you're younger than Mom," Lola says.

"Yes."

"You're like a boy toy." Are those Greg's words? It sure sounds like it to me.

Tarek laughs. "Something like that, yes."

I should be glad they seem to be developing some kind of rapport. Lola is trying not to smile. See, he's irresistible. So why do I feel annoyed?

Because he's winning her over at my expense. He just contradicted me, saying it's not about her age when, in fact, it is. Also, he's letting her think that we're not a real couple, that he's no threat to her father when, in fact, he is. I'm tired of men colluding with my daughter against me. It's time for Lola to face facts.

"This is a relationship," I say, gesturing between Tarek and myself. "Your dad doesn't like that, but since we're separated, he doesn't get a vote."

"Do I get a vote?" Lola asks. "Because I vote no."

"I'm sorry, but no, you don't get a vote either. I'm your mother and I have the right to make my own decisions—"

"You are such a hypocrite!" Lola fumes. Greg must have taught her that word, or at the very least he's been calling me that where she could overhear. I'll make sure to document when we get home. "You say you're sorry when what you mean is, 'I don't care what you think.'"

"I do care what you think."

"You just want me to think what you think. You want me to think this is okay. And I don't. I never will." She pushes her chair back and stands up. The next table is staring over, like they probably have been ever since Lola shrieked about me having sex with another man while being married to her father.

"Sit down, please," I say, low but commanding.

She hesitates, unsure how far she should take it, how far I might go in response. She must not be ready to find out because she sits. Perches, really. Her expression is faraway and closed off. It's telling me that I might control her body but I don't control her mind.

"I'm just asking you to give Tarek a chance," I say, tears pricking my eyes. "He's someone that I care for very much, and once you get to know him, you'll see why. My feelings for him don't change how I feel for you, Lola. I love you more than anything, and I always will."

She doesn't seem to register what I'm saying. For all intents and purposes, Lola has left the building.

I sigh and turn to Tarek, expecting sympathy or at least

support. I'm surprised to find that his face is closed off, too, like he's blaming me. He said this was too soon; I said we had to strike now before Greg poisoned her against us totally.

Lola's reaction proves this wasn't too soon at all. It's already too late.

FORTY-EIGHT

GREG

"Doesn't it feel good to be out in the sunshine, moving your body?" Sidney asks. I groan loudly in response. It's not really funny but she laughs. She's the reason I'm in any shape to even attempt humor. "Come on, Dracula. Pick up the pace."

It's not the worst thing to be sober at noon, in the workout clothes that have been gathering dust, on the waterfront path outside my apartment that I've refused to use until now. Madeline had made it such a selling point, stressing the walkability (and runnability) of my new neighborhood, in contrast with my old neighborhood. Our neighborhood, as a family.

"Uh-oh," Sidney says, noting my change of expression. "Where did you go?"

"Nowhere that's healthy for me." Sidney's all about health these days. Mine, in particular, which has definitely suffered over the past couple of months. That's why Sidney insisted we take this walk today.

She's also insisted that I start exercising again. I told her I can't, Madeline's the one with the full gym, but Sidney gave me an incredulous look. She wasn't taking no for an answer. She made me call my trainer, who's going to meet me in the gym of my complex tomorrow morning.

Do I want to start working out again? Fuck no. Was I touched that she cares whether I do or not? Fuck yeah. It was such a Madeline thing to do, caretaking in that way. The Madeline I used to know, and love.

Sidney also got me to sign up for a meal delivery service, one I'd never heard of that's all about clean eating. When she told me about it, we were sitting on the couch and she patted my growing paunch. I should have been offended or embarrassed but, instead, I appreciated the intimacy. Who'd have predicted that Madeline and I would be at each other's throats and her best friend would become my lifeline? Definitely not me.

As we walk along the shoreline and Sidney chatters on about her latest interior design client, I'm trying not to think about my fledgling business. Three upcoming contracts have already been cancelled, and Lucas hasn't received a single new inquiry about my services in days. I've never been the architect for the masses; I cater to the tech elite, the 1 percent of the 1 percent. It's now clear that Peter Tramboni's put out the equivalent of a professional hit on me. I'm dead to the upper echelons of Silicon Valley.

Once I'm feeling strong enough, once I'm creatively and socially vital again, I'll network my way to a new and diversified client base that's not dependent on any one referral source. I could even start with Sidney. She knows rich people. Well, people who would be considered rich in any other burg in the U.S. except ours.

So that's my mission. Get healthy and find my mojo again. I'm exhausted just thinking about it. "Want to sit on that bench?" I ask Sidney, pointing.

She laughs. "We haven't even gone a mile!"

"A journey of a mile starts with a single step," I say.

"A journey of a *thousand* miles starts with a single step," she corrects, with another trilling laugh. She's got an amazing laugh, and such incredible positive energy. Lately I've wondered what would have happened if I'd gone for her all those years ago instead of Madeline. I had the sense that night that she was much more into me than Madeline was. But we've never had any physical chemistry. She's technically attractive, I'm just not attracted to her. Plus, I've always wanted a family and she never did.

When your whole world blows up, it's easy to lose untold numbers of hours playing the What if? game, imagining all the roads not taken, all the different lives you could have led, all the potential permutations of self. Who could I have become without Madeline? Is it possible I'm still becoming, at my age?

Well, I'm not dead yet, so there's that.

Sidney and I take the bench, staring out at the cornflower-blue water dotted with sailboats, kayaks, and paddleboards. On the other side, it's a mix of the industrial and the residential, that Oakland eclecticism. This is the lateral view of San Francisco; up in the hills, I used to look down on it. But really, that's just an illusion. I'm starting to realize how many illusions I've labored under for years.

These days, though, I haven't been laboring at all, something that Sidney and Lucas are worrying about more than I am. There's an air of unreality to my daily existence. I mean, I know I need money, and therefore I need to work. These are immutable laws. But somehow my peripheral awareness doesn't translate into action.

At least I still have Lola to ground me. Her love keeps me from drifting off into the ether. She's my only purpose. I have to protect her.

"Can you believe Madeline introduced Lola to Tarek?" I ask Sidney. "How selfish can she get? It's like she didn't even consider how that might affect Lola."

Sidney's posture goes rigid. It's clear that, once again, she's having to find out Tarek-related news from me rather than from her supposed best friend.

"You're getting iced out, too?" I say.

Sidney stares off toward the horizon. "It does feel a little bit chilly these days. But I guess I can't entirely blame her. I mean, I'd be telling her to pump the brakes with Tarek and she obviously doesn't want to hear that. Not from me, or from her attorney."

"Esther Kahn has been telling her to pump the brakes?" As in, Tarek (a.k.a. Mr. Perfect) is bad for Madeline's case?

Sidney nods. "The heart wants what it wants, isn't that the line?"

"It's a line, all right." My jaw tightens. So her heart didn't want to preserve our family? "All I know is, Hugh's going to rake her over the coals for this one. Madeline and I are supposed to consult each other on all major decisions concerning Lola. Meeting the guy your mom's been having an affair with is pretty major."

Some might say I have no room to complain since I was the one who burst in and exposed Lola to her mother's sex life. But I can claim that was accidental. Madeline intentionally introduced Lola to Tarek without giving me so much as a heads up, and it caused Lola distress. Lola's told me so herself, and she'll tell the judge, too. Does Madeline care more about her boyfriend than her own kid? It sure looks like it.

"I used to think that Madeline was one of those mama bears," I say. "The kind who would always put Lola first, no matter what. Who'd defend her to the death."

"She is." But Sidney's tone lacks conviction.

"If Madeline stopped fucking Tarek, do you think she'd come to her senses? Or do you think she's changed, for good?"

"I can't do this anymore," Sidney says, now visibly upset.

"You can't use me like this. You need to find someone else to talk to."

So despite everything, Madeline's still got dibs?

"We can't keep talking about Madeline. Seeing you behind her back already feels," Sidney searches for the word, "icky. I'm here to help you get back on track and then I need to distance myself."

"Until when?"

"Until you and Madeline have made peace with each other."

"With how things are going, that could be a very long time." I'm caught off-guard by just how bereft and frightened I feel. I hadn't even realized how important Sidney has become to me. But we text multiple times every day, and see each other every few days. Pathetic as it sounds, just knowing that someone like her cares for me is buoying. Madeline might not think I'm worth a shit anymore, but Sidney does.

"No more pining," she says. "No more self-pity. You're not going to be summoned back to the mother ship. This isn't purgatory. This is your life."

What a vile thought.

"Get out of your head and get active. Work, for God's sake. And have you reached out to any of your other friends?"

"I don't have those."

"What about the couples you and Madeline used to hang out with? Some of those people really liked you. Madeline suspected they liked you more than they liked her."

"Huh. She never told me that." Even when she encouraged me to text the husbands to play golf or engage in some other manly pursuit, she didn't include that little nugget. Maybe she couldn't spare even that much vulnerability.

I'm starting to think that Madeline's spent her life doing constant impression management, even before the lawyers, even with the people who are closest to her, like Sidney and me. I'm sure she's doing it big time with Tarek these days. He probably has no idea who she really is.

"She has occasionally rubbed people the wrong way as far back as college," Sidney says. "But it's not her fault. Looking like she does, being as self-possessed and self-contained as she is, it can come off like she thinks she's better than other people."

"She does think she's better than other people." If I want to keep custody of Sidney in the divorce, it might be time for some radical honesty. "She thinks she's better than you."

Sidney stiffens. She looks like she's going to change the subject and then she can't resist asking. "What do you mean?"

"She's said before that your life seems a little bit empty and shallow. She thinks it's strange that you and Jared never seem to need each other, that you operate so independently. One time she said, 'It's like they're already separated but Sidney wants to hang onto that joint bank account.'"

Sidney's eyes flash. "She thinks I'm a gold-digger? Are you fucking serious?"

"She'd never say it like that."

I can tell by Sidney's face that she's catching my drift: Madeline might be too self-possessed and self-contained to say certain things but she can damn well imply them.

I haven't fully let loose before with Sidney; I've always maintained a certain decorum given their relationship. But maybe Sidney is ready to finally see the painful truth about Madeline, too.

It's possible we'd all be better off without her: me, Sidney, and Lola.

Any guilt I had about helping Lola discover Tarek has dissipated since Madeline pulled that stunt at the restaurant, just springing him on Lola without warning Lola or me first. Talk about shady.

But Lola wasn't having it. I was so proud when she described how she held her own. How she held her mother accountable. She's really growing up fast. I know she'll never accept Tarek, not after what Madeline's done.

If Madeline had handled this divorce in an upstanding way, it all could have been different. But she only has herself to blame.

FORTY-NINE

MADELINE

"I've been patient," I whisper angrily into the phone, feeling like I'm being held hostage in my own bedroom. "I've been loving. But there has to be a limit. There have to be clear rules and boundaries. Lola's behavior is completely unacceptable. She won't look at me, she won't speak to me, she leaves the room when I enter. She's continuing to insist that all our communications be via text and that it's about nothing but logistics. I got a text from her earlier tonight informing me that she'll be going to Bliss's house after school and I should pick her up from there. She doesn't seem to think she needs my permission anymore, for anything!"

"Do you ever say no about her going to Bliss's house?" Tarek asks, his tone both reasonable and of reasonable volume. Sure, he lives in a neighborhood where there are gunshots every other night but at least he has his dignity. I'm the one barricaded in my room, afraid to be overheard by my daughter. Afraid of what she might transcribe and text to her father, and how it could be held against me in a court of law.

I envy Tarek. The thing you never think about before you

have kids? That you'll never be unencumbered again. Not for as long as they live.

"Whether I'd say no about her going to Bliss's house isn't the point." I have to remind myself that he's not dense; he's simply ignorant. He's never been in anything close to my position before. Frankly, I never imagined I would either. "The point is, she shouldn't be dictating the terms of the relationship. If I let her get away with it now, where will this end?"

"What do you mean, there's a limit?"

"What?" I ask, confused.

"You said you've been patient and loving but there has to be a limit. Why?"

"You misunderstood. There's no limit on love, but there have to be limits on what kind of treatment I'm willing to accept." He's actually trying my patience right now. Normally, I appreciate his Dalai Lama routine, that he wouldn't even kill a spider because he thinks it has a soul. But does he really think I should interact with Lola exclusively via text just because she says so?

"At a time like this, it's not about rules or structure. It's about trusting that Lola knows what she needs."

I've been feeling a little bit judged and criticized ever since the failed dinner, but this is another level. "It seems like you're having an easier time being compassionate toward Lola than you are towards me."

"True," he responds instantly. "Lola didn't choose any of this."

"I chose to get divorced. I didn't choose to be embroiled in a custody battle. This is all Greg's doing."

He's quiet a few beats too long. "If I were a child, I wouldn't like having some strange man foisted on me either. Of course Lola feels loyal to her father."

"You're not a strange man. You're the man I love."

Another pause.

"And I'm the woman you love, right?" He hasn't been nearly as verbose about his feelings for me since we emerged from our bubble into cold, hard reality. I can't help wondering if I'm not as lovable now that he can see what's he's really getting, the package deal that is Lola and me.

"Of course," he says. I wish we were on a video call so that I could have visual confirmation.

"I don't think just any child would be acting like Lola is, though. To me, she looks like a girl being worked over by her father. Greg must make her feel like she has to choose between us. Then he empowers her to disrespect me. She knows she has his backing."

"At dinner, her issues with you sounded like her own. She's intelligent and strong-willed. I wouldn't assume that she's just a mouthpiece for her father."

It seems like Tarek is the one making an assumption that I'm screwing up Lola by being with him. Which is pretty strange, when you think about it. He should be invested in seeing Greg in the worst light. Instead, he's siding with Greg and Lola. Sidney's been peculiarly close-lipped and inaccessible. I'm starting to think everyone's turning against me.

"Do you think we're doing the wrong thing by being together?" It has occurred to me that my relationship with Lola could be immeasurably improved by ending the one with him. Esther thinks the court will look at me more favorably, too.

"I've wondered that myself," he says, and my heart sinks. I'd asked the question so that he'd say we're meant for each other and a love like ours could never be wrong, not when I tried to do it all so cleanly. Why isn't anyone giving me credit for not having an affair? I ended my marriage like you're supposed to, yet somehow I'm still the bad guy.

"You still there?" he asks.

"I am," I say curtly.

"Are you upset with me?"

"No, just upset. I've tried so hard my whole life to be a responsible, decent human being. How would it be fair for me to give you up?" I realize my aggrieved voice has become loud. I remind myself of the excellent soundproofing, and how far away Lola's room is.

"Parenting is the opposite of equitable. Talk about an uneven distribution of labor. All the sacrifices. The inevitable power struggles. That's why it's never appealed to me."

"But stepparenting is different," I say. "You can influence a child without being beholden." He doesn't answer. "Well, I'm not ending things. That's not the lesson I want to teach Lola. I never gave into her tantrums when she was a toddler and I'm not going to start now."

"It didn't look like a tantrum at dinner. She kept her composure. Very much like her mother."

While I appreciate the compliment, it feels like Tarek is overestimating Lola. She's her father's puppet, I can tell. Greg can't stand the idea of me being happy on my own, or with anyone else. He's trying to blow up my relationship with Tarek, and if I'm not careful, it might work.

We say our goodbyes. I tuck myself into bed, only to toss and turn for the next hour. I can't escape the feeling that I'm in this alone. After all, I'm fighting to stay with Tarek and he sounds like he'd be okay with throwing in the towel.

Finally I put in my earbuds and listen to a podcast on co-parenting with a narcissist. If I can't be well-rested, might as well be productive and proactive. Plot my next move.

By morning, I'm exhausted and irritable. In the break room, while everyone's standing around eating the crullers that a pharmaceutical rep dropped off, they start to trade cute kid stories—not about the patients but about their own children. I realize for the first time that I'm the only person on the staff who's split from their spouse, and also most likely the only one whose kid hates her.

I turn on my heel and exit without another word. Then the embarrassment sets in. For me, this is the equivalent of a full-blown meltdown. And it's all because of Greg. He's done this to Lola and me.

Back in my office, I return to the twelve tabs that are open on my computer screen. They're all about parental alienation syndrome. I learned about it from last night's podcast binge. Parental alienation is when one parent behaves in a way that's likely to turn the child against the other. The child is being manipulated but often, so are others in the community. The hope is that those other people will amplify the message that the targeted parent is unloving, unsafe, and unavailable. Good thing that Sidney is staying far away from Greg. I could see him going to work on her, tenderhearted as she is.

The tactics involve interfering with the targeted parent's communication with the child; erasing and rewriting the child's history with that parent; encouraging the child to betray, spy or keep secrets from the targeted parent; making the child feel she needs to reject the targeted parent; and undermining that parent's authority and rules.

It could not be clearer: I'm the targeted parent. Greg is deliberately alienating me from Lola. It's the only explanation that makes sense. How else could my relationship with her have gone to shit so quickly?

I forward a bunch of the links to Esther before I hurry off to the exam room. I would never snap at a patient or a parent but, I have to admit, I'm distracted and forgetful. Rather than trust myself to make a complicated diagnosis, I tell one of the parents that I'll refer their child to a specialist. Typically, parents love this. It makes them think they're getting the very best care possible. None would imagine that it's a sequela of my divorce, a way for me to cover myself and make sure that nothing's falling through the cracks.

At lunchtime, I call Esther's office and leave a message,

saying it's urgent. She calls back forty minutes later when I don't have much time to spare before my next patient. I cut to the chase. "Have you read the articles I sent?"

"You're not my only client," Esther says, "and I don't need to read your articles. I'm well versed in the concept of parental alienation syndrome." She sounds infuriatingly casual. "Many of my clients come to feel that's what's going on in their cases."

"Well, in my case, it's true."

"What did Greg do now? What's the emergency?"

"He's turning my daughter against me. She and I are still communicating exclusively through text, even when she's in the same house with me. Even when we're in the same car."

"Is there anything new? Can you prove that Greg is behind it?" Esther doesn't sound impatient, exactly, but she's something.

"How could I prove it? She won't tell me anything!"

"Correlation is not causation."

"You're the one who said he was a narcissist!" I burst out.

"Well, most men are. And you're the one who introduced Tarek to Lola without consulting your co-parent. Or your attorney. I just loved learning about that from a gloating Hugh Warshaw. You know it's going to make an appearance in his next court filing. So, is there anything else?"

"I guess not." Did I seriously just get a dressing down from Esther when she should be up in arms about Greg's behavior? As I hang up, I'm hit by a fresh wave of betrayal. Not only that, I feel abandoned. I can't believe I'm the only one seeing this, that I'm the only one who's outraged. I've never been this alone.

Well, I just need to shore myself up since no one else is going to do it for me. That's what I learned growing up when my parents were more consumed by their hatred of one another than their love for me. I've put so much thought, energy, and planning into Lola but somehow it's still not enough.

I think of what she said at that dinner with Tarek, how she

made me sound like a complete phony. It's true that I don't share my every thought and feeling. I never thought there was anything wrong with that but apparently Lola does.

Something has to change. Because I can't lose Lola. I will not lose Lola.

But I can't lose Tarek either.

So I have to win, at all costs.

FIFTY

GREG

It's full-on guerrilla warfare, and Lola's in my foxhole, not Madeline's.

I never asked Lola to do reconnaissance but she's really into it. The iPhone that Madeline bought her without my permission has turned out to be incredibly useful. Lola loves texting me updates. She's expressed a strong suspicion that Madeline and Tarek are having problems, and that Madeline isn't doing a very good job at work these days because she can't seem to focus with all the stress. I have a strong suspicion of my own that Lola's been listening at Madeline's bedroom door or maybe even reading Madeline's texts. Still, I write it all down. Let Hugh and the judge decide what's relevant.

Do I occasionally have twinges of conscience? Sure. But I've realized that Madeline would do the same thing to me, in a heartbeat. She won't get the chance, though, because she's fucked up so badly that her own child is out to get her.

"Lola's my angel, she really is," I say to Hugh. "She's my saving grace. I tell her all the time."

"You sure it's a good idea to tell her that?" Hugh's hair is especially explosive today, making it hard to take him seriously.

"Is it a good idea to tell someone how loved they are?" The question's rhetorical, but actually, that did backfire when I did it with Madeline for all those years. "All I'm saying is, Lola and I are closer than we've ever been, and that might be because Madeline's always been in the way. She'd say that it was my fault for not spending enough time with Lola since I worked so much but really, Madeline preferred it that way. She wanted Lola all to herself."

"Uh-huh." Hugh's eyes are practically glazing over as he plays with a paper clip. He's heard this before.

"Lola doesn't even care about Madeline's pain. Which has to tell you something. Lola's sympathies are entirely with me. She knows I'm in the right and Madeline's in the wrong."

Hugh appears to wake up. "Be careful with that kind of talk. You shouldn't be saying it in front of your kid, and you definitely shouldn't say it in front of the judge."

"Why not?"

"It sounds like you're enjoying the rift between Lola and her mother. Like you're encouraging it."

I shake my head. "It's not like that at all."

"I hope to hell it's not. You need to present in court like you value Lola's relationship with her mother. Like you hate that the custody battle initiated by the plaintiff has had an adverse effect on their relationship. You've tried to mitigate the damage but, well, Lola's her own person."

"Got it."

"And don't ever let the judge know that you've been mooning around your kid, making her think she needs to save you."

I glare at him. "Where'd you get that idea?"

"A little birdy named Greg just told me. Keep Lola out of the middle, okay? It's not where she ought to be."

I didn't come here for a lecture. I have important information. "I reduced my hours at work. Since Lola and I are getting along so well, the extra time will be good for her. It's good for me, too."

"Level with me. Was this reduction voluntary?" From his face, he's already guessed the answer.

"I work for master-of-the-universe cocksuckers. It was only a matter of time before I ran afoul of one of them. It happened to be the biggest cocksucker of them all, Peter Tramboni."

Hugh does a double take. "You crossed Peter Tramboni? He's like the Godfather of Silicon Valley."

"You're exaggerating. Nobody's going to wind up wearing cement boots and sleeping with the fishes." I expect him to smile, but he doesn't. "I was a little late on some designs for his fourth vacation home and he went apeshit. He must have told a few of his cronies, but this is just a temporary setback. I'll regroup, and in the meantime, I get to spend some extra time with my daughter. I'm happy about it, actually. You can tell the court I'm a recovered workaholic."

"Esther Kahn's going to tell the court you're unstable and can't hold a job." He shakes his head, irate. "You've been kissing this guy's ass for how many years now? You couldn't do it just a little longer?"

"I'm great at what I do. I can have a new clientele in no time. Just spin this as a change in my business model for the betterment of my daughter."

"I don't tell you how to design buildings, do I? Don't tell me how to spin." Hugh's drumming his hands on the desk, looking peeved. "We'll need to get out in front of this, that's for sure."

I don't appreciate his attitude. I'm not the problem here. "Listen," I say, "Madeline's the reason I've been creatively constipated, which is why I couldn't meet Peter Tramboni's deadline. She's the reason I couldn't keep my cool when I talked to him. In other words, she's the reason my income isn't what it should be. Let's make sure this costs her, okay?"

"Leave it to me," Hugh says tightly.

"Maybe I should let Antonio do that background check on her like he suggested. He can probably dig up something worse than this. He didn't find anything on Tarek but I'm not divorcing Tarek."

"Who's Antonio?"

"I'm sure I told you about Antonio." Oops. I hadn't told him. Because I didn't want Hugh or anyone else to know about the stakeout of Madeline's house, which led to Lola's discovery of Tarek.

"Who's Antonio?" Hugh repeats ominously.

"A private investigator I consulted with."

"You consulted with him, or you hired him?"

"Maybe I hired him. I mean, I did hire him." I could avert my eyes but instead I look at Hugh challengingly. "Madeline's been lying this whole time and I needed to know the truth. Antonio confirmed that Madeline and Tarek had started sleeping together."

"Wait, so you knew they were sleeping together before you barged into her house without knocking?"

Shit, he's quicker than he looks. "It's my house."

"She lives there, it's her house." Hugh narrows his eyes at me. "Did you know Tarek was there the day you barged in with your child in tow?" Then he closes his eyes. "No, don't tell me. I don't want to know."

"Antonio only worked a few hours here and there. It's not like he's been going through her garbage. But maybe he should start?"

"Has he been watching Madeline's house? Is it possible her neighbors saw and told her? Or that she's seen him?"

"If she knew, she would have confronted me."

"That's your style, not hers." He looks disgusted. "She's playing chess. You, my friend, are barely capable of checkers these days."

I stand up. "You love Madeline so much? Go be her lawyer."

"Listen carefully. Your judgment is impaired, and you have to run everything by me before you do it. Before you hired a private investigator, we should have talked about how that fits into our strategy. If it had, I would have done the hiring. Then it would have been shielded as attorney work product. Do you realize that if Madeline finds out, her attorney could use it against us? The judge isn't going to appreciate you paying a pro to tail her. You'll seem unbalanced. Are you unbalanced?"

"Of course not."

"I've never heard the name Antonio. And if I were you, I'd get rid of all traces of his existence. How'd you pay him?"

"Cash."

"So there's no paper trail? No way for the forensic accountant and Esther Kahn to trace him to you?" I shake my head. "Well, at least you're not a total fucking idiot. In the future, I'll decide if we need a PI, and if we do, I'll handle it. I'll hire someone whose testimony will hold up in court. Get rid of this guy, you hear me? And get your shit together, yesterday."

"It's not as dire as you're making it out to be. Lola wants me, not Madeline, and now I've got a lot more time to devote to her. Can you get Lola in front of the judge?"

"Leave the strategy to me, all right?" he nearly growls.

FIFTY-ONE

MADELINE

Greg looks good, I have to admit that. He's wearing one of his thousand-dollar suits and it's neatly pressed. He finally got a haircut. His skin's freshened, too; I'm guessing he had a facial and a round of fillers.

But I'm looking good, too. I had a facial (no fillers) and my makeup is subtle perfection. I'm in a Balenciaga sheath dress with a blazer. If the judge is going to decide based on appearances alone, it's probably a real toss-up. 50/50 custody for sure. Hopefully, he's willing to scratch the surface and see who Greg really is. What he's actually capable of.

Oh, but if you get bonus points for your attorney, I'm definitely taking this. Hugh is rumpled and wrinkled in a way that strikes me as deliberate. He's communicating that he can't be bothered. And that electrified hair—is he pretending to be a mad genius? He's either got rosacea or the broken capillaries of an alcoholic. Meanwhile, Esther is impeccable in a tailored pantsuit with that incredible black curtain of hair.

She hasn't been the warmest toward me this morning. I think she's unhappy with the personal choices I'm making, choices that she's now having to defend. But that's why I'm paying her. I have to go with my instincts, even if she seems doubtful, or Tarek does. I have to trust myself even if no one else seems to.

The bailiff calls our case and we take our seats: Greg and Hugh at one bronzed table, Esther and me at the other. The judge hasn't said a word to us yet. He's been reviewing paperwork. He's over sixty with gray wispy hair and little half-glasses. He's straight out of central casting.

He looks up. "So we're here today because the respondent has filed an emergency motion to increase parenting time with the minor child."

"Your Honor," Esther says, her voice silky, "this is not an emergency situation. The respondent has a million-dollar business and adequate savings, which means there would be no hardship associated with waiting for this motion to go through the normal channels, and there are no safety risks to him or to the minor. In other words, this is non-urgent. The motion is intended to establish dominance, as respondent and his attorney have been trying to do throughout the entire process. That's why it's escalated to this point despite my client's fervent desire to reach a fair and expeditious settlement."

"Your Honor," Hugh says, "there is a risk of psychological harm to the minor, as I've laid out in the brief. The plaintiff's judgment has been compromised. She's acting in her own interests rather than those of the minor child. Introducing her new boyfriend without consultation with or even notification to my client has resulted in emotional distress to the minor."

"Yes, a protracted divorce is distressing," Esther rejoins. "The slander of one parent by the other is distressing. While I'm not yet ready to present a full case, there are early indications of parental alienation syndrome. The minor has historically been closer to her mother than her father but since the separation, there has been a stark realignment."

"Due to the mother's behavior," Hugh says. "You reap what you sow."

"Enough," the judge says, though his tone is mild. "Let's keep the Biblical references and the hyperbole to a minimum. I'm interested in evidence. Mr. Warshaw, what is your evidence that the minor is in emotional distress and that it's been caused by the plaintiff?"

"I have a recording of the minor describing the trauma of overhearing the plaintiff engaging in sexual acts with her boyfriend and then later being introduced to him without any warning, as well as the anxiety of bearing witness to the increasingly turbulent relationship between the plaintiff and said boyfriend. While my motion had requested a 50/50 parenting split, I'd like to amend that now. In light of the extreme psychological impact that the plaintiff's negligence and poor judgment has had on the minor child, my client is now seeking full custody."

Trauma? Extreme psychological impact? Negligence? Poor judgment? It's like they're talking about some other family.

My mouth falls open. I look toward Greg, who is staring straight ahead. For once, he's the expressionless one.

"Your Honor, this is highly unorthodox as well as defamatory," Esther says. "We were given no advance notice about the request for full custody or about the existence of this recording. It hasn't been authenticated. We also have no idea how it was obtained, what sort of coercion or force may have been brought to bear. In fact, I would say that this recording supports the idea of parental alienation syndrome. It's clearly manipulative."

"I don't know that I'd say 'clearly,' but you are on thin ice, Mr. Warshaw," the judge says. "I will not be listening to that recording at this time."

Wait, would he listen at another time?

I can't believe what I'm hearing. Even if the recording was suggested by Hugh, Greg is the one who decided it was appropriate to ask Lola to talk about me while being taped. Or did he do it without her consent? I have a ton of questions but I've been told in no uncertain terms that Greg and I aren't to speak. We have to solely rely on our attorneys.

Seeing Hugh in action, I realize that all my fears are well-founded. He has the ethics of a graverobber.

But Greg's the one I'm worried about. No, I'm worried about Lola. If her dad would use her like this, would get her to badmouth me on tape, then what won't he do?

"On the recording," Hugh says, "the minor expresses her desire to live solely with the respondent. This is certainly relevant to today's proceedings since my client has reduced his hours for the express purpose of increasing his availability to the minor during her time of need. That's how dedicated he is to her well-being."

And I'm not? I glance at Esther. She'd better defend me, vociferously.

"My client has always maintained hours conducive to quality time with the minor," Esther says. "She didn't require divorce proceedings as a reminder of how important her child's well-being is. Her priorities didn't need realigning."

"Careful," the judge says. "Them's fighting words."

"While I'm trying to tread lightly here," Hugh says, "and I of course accept Your Honor's decision not to listen to the recording at this time, I do want to point out that the plaintiff's supposed commitment pre-dated her involvement with her current boyfriend. The minor talks about that on the recording, how much her mother has changed and therefore how much their relationship has changed since his arrival on the scene."

"Since I'm not going to listen to the recording, I can't substantiate any of that," the judge answers. "Please stop referencing facts that are not in evidence."

"The fact is, there is a new boyfriend," Hugh says. "The fact is, the minor is extremely unhappy with the state of affairs, no pun intended, and the relationship has become so strained that the minor refuses to speak to her mother. The minor has asked that she and her mother communicate only by text when they're in the same house."

"Is this true?" the judge asks Esther.

She does a nod and adds quickly, "Further indication of parental alienation syndrome."

"I don't know quite what any of this indicates right now, but I am concerned. We're talking about a ten-year-old, correct?" Both attorneys nod. The judge looks back down at the paperwork and then up at Hugh. "Is there anything else for me to consider at this time?"

"If the minor is going to be living full-time with my client," Hugh says, "then obviously we'll seek a commensurate reduction in child support. As in, my client should no longer be paying any child support."

"Your Honor, how could my client possibly afford—" Esther begins.

But Hugh is the one to finish. "Without the child support furnished by my client, plaintiff wouldn't be able to afford the family home where she's currently living. That's why I'd request that plaintiff be ordered to vacate the family home so that my client could live in it full-time with the minor."

I'm aghast. I might not like the family home much but to be evicted from it—this is outrageous.

"This is outrageous," Esther says, reading my mind.

"What's outrageous is how the plaintiff initially manipulated the respondent so that she could stay there in the first place," Hugh says. "Also outrageous is that the plaintiff paid the last month's mortgage and all household bills with one of their joint credit cards and then proceeded to pay only the minimum balance."

"Because the respondent had halved their agreed-upon child support," Esther cuts in.

"Plaintiff's counsel is making my argument for me. As I've stated, the plaintiff can't afford the family home in which she resides—a home that, by all accounts, she doesn't even like—so once full custody has been granted to my client, there would be no reason for her to remain. If she vacates and my client takes possession, it's a win-win."

"This is crazy!" I can't remain silent any longer. Sure, Lola's angry with me these days but there's no way she wants to spend 100 percent of her time with Greg. "They're twisting everything! How is it legal for them to just lie like this?"

Esther shushes me and addresses the judge. "I apologize for my client's outburst." I can't believe that I'm the one having an outburst while Greg is sitting there with complete composure. Is that a slight smirk on his face? It's hard to be sure in profile. He's still staring straight ahead. "Since this is the first I or my client are hearing about any of this, we're not prepared to respond at this time. I would ask that you continue this matter, along with all the others from the respondent's motion. This was never an emergency, Your Honor, and the respondent should be sanctioned for treating the court with such blatant disrespect."

"I don't know about blatant," the judge says. "What I do know is that the accusations are flying fast and furious from both sides, and I'm worried about the minor getting caught in the crossfire. So I'll decline to rule at this time, and I'll decline to hold anyone in contempt. But in the future, if anyone's emergencies aren't emergencies, there will be a price to pay. I'm going to order a 730 custody evaluation. Participation by both parties is mandatory," he looks sternly at me and then at Greg, "and I'll expect full cooperation. I want to get to the bottom of what's really going on here."

I nod solemnly, back under control or at least able to give the appearance of control. I should never have let Greg and his cretin attorney goad me into misbehaving in court. Hopefully the judge won't hold it against me. But I'd been caught off-guard. I thought we were here to discuss 50/50 custody. I had no idea that Greg would ask for full custody and try to justify it by basically alleging that I'd abused Lola, with a recording to supposedly back it up. I keep thinking he can't stoop any lower, but look at him, slithering.

Greg and Hugh exit the courtroom first, while Esther holds my arm. "Let them go," she whispers. "Don't confront him. Don't give him what he wants."

She might be right. He's been trying to get a rise out of me ever since this started. But I am so tired of the high road.

Once Esther and I have parted ways, I walk briskly toward the parking lot. I decide that I won't try hard to find him there, that if he's already gone, he's gone. But if I get lucky and I do happen to see him...

Yes, there he is, up ahead. Sauntering. He's probably excited by the prospect of the custody evaluation. He must think that Lola is going to parrot exactly what he's told her and, as a result, he'll come out on top. What he doesn't seem to realize is how transparent his alienation tactics are. He's about to expose himself.

Dealing with professionals is my domain. He's on my turf now.

But I'm not going to tell him that. I want him juiced up and overconfident. "Hey," I call. He stops and turns around, waiting. The cocky expression on his face is one I haven't seen in so long. I've gotten used to the beaten-down puppy dog.

"Court wasn't as bad as I expected," he says.

"Do you really like playing this dirty? You actually want me thrown out into the street? I'm the mother of your child."

"Don't be so dramatic." Now he's definitely smirking, before his face goes alarmingly cold. "Hugh was telling the truth. You never liked that house anyway."

"It's my home. It's Lola's home."

"And once you're out of there, it'll still be Lola's home. You tricked me into giving it to you."

"I never tricked you." So when Hugh talks about me coercing Greg, it's not just hyperbole. It's really what Greg has come to think. He's convinced himself of it. "And I would never intentionally hurt Lola. Can you say the same?"

He shakes his head as if he doesn't even need to dignify my question, as if his dedication to Lola is a given. "My blood, sweat, and tears went into that house," he says. "It's not just another asset."

"I never said it was."

He moves in close to me and spits out, "You are not going to move your boy toy into the house that I built. Do you get that? I'll burn it to the ground before I let that happen."

I'm stunned. I can tell from the look in his eyes that he thinks I'm truly evil, and I feel the same way about him. I never thought that he was capable of this degree of entitlement, that if he can't have something, no one can.

Does he feel that way about me, too? And about Lola?

He whispers, "Why did I ever think you'd respect me? You don't give a fuck about fathers. Just look what you did to your own."

No. He can't possibly mean...

If he knew, it would have come out by now. Greg's not strategic. He's far too emotional to keep secrets.

But then, if the past months have proven anything, it's that I don't know Greg at all.

FIFTY-TWO

GREG

Sidney and I are on my couch with all the blinds drawn. I know she would have preferred the balcony but we just can't risk it right now. What if Madeline's got her own private investigator? I don't want to get Sidney in any trouble. She says she's only sticking around until I'm back on my feet but who are we fooling? That's not happening anytime soon.

"Hugh's motion wasn't malicious," I explain. I take a sip of the smoothie Sidney made, pretending it's liquor. "Lola wants more time with me, and I want that, too. This Peter Tramboni thing happened at just the right moment. And you and I both know that Madeline's never appreciated that house. Not like I do. Not like you do." Sidney nods. Now there's a woman of true discernment. "I don't know why she was acting so stricken. It would be plain unfair for her to stay there when I'm awarded full custody."

"She was just in shock, I think." Sidney is clearly uncomfortable. I won't make her talk about this for too long but it's important that she has all the facts.

"I'm trying to do what's best for Lola. Now this," I wave the sheaf of papers, "this is malicious. Madeline isn't afraid of me. She's playing weak to get her way."

Sidney says nothing. She can't even attempt to mount a defense, because this is indefensible. It's a draft motion from Esther Kahn. A blackmail attempt by Madeline.

It says that all transfers and exchanges of Lola are to take place at a safe, neutral location rather than at one of our homes because Madeline doesn't feel safe being alone with me, in light of my threat to burn down her house. That's my house! Or it will be again soon. Why would I burn down a house that I want to reclaim? It makes no sense. Madeline knows that I was just blowing off steam.

Esther told Hugh that if I don't agree to the public place stipulation, then she'll file this motion and she'll submit the supporting materials to the judge—i.e. the recording that Madeline made of our conversation in the parking lot. As in, Madeline tricked me into saying something I didn't mean so that she could record me.

I told Hugh that's entrapment, and this is extortion. He said, "Yep, but it's all legal." He advised me to cave now and try not to give Esther any reason to enter that recording into evidence down the line. "Though she's going to try to find a way. These are her warning shots." So I caved, even though this whole thing serves Madeline's interests, not Lola's.

What I whispered to Madeline couldn't be heard on the recording, and I'm debating whether to tell Hugh what she did to her father. As of this moment, there are still a few lines I wouldn't cross. But that could change so she'd better tread lightly.

"Maybe she's hoping I'll burn down the house," I say to Sidney. "Then she can have Lola all to herself plus the insurance money."

"I can't believe that."

"So you think she's telling the truth? She really is afraid to be alone with me?"

Sidney looks troubled. "I don't know what's real anymore."

I know the feeling. Tears suddenly fill my eyes as I stare into hers, asking, "With all I've done, what kind of man do you think I am?"

She holds my gaze, and something surprising happens. I mean, all these years, there's never been a hint of romance between us. These past weeks, all my energy's been funneled toward survival; none of it's been libidinal. But right now, it's like Sidney and I are magnetized, our heads moving infinitesimally closer to one another, so slow that it's like we're each daring the other to stop. When we're within a few millimeters, she comes out of the trance, pulling back and then leaping to her feet.

"I'm sorry," she says, grabbing her purse and heading for the door.

"No, I'm sorry." I feel panicked. What if she tells Madeline? "I don't even know what that was. We can just pretend it never happened, right? Please, don't go—"

She won't look at me. Then she's gone.

FIFTY-THREE
MADELINE

"You don't have to talk," I tell Lola, "but I need you to listen."

Lola sits back against the sofa, her gaze impudent. Which is pretty much what I expected, but at least it's no worse than usual.

It's amazing how much enmity she's stored up toward me when I've been so careful to be appropriate and avoid badmouthing Greg. He's upped the ante, though. I'm not sure exactly what he knows about my father but I need to act quickly. This is a pre-emptive strike. I have to damage his credibility with Lola before he entirely destroys mine.

"There's a change you should know about," I say. "Your dad can't come to the house anymore to pick you up or drop you off. We'll be meeting in public places and then you'll go from his car to mine, and vice versa. He and I won't be interacting at all."

I can tell she's dying to either ask why or to make a snarky comment. But she's a stubborn one, so she says nothing. Not even, "Can I go now?" I could be impressed that she's so principled except that the principle is to make me as uncomfortable and miserable in my own home as possible.

"The reason is that I don't feel safe around your father

anymore," I continue. Lola's eyes flick over to me, disbelieving and derisive. "I know, I never expected this either. I never thought he could be so aggressive but I have to face reality. I need you to face reality, too."

She angles her body away from me.

"I've always protected you from adult subjects but it's time to tell you the truth. Your dad's been trying to drive a wedge between you and me. That's why he brought you back that day to get Blob. He knew Tarek was here. He wanted you to find us. He wanted you to turn against me."

She doesn't move a muscle. Could that mean she's really listening?

"Your father's become dangerous. On some level, he must know it, too. That's why he agreed to do the exchanges in public places instead of waiting for a court order. He doesn't trust himself alone with me. He's that angry, and that vengeful. Vengeful means you want to take revenge on someone."

She shakes her head, squeezing her eyes shut like she's trying hard not to see what's right in front of her. I wish I didn't have to do this to her, but he did it first.

"I'm sorry. The last thing I want is to hurt you." I'm looking at the proof of parental alienation syndrome in Lola's posture, in how she's turned away. First, Greg destroyed her trust and respect for me, and now he wants to severely limit my time with her so there's no chance to rebuild. I don't care what I have to do, he will not get full custody.

"What about Tarek?" Lola's tone is so mean and mocking that I almost don't recognize it. Also, I haven't heard her voice in days. "Did he break up with you yet?"

I pale at the accuracy of her cruelty. The last time I saw Tarek, it was like dying embers. We didn't even have sex, and we were avoiding most conversations. He's not on board with my choices, and his sympathies clearly rest with Lola and even maybe a little bit with Greg. I still love him and we haven't discussed a break-up but I'm not sure we can survive his disloyalty.

Lola shouldn't know anything about that, though. I certainly haven't discussed it with her. Really, I've taken pains to avoid being overheard. This intensifies my sense that I have a spy in my house.

But I'm still her mother. I need to do what's best for her even if she hates me. Temporarily.

I have to loosen Greg's hold on her somehow, which is why I play her the recording from the parking lot. Anyone can hear that I did nothing to provoke such extreme aggression. You can't make out his comment at the end about me not respecting fathers.

He's dead wrong about that, by the way. I start out respecting fathers, until they lose it.

The recording ends. Lola turns back to me, her eyes full of wonder like she can't believe what she's just heard. And I think this is it, I'm finally going to have my girl back. She looks me full in the face and says, "You are the worst." She pauses to let it sink in before asking, "Can I go now?"

All I can do is nod. Then when she's out of sight and down the steps, I burst into tears. Because it's just possible that she's right.

FIFTY-FOUR

GREG

Lola needs a therapist. I sent you a list of names.

Oh, Madeline. She still thinks that after everything, I'm going to bow down when she tells me what Lola needs? That I'm going to trust another one of her lists?

Madeline's the one who needs a therapist, anyway. She's gone completely off the rails. When Lola described their conversation—the one where Madeline tried to turn Lola against me by saying that I was trying to turn Lola against her, say that three times fast—I wasn't even angry. It was just too desperate. Too pathetic. Don't get me wrong, I didn't feel sorry for her in the slightest. At this point, she deserves everything she gets, including Lola's hatred.

There's nothing wrong with Lola's mental health. She's handled all this like a champ. She knows her own mind, and she's absolutely correct: Madeline is the worst.

Madeline called me manipulative when obviously it's the other way around. She'd been intentionally poking me in that parking lot so she could make a recording and then force Lola to listen to it. It was a heinous, vile miscalculation and it's back-fired spectacularly. Madeline exposed herself.

And now she doesn't like Lola's thoughts and feelings so she wants to send her to a therapist and have them changed. I'm not about to let anyone brainwash my amazing, resilient kid.

Fortunately I've learned a few things over the past months about the legal system, and the importance of perception. If I flat-out refuse, then Madeline looks like the more concerned parent and I look uncooperative. So instead, I message through the app:

I'll start researching therapists myself.

> *That's fine. Please send me your top three choices, and I'll send you mine. We can interview each other's and reconvene.*

Reconvene. Was she always this much of a pill?

Sure, let's reconvene.

> *We should agree on a deadline. How long will it take you?*

Three weeks.

> *Two.*

Was she always this much of a ballbuster? I don't know why she thinks she gets to dictate every timeline.

Two and a half.

> *Deal.*

We're parodies of the bitter divorcing couple. The irony is,

Madeline's finally turned me into a planner. Like right now, I'm planning to get her a list of three choices who have long wait-lists, and then I'll take my sweet time scheduling consultations with her three choices, and then I'll make sure we can't agree on anyone, and then we'll do another round of names with the same result. Somewhere along the line, she'll probably have her attorney file a motion to compel me but that won't be heard for months. Perhaps then Hugh can file his own motion to suggest a new elaborate vetting process. This can surely continue until the new year.

I'm not dragging my feet anymore to get that woman back. I'm fighting for my life here, and for Lola's.

The custody evaluation will have been completed long before then. I'm clearly the better parent, and while my work schedule permits, it would benefit Lola to spend more time in my care. Once I've developed a whole new referral network and I have more commissions than I know what to do with, I'm thinking I'll bring Lucas on as a full associate. Maybe I'll even add on some other associates. At some point, I'll have to hire someone to help with childcare, but a paid professional would be a big step up from Madeline.

So I've got big plans all right. What I haven't decided is how Sidney fits into them. It's been awkward between us for the past few days. We haven't seen each other or talked about seeing each other; our texts have been impersonal and infrequent. For a while now, I've been self-absorbed—well, absorbed by the destruction of my family—so I've probably missed a lot of cues. It's possible that Sidney has had growing feelings toward me for a while. I'm not sure what I feel for her.

While she's not as beautiful as Madeline, she is more fun. Unlike Madeline, Sidney is genuinely kind. She'd be an excellent stepmother, and Lola already loves her. What if I could love her, too? What if the three of us could become a family?

It's an appealing thought, since I really value partnership

and could use someone in my corner, posthaste. But there are some drawbacks. Obviously, Madeline would feel betrayed and it's hard to imagine the three of us sitting in the bleachers for Lola's soccer games any time soon. The four of us, if Tarek sticks around. But Madeline and Sidney haven't had a true friendship for a while, if they ever did. Madeline might not even be capable of it. Best friends don't lie, withhold, and use each other.

Then there's the matter of Sidney's husband. Jared and I are barely acquaintances but he's always struck me as a decent guy and from what I know, he's always treated Sidney well. Can I really be okay with wrecking someone else's marriage, after what I've been through with Madeline's infidelity? He doesn't deserve that.

What I'm learning, though, is that it's not about what you deserve. It's what you have to accept. I didn't deserve what Madeline's done to me, and Lola certainly doesn't. But we're surviving, and Jared would, too. It's not like it would even alter his lifestyle much. He and Sidney barely see each other, which is why I was able to swoop in so easily.

The more I think about it, the more I'm feeling like yeah, it could really work between Sidney and me. The impediments aren't that big, really, and there's one very large incentive.

The custody evaluator has already asked me for a list of collateral contacts, and Sidney's one of the names I've supplied. Madeline's surely included her, too. If Madeline's best friend of twenty years says that Lola's better off with me, then Madeline won't stand a chance. This could put me in the driver's seat once and for all.

FIFTY-FIVE

MADELINE

"Hi, Lucas," I say. My smile is tinged with wariness, given that I'm at war with his boss. I've always liked Lucas. He reminds me of me, actually. He's a real workhouse, and he's developed a pleasant persona though he's not a natural extrovert.

"Could I come in, please?" he asks. "Just for a few minutes? I was hoping we could talk privately."

I really don't like people showing up at my door but Lucas is practically pulsing with anxiety. I feel bad for him, having to still put up with Greg every day. "Did Greg send you?"

"No. He doesn't know I'm here. Would you be able to keep this just between us?"

"It depends what you have to say." But I'm curious enough to step aside and let him in.

He does a sharp intake of breath as he looks at the view. "It gets me every time," he says. "This house is a masterpiece."

He must not know many details about the divorce or about me if he thinks that complimenting the house is a good jumping-off point. "Thank you," I say, taking a seat at the dining room table rather than on the sofa. I debate whether to offer him anything to drink but decide against it. I'm not Greg's hostess wife anymore.

Lucas sits opposite me, smiling nervously. "I'm not sure I should be here but I don't know what else to do. Greg is such a tremendous talent, he's a real artist, which means he has that artistic temperament. Do you know what I mean?"

"You mean he's volatile?"

He tilts his head in acquiescence. That is what he meant; he just didn't want to say it.

"That's why you were so good for him," he says. You kept him on an even keel. Without you—"

"You're not here to suggest I get back together with Greg so he can keep designing his masterpieces, are you?" Lucas truly has no idea what's been going on between Greg and me.

"No, no, I would never suggest that."

"Then what?"

"I know you're a good person. Greg is, too, even if he can be a little..." Lucas trails off. "He's an artist, that's all."

"I'm still not sure what you're asking."

"This Peter Tramboni situation has been unfortunate, it's a definite setback, but it shouldn't be career-ending, not for someone like Greg. He could build a new client base, no problem, if his head and his heart were in it."

I nod slowly. I don't want to let on that I was completely unaware of the "Peter Tramboni situation" since Lucas is talking like it's common knowledge.

Greg must have lied to the court. Hugh presented the reduction of hours as something that Greg was doing for Lola's welfare when, really, it sounds like Greg's been screwing up royally. He's perched on the edge of a professional cliff, from what Lucas is saying.

"He has so much potential," I say.

Lucas looks relieved. "I'm so glad you agree. I was thinking that maybe if you took it easy on Greg, or even told him that you still believe in him, despite everything, that could help him to refocus." Bless his heart, he hasn't a clue. "Greg's not like you or me. He's much more fragile."

"So true," I say. He has a fragile ego and a mean streak a mile wide but he's convinced Lucas to take up his mantle. Lucas is reminding me of how sympathetically Greg portrayed himself to Dr. Vaughn, how he acted like a wounded bird when, really, he's a vulture. For so many years, I had that same blind spot myself.

Lucas is looking brighter. "There's also Lola to consider. If Greg's business tanks, then that's less for alimony and child support. It would probably be hard to stay in a house like this, with the mortgage and the cost of upkeep."

What a tragedy it would be, to have to sell this place. "Do you think there's any chance that Greg could just go back to Peter Tramboni, tail between his legs?"

"I was hoping that would be the case. I even reached out to Peter myself. I tried to explain how Greg works, that he's like Picasso, but Peter says that once his trust is gone, it can't be regained. I don't know any details but I guess their fight got pretty nasty."

"It sounds like Greg's made himself an enemy." It's hard for me to keep a straight face.

"I think he has, which is why everyone in Peter's circle cancelled their contracts."

This is getting better and better. Maybe we can subpoena Peter Tramboni as a witness? I'm sure Esther would be tickled by the idea of deposing a scion.

Lucas has basically confirmed that Greg is mentally unstable. He's also demonstrated poor impulse control and, for all I know, he showed the potential for violence toward Peter Tramboni. Their fight did get nasty, according to Lucas.

I feel for Lucas, though. He's a sweet kid, and he's just

handed me his boss on a silver platter. I'll try to keep his name out of this, if I can.

I've been so down these past few days, given what's been going on with Lola and with Tarek. Sidney's MIA. I meet with the custody evaluator this week, and while I know how to present myself to a fellow professional, the results are far from assured.

But now, things are looking up.

"Thanks for coming by," I say, sincerely.

FIFTY-SIX

GREG

"I appreciate you coming over," I tell Sidney. She's sitting far away from me on the sofa, looking jumpy. "I'm a little stressed about meeting with the custody evaluator tomorrow. His name's Wilfred von Holten. Sounds like a real barrel of laughs, right? Like a failed presidential candidate from 1912."

"What's involved in the evaluation?" Sidney asks.

"He's going to interview Madeline, Lola, and me separately. He's also going to observe Lola with each of us. I guess he's supposed to figure out what Lola needs and then assess how well Madeline and I can meet those needs. He talks to people like you. Then he writes a report with recommendations about custody and submits it to the court."

"You don't have anything to worry about. You're an incredible father. You and Lola can talk about anything. She barely speaks to Madeline."

I smile. "From your mouth to Wilfred's ears." I'm of course hoping that Sidney will be able to sway Wilfred in my favor but I wouldn't ask directly. After I say what I have to say, though, she'll probably want to do what she can.

"Stop looking at me like that," she says.

"Like what?" Though obviously I know what she means. It's been a long time since I've tried to seduce a woman but I've got some game left.

"I shouldn't be here. I just keep thinking about what happened the other day."

"What almost happened."

"What I wanted to have happen, that's the problem. I came really close to telling Jared the truth when we were FaceTiming."

"What stopped you?" I study her face. I realize I've never seen her without makeup. Without artifice, though, really, she's much more real with me than Madeline has been lately. Or ever.

Sidney sighs and looks down at her hands. "I don't want to hurt him if I don't have to."

Speaking of game, she's just put the ball squarely in my court. I move toward her on the couch. "I think you might have to."

She lifts her eyes to mine. They're shining with excitement and fear. "For a while now, Jared and I haven't been on the same page. I've started to have these pangs. You know, regret about what I've missed out on. I think I might have chosen Jared and this sort of half-marriage because I didn't have the guts to commit to anything fully. But spending all this time with Lola has made me realize that I would have liked to be a mother."

"You still can be. Maybe even to Lola." I smile. She smiles back hesitantly.

"I love Lola. But do you think it's too late for me to have a baby myself?"

"You're, what, forty?"

"Forty-one."

"For the Bay Area, you'd be a young mom. Babies having babies." She laughs. "No, really, you've got the energy of a twenty-five-year-old. You can do anything you want."

"Jared is adamant about staying child-free."

I honestly haven't thought about whether I'd want another kid. Madeline vetoed the prospect years ago. "Sometimes people start out with a perfect fit and then one of them starts growing."

"Like that Shel Silverstein book, *The Missing Piece*."

"Exactly. I love that book." I've actually never heard of it, but she's grinning at me like she can't believe her good fortune.

Then the smile slips from her face. "I wish the circumstances were different. I mean, I want to be happy, and I want Madeline to be happy. What would she think if she knew that you and I have feelings for each other?"

"Could she have made it any clearer that she's not into me anymore? That she sees absolutely no future with me?" Despite everything, I find myself hoping that Sidney will disagree. Call me crazy but if there was still a sliver of a chance with Madeline, I just might have to take it. Assuming she did a lot of penance and we did a lot of therapy.

"That's true," Sidney says. "She's been over you since long before you separated."

I'm aiming to conceal the hurt and I must be doing a good job because suddenly Sidney's all over me. Her hands, her lips, her tongue. If only I were swept up in that same intensity of desire but God help me, what I'm thinking is *I just hope this helps with the custody evaluation.*

FIFTY-SEVEN

MADELINE

So far, it's going great. Wilfred is a true gentleman, soft-voiced, wearing a sweater vest in an office with an oceanic color palette. I have the sense that his resemblance to Mr. Rogers has been intentionally cultivated. That's not to say he seems affected. It's more that he's playing to his strengths, which I can absolutely respect.

I'm tense as can be but I know how to appear at ease as he leads me through questions about my childhood and the transition to adulthood. Fortunately, he lets me talk in broad strokes about the brutality of my parents' divorce rather than pressing for details, and he seems to understand the distance that I now keep from both of them. I fly back to the East Coast once a year so Lola can see her grandparents and that's about it.

"Ultimately, I chose my mom," I say, "but I've always carried resentment that she made me choose. I could never fully trust her again because I knew that if it came down to it, she'd put her own interests ahead of mine."

"That's the sad legacy of divorce for too many children," Wilfred says.

"I would never do that to Lola. I want her to have a healthy attachment to me and to Greg." Well, I did, once upon a time.

"Did you feel like your parents hated each other more than they loved you?" Wilfred asks, and I find myself flinching like he hit me. I've never heard it said out loud like that before.

"Yes," I say. "That's exactly what it felt like." I should stop there—Esther and I practiced keeping my answers brief—but I'm surprised to find that I don't want to. "I was just a little older than Lola when my parents announced they were getting a divorce. Actually, they didn't even tell me together. My mom told me, and then my dad did later, like they couldn't even coordinate that much. I was so relieved. I'd been listening to them fight my whole life, and I thought it was almost over."

"But it didn't turn out that way." Wilfred's face is all sympathy.

"No, it didn't." My eyes cloud over at memories I've long suppressed. "It was the end of one kind of fighting and the beginning of another. When they were together, in private, there was no one to declare a winner. Now they each wanted to be publicly vindicated. They wanted me to take their side and say they were right, and they wanted the judge to say it, too. They couldn't decide anything on their own. They were constantly going back to court, like they were addicts who needed a fix. It was exhausting even to watch it. It consumed them. I sometimes wonder if they could have actually bettered their lives—bettered my life—if they'd channeled all that energy into something productive."

"You're very astute. People can get so caught up in the heat of battle that they don't recognize the impact of the choices they're making. They stop being actors and become reactors."

I nod slowly. "Maybe that is what happened with my parents. They were so easily set off by everything the other person did. They loved placing blame. Like my mother had this notebook that she would carry around everywhere so she could write down anything my father did wrong. She liked to read from it in court."

How had I forgotten about my mother and her notebook? It seems uncomfortably close to my own record keeping.

But I don't take pleasure from besting Greg. I'm just doing what's necessary.

Would my parents have said the same thing?

"It's not easy for you to remember," Wilfred observes.

"There was a lot of pain in my childhood." Tears spring to my eyes.

"You don't want that for Lola."

"No, of course not." I'm tempted to declare that it's not me, I'm not the reason it's gotten to this point, Greg's the one, but placing blame would just make me look like the hypocrite that he seems to think I am. The hypocrite that he's convinced Lola I am.

Wilfred lets me off the hook. He jumps forward in time, quizzing me about other relationships throughout my life. I'm on firmer footing, going into areas that Esther and I have rehearsed.

"I can see now that I used the wrong criteria to choose romantic partners," I say. "I grew up feeling unsettled and unstable and I must have thought that being financially secure would fix everything. So I always went for men with high earning potential." Until Tarek, that is.

"That's not an unusual criteria, given how expensive it is to live in the Bay Area," Wilfred says.

"I've tried to do right by Lola, to give her everything I never got. I know I've made some mistakes, but I still can't believe I'm in this position. I love her so much and these days she seems to hate me."

"I think 'seems' is the operative word."

He hasn't met with Lola yet so he really can't know. I wish I could spell out Greg's role in that hatred but Esther's warned me not to throw too much shade at Greg and definitely not to mention parental alienation syndrome. I have to be self-aware and self-reflective since I know Greg won't be, and I need to drop enough breadcrumbs for Wilfred to follow.

He asks about Lola's developmental history, milestones, interests, and hobbies. I'm able to speak with equal parts authority and tenderness as I recollect memories from earlier years. I worked part-time for the first five years of Lola's life so I wouldn't miss much, in comparison to Greg. I know this is where I'll shine. I think of pointing out Greg's notable absence but then decide against it. He should be the one to hang himself.

Wilfred starts asking about my parenting style versus Greg's, and about what it's been like to co-parent since the split. Esther's prepped me well. We did a role-play where she asked me many of these same questions. I practiced giving answers that avoided black-and-white thinking, exaggeration, and the vilification of Greg. Instead, I'm using tempered, moderate language and supporting any contentions with stories and examples. I make sure to convey appropriate but not excessive emotion, with matching facial expressions and body language. I'm organized and I never ramble. "Custody evaluators are like anyone else," Esther told me. "They like people who make their jobs easy."

The key, according to Esther, is to demonstrate clear patterns of behavior and to stay focused on how Greg's negative behaviors have affected or could affect Lola, not on how it makes me feel. I don't level any charges about Greg bursting into the house on purpose when Tarek was there but I do mention some of what went on in co-parenting counseling, the disparity between his promises and his attorney's actions—basically, all the lies that can be documented. I share my fears about inappropriate conversations between him and Lola, adding, "Though I could absolutely be wrong about that."

Wilfred's eyebrows are knitted together in concern, which is encouraging.

As we continue, I'm getting more and more positive signals. He finds me trustworthy, persuasive, and attractive, I can tell. But really, this was never the part that had me worried. I'm afraid of what Lola will say to him behind my back, and what she'll say to my face when he's there to observe.

"Well, this has been very enlightening," Wilfred says. "I really appreciate how forthcoming you've been, and how willing you are to own your challenges and flaws. Too often, people try to present some perfect version of themselves. But I want to make sure you know who you are, and what your learning edges are." He smiles. "Now, should we start the psychological testing?"

I smile back and scoot my chair forward, close enough that he can get a whiff of my perfume. "Yes, please."

FIFTY-EIGHT

GREG

It's hard for me to trust a professional with an office that looks like it came preassembled from IKEA. But I don't have a choice. The judge selected Wilfred and ordered Madeline and me to meet with him ASAP.

The timing's no problem. I want this done and over with as soon as possible. Hand me my victory, please.

I'm calling him "Wilfred" because he doesn't have a PhD. He's no doctor. He has an MSW, a dubious-sounding credential that I meant to Google and forgot.

"Listen, I understand what you're doing here," I say. "I get it. You want to hear all about my childhood and my parents so you know what kind of role models I had. The fact is, they weren't the greatest. There wasn't a lot of love in our house. It was more like, they tolerated each other. But they were under a lot of stress, working long hours and barely scraping by. I vowed that I was going to do work that I love, work that paid well, and have a wife that I adore, and I had all that. I used my own childhood for inspiration and motivation."

Wilfred is watching me expectantly, like he's waiting for more.

"Dad was just slightly alcoholic. Mom was, too. I guess you could say that they enabled each other." I've been brushing up on my pop psychology speak because of how well Madeline deployed hers during the sessions with Dr. Vaughn. I still think that Dr. Vaughn liked me better but that remains to be seen. Wilfred is going to be talking to her.

"What do you mean, they enabled each other?" He has this slow and grating manner of speaking. And he's wearing a sweater vest. I feel like I've shrunken down to the size of a ten-year-old myself just being in his presence.

"They didn't stop each other from making bad decisions, but they also weren't judging each other for their problems. I never judged Madeline. Not for how controlling she was, or how regimented. I would have stayed married to her forever but she fell for some other guy. You know that, right? About her affair?"

"Did your parents stay married?"

"Yes. They're still married. Maybe that's where I get it from, my sense of commitment. Madeline's parents had the nastiest divorce I've ever heard of, so that could be where she gets this from, eh?" I smile. He doesn't smile back. I've been trying to talk to him man to man but, apparently, he wants to relate on some other level entirely. "I'm just saying, she grew up in the war zone of her parents' divorce and still didn't take measures to protect her daughter from the same experience. I'm no psychologist, but I feel like that's significant." He's no psychologist either; he's an MSW, whatever that is.

"When I ask about you, you often bring it back to Madeline."

"I guess that's because this all comes back to her. She wanted this divorce, and she wants to control every aspect of it. She wants to decide how we'll divide the assets and how we'll divide our time with Lola. She's always sure she knows best. Have you met with her yet?"

"Let's talk about Lola." Wilfred asks a series of questions about Lola's milestones. They seem tailor-made for Madeline. I almost want to ask if she put him up to this but that probably wouldn't go over well. He and I aren't exactly bonding.

But that doesn't matter, since Lola and I are. He'll see that when he observes us together, and Lola will tell him nothing but good things about me when they meet privately. Lola's also going to back up everything I say about Madeline being a phony and a liar and a terrible role model who puts her sex life before her own child's emotional needs. After the night I spent with Sidney, she'll back me up, too.

I answer Wilfred's questions to the best of my knowledge, which isn't extensive. "I imagine Madeline will ace that little exam," I say. "But what's important is connecting in the present with Lola. That's something I can do and Madeline can't."

Wilfred wants to know about the women I was with before Madeline, which seems odd, but all right, I'll play along. I explain that Madeline was different than all the others, that I liked how she made me work for it, that she wasn't some flighty artist type. She had a good head on her shoulders and she knew how to support a man's dreams. I have to admit that, without her, I would still be at my architecture firm and I never would have struck it rich. Well, it was her and Peter Tramboni but I'm hardly going to mention that dick.

"Madeline and I had an arrangement that worked for a long time," I say. "But the thing is, she's secretive. I never knew when it stopped working for her. Or maybe it wasn't about our arrangement at all; it was about her wanting some other dude."

Wilfred looks uncomfortable.

"Look, I know her affair doesn't make her a bad mother. But her preoccupation with another guy did make her a bad mother. Just ask Lola."

"Are you having conversations with Lola about her mother's activities?"

"Only when Lola brings it up, and only in the most appropriate ways. I keep it very neutral. But Lola's upset, understandably. Her mother blew up our family. Madeline wouldn't even do couples therapy, did you know that?"

"I think we should confine ourselves to—"

"I'm not saying I was the perfect husband. I worked long hours, that's true, but I worked downstairs. I was always around. If she'd asked for help, she would have gotten it. If she wanted me to change, I would have. I never would have stepped out on her like she did to me. I built the family I always dreamed of, and I loved it." Dammit, I've started crying. "Pass me that box of tissues, would you?"

He does. Unlike Dr. Vaughn, he seems unmoved by my vulnerability. If anything, it's making him even more uncomfortable. Maybe that's why he does evaluations and not therapy.

"I didn't want to end up like this, you know?" I say, blowing my nose.

"No one does." He consults his clipboard. "I have more questions for you, and I'd appreciate if you'd limit the scope of your answers."

"Meaning?"

"Please answer each question without any additional commentary."

Sheesh. This guy's a real paragon of compassion. I glance at his hand. No wedding ring. "Have you been through a divorce yourself?"

"Let's limit the scope of your questions, too."

I have the sense that it doesn't matter what I say. Madeline's gotten to him first.

It's like fireworks are going off inside me. I know what Hugh said, that nobody wants to hear about what a sixteen-year-old did after being put through the wringer of her parents' divorce, that if anything, the court might be more sympathetic to Madeline now for what she experienced then. But Hugh doesn't know everything, and Wilfred's a real buttoned-up type. Once I tell him what Madeline did to her own father, he'll take everything she's said to him with a grain of salt. He'll know that she's not as she appears.

"Before we get back to the questions," I say, "I've got a story for you."

FIFTY-NINE

MADELINE

Tarek only comes over to my house when Lola's with Greg but even so, it's tense. He seems more worried than I am about us being unceremoniously interrupted. When we're at Tarek's apartment, I'm just as distractible. I'm more aware of his poverty (I know, it's by principled choice but lately it seems more sanctimonious than romantic). And when we're in public, I'm constantly looking over my shoulder. I don't want anyone who knew Greg and me as a couple to start speculating about the other man.

In other words, no place feels safe or comfortable anymore. Greg's seen to that.

Tonight, Tarek and I are trying out a dive bar. Everyone's at least ten years younger than I am, and I'm definitely feeling my age. Tarek, on the other hand, fits right in. He's even put quarters in the hipster jukebox and it's spitting out songs I've never heard.

At least the lighting is dim so it'll conceal the crow's feet that have deepened since all this started. Well drinks are $5. I'm having a rum and Coke, which was my college favorite. An upper plus a downer = the perfect buzz.

I'm on my second. Still no buzz.

"It was just so humiliating," I say. "Having this social worker sit on the couch, scribbling notes, while Lola and I sat at the dining room table. Before he got there, I had to threaten her just to get her to play a board game with me—Chinese checkers, which she used to love, by the way—and after he'd arrived, she actually said, loudly, 'You're the one who said that if I didn't play, I wasn't going to see Bliss for a month.' That's a lie, I said a week, but if I'd corrected her, then it would have shown that I had, in fact, threatened her."

"Why did you threaten her?" He takes a sip of sangria. This bar prides itself on its sangria, and Tarek's philosophy is that you always get the house special/local delicacy. That's how he approached his time in Gambia. Or was it Gabon? I can't ask him because he'd think I'm racist.

"Because otherwise he would have watched us sitting at that table either in total silence, or with me asking questions and her ignoring me."

"But that's reality. That's your relationship with her these days."

"I'm trying to make an impression, Tarek." I shake my head in frustration. "I'm trying to hang onto my child. Do you have to criticize every move I make?"

"Did I criticize?" His tone is mild.

"You never do it overtly. It's this undercurrent. I feel your judgment all the time."

"That might just be your own conscience."

"See? That was judgmental." Or maybe he's right, and I am making him the voice of my conscience, my very own Jiminy Cricket. No wonder I don't want to fuck him anymore. Frankly, I don't want to do anything anymore, with anyone. "I think I'm depressed."

"I would be, if I were you."

I toss back the rest of my drink because the alternative is to toss it in his face.

"Hey." He touches my arm lightly. I realize that's the first time he's done that all night. It wasn't so long ago that we couldn't keep our hands off each other. "All I mean is, I'd be depressed if I were being treated the way you are by my ex and by my daughter."

Tears fill my eyes. I've just wanted someone to get it. "I have no idea what Lola said to the evaluator, but I know what I saw. When we were sitting at that table, she relished it. She loved watching me squirm."

"I can't imagine that's true."

"No, it is! It is true!" So much for someone getting it. "Meanwhile, I'm fighting tooth and nail to keep custody. Why am I fighting so hard? Maybe it's time to just let Lola go. Maybe she and Greg deserve each other."

Tarek actually flinches. It's like he's never heard anything so despicable in all his life.

"I obviously don't mean that. I'm just venting."

He looks down at the bar as if he wants to disappear. Or wants me to. "Sometimes when I listen to you, I can barely recognize the woman I fell in love with."

"Well, you know that? Divorce is disfiguring. Try it and you'll see."

"You've gotten so far from what you said initially. Back then, it was all about collaboration, and making sure it stayed amicable for Lola's sake."

"Yes, I meant that. But Greg's trying to take my daughter away from me. I have to fight back."

"I'm not sure who the aggressor is anymore."

"It's Greg. It's always Greg."

Tarek looks unconvinced. "I'm just afraid that you're the one who's driving Lola away. That she's seeing what the divorce has done to you and she wants no part of it."

I can't do this anymore. I don't have the strength to try to be understood. I stand up. "I'm going home."

"You can't drive."

"Sure I can." What I can't do is stay with him another minute, especially since he's only trying to keep me here to stop me from driving drunk, not because he wants to be with me. "I'm not even buzzed."

I need a boyfriend who'll support me, and a child who'll speak to me. I need a best friend who'll return my texts and an ex who's not trying to ruin my life. Or am I trying to ruin his?

I think of what Wilfred said about actors and reactors. I wish I knew which one I was. Tarek's not the only one who doesn't recognize me anymore.

Has the entire world gone mad? Or is it really just me?

SIXTY

GREG

Sex with Sidney is a revelation, only not in the way I'd hoped.

In the postcoital moments, like now, it brings up painful memories of being with Madeline. She and I made love just a few days before she told me it was over. When she came onto me, I was surprised because it had been so long since she'd seemed remotely interested, let alone initiated. Of course, as it turned out, it hadn't been making love for her at all; it had been a kiss-off. A way to end things on a good note, probably. That's always been important to her. The social graces, the niceties. I've always told myself that she wasn't capable of true passion, which was why finding out about Tarek had been such an enormous blow.

But you want the truth? As long as she stayed, as long as she went through the motions, I was all right. I felt lucky to have a wife that I worshipped. No one else I know has that, except maybe Jared, and he and Sidney have only been able to maintain their honeymoon phase because they practically only have honeymoon sex. They meet in exotic places to keep it spicy, and at home, they barely look at each other. I'm finding out all sorts of tidbits like that during pillow talk with Sidney.

I enjoy the pillow talk. I even enjoy the sex on a purely physical level. But the emotion's not there. Not yet anyway. Hopefully that'll develop over time. I can grow to love her. Because I'm not just using her. I'm a long-haul kind of a guy.

I already appreciate the hell out of her. I mean, she came through in a big way with Wilfred. From what she told me, in their interview, she skewed things in my direction without skewering Madeline. She wanted to make sure she looked both conflicted and unbiased. "If I was too much on your team, I'd arouse suspicion," she said. In some ways, she's smarter than me, just like Madeline.

She's up on one elbow, smiling down at me with such abject devotion that I feel a little bit dirty for all these Madeline thoughts. She brushes the hair back from my face. "I liked it a little longer," she says. "It made you look rakish."

I laugh. "Rakish? I haven't pulled up a weed since I was a kid. I've been living on a slope, remember?"

She laughs, too. It's just so easy between us. It's nice not having so much baggage. "I've always wondered what it would be like with you. Madeline told me you were technically amazing."

I'm startled that Sidney can invoke Madeline casually, as if all her guilt has already ebbed away, like Madeline is my ex from olden times and not her recent best friend. I'm also startled that she doesn't realize hearing things like that can still hurt me.

Technically amazing. That's like saying that Madeline felt nothing.

Sidney leans in for a kiss, and I comply. Afterwards, she falls back against the pillow with a rapturous expression. "You are amazing, in every way! Pinch me, I need to know if I'm dreaming."

"You're not dreaming." I feel a little sick, actually.

I'd started out in high spirits, celebrating my impending

victory. It couldn't have gone more perfectly this afternoon. Even old Wilfred had to crack a smile when he watched Lola and me together. Lola had her private interview yesterday, and she told me in detail all the positive things she'd said about me and all the negative things she said about Madeline. It's not like I coached her ahead of time; she just happens to see in Madeline what I do. She's seen through her mother.

I'm not sure the victory is going to feel that sweet. I may win, but I haven't won Madeline back. She's always been the ultimate prize.

She can claim that her intransigence hasn't been because of Tarek, that all this has been some voyage of self-discovery, but come on. According to Lola, he's still hanging around. While apparently he doesn't approve of how Madeline's been handling the divorce, they're weathering the storm. So Madeline is willing to take constructive criticism from Tarek? She never would have taken it from me.

I wish I could give up on Madeline once and for all, but in my entire life, no other woman has ever come close. Call me crazy but sometimes I still think that if Tarek was out of the picture, Madeline and I could have a chance. I'm not scared to do the work. I've overseen complete demolitions and reconstructions. Couples get remarried all the time. Madeline and I would need to get on our bulldozers and, more importantly, our excavators, say what we've always held back, and start building a whole new foundation. If after everything she's done to me, I can still love her like I do, then that proves we're meant to be.

Sidney hasn't told Jared yet, so she hasn't passed the point of no return. Maybe where Tarek's concerned, I just have to get creative.

SIXTY-ONE

MADELINE

"I really need you," I say, wishing it hadn't come to this, that I wasn't pouring my heart out in a voicemail. "I'm starting to wonder if you blocked my number since you haven't answered my texts. I know I've been a lot. I talk about myself too much. But I really want to know what's going on with you. It must be something big or you'd be here for me just like you always have been. I took you for granted, and I'm sorry.

"We've been friends for twenty years, Sid. I've been self-centered lately, but you know that's not the real me. I can do better. Please call me back. We can talk through anything. If you're mad at me, just tell me. Or if it's something else, something with Jared or work or whatever, then we'll talk about that. I'm here for you."

I'm about to hang up when an unfamiliar wave of self-loathing nearly bowls me over.

"I wouldn't blame you if you're just sick of me. I'm sick of me, too. Sick of all my talk about Greg and Lola and the custody battle. And in all my talking, I haven't been honest with you." I take a deep breath. "I should have told you everything about Tarek. Before I started sleeping with him, and afterwards. I guess I didn't want you to judge me. No, I didn't want you to stop me. And now that it's all falling apart, now that he's let me down or maybe I've let him down, I don't even know anymore... I'm just so ashamed."

I rub at my eyes, surprised to find them dry. "For months, I told you that leaving Greg had nothing to do with Tarek. I even convinced myself that it was all a declaration of independence. Self-actualization, did I really say that? But it was all for Tarek, and he's turned out to be a fair-weather boyfriend." He answers more of my texts than Sidney has of late, but that's not saying much.

"I didn't want to be so shallow as to break up my family for another man. But the truth is, I am. I was too weak to end my marriage without a life raft. I was too weak to be on my own. Except I'm going to have to get a lot stronger because Tarek is on his way out the door and Greg's probably going to be granted full custody. Lola hates me, and the custody evaluator must have been able to see that." Finally, the tears start. "I'm about to be thoroughly alone, Sid. Do you think I deserve that? Is that why I haven't heard from you?"

I wish I could sob because then Sidney would know what an absolute mess I am, and maybe that would turn the tides. But despite everything, that's not who I am.

"I don't know how it all got so out of hand," I tell Sidney— well, Sidney's voicemail. "I don't know where you are or what you're doing but I hope to God I hear from you. Otherwise..." I can't finish the sentence; it would sound too melodramatic. But that doesn't make the fear any less real.

SIXTY-TWO

GREG

"I had to do this in person," Hugh says. His hair looks as wild as I've ever seen it while his desk is unusually neat. His expression is inscrutable. "The law says that you and Madeline don't get copies of the custody evaluation report, that it's got to go through your attorneys. So I have it here, up on my screen." He doesn't turn it toward me. It's for his eyes only.

Why all the build-up? Why not just tell me the good news? I've been thinking that once I prevail in the divorce settlement, Madeline will see in no uncertain terms what this is really going to cost her. I mean, it's already cost us thousands of dollars but I can forgive her for that. Madeline is nothing if not practical so I'm thinking that after the judgment comes down, she'll be open to the idea of reconciliation. Maybe I won't need to do a thing about Tarek after all.

"Wilfred's always been a fair-minded, level-headed guy." Hugh's looking at the computer, not me. "I've never seen him excoriate someone like this."

"Madeline can rub people the wrong way." Even Sidney said so.

He shakes his head. "Not her. You."

"Wait, what?" I had this in the bag. Given what I revealed to Wilfred about Madeline's past and with Lola and Sidney on my side, I'm in a can't-lose position. "There must be some misunderstanding."

"Wilfred's a very clear writer. Not a lot of clinical mumbo jumbo." Hugh scans the screen. "Nope, no misunderstanding. He's determined that this is a parental alienation case, which is pretty much our worst-case scenario."

"What does that mean, parental alienation?"

"He wrote that he doesn't diagnose parental alienation syndrome lightly, but this is a clear-cut case. He says you're text-book. You've poisoned Lola against her mother."

I feel like leaping across the desk and I'm not sure if it's to get at Hugh or that computer of his. "This is bullshit! Lola made up her own mind about Madeline."

Hugh is skimming. "Wilfred says that Lola initially presents as very mature for her age with an advanced vocabulary but is developmentally and emotionally younger. According to the psychological testing, he found her to be unusually suggestible. He said that she was using the exact same phrases you did to describe Madeline, which is a red flag."

"I never told her what to say."

"You may not have, but at a minimum, you talked about Madeline where Lola could overhear and, more likely, you talked about Madeline to her in ways that were highly inappropriate."

"That's what the report says?" I glower.

"That's what I'm saying. Throughout, I've told you not to put Lola in the middle. You don't tell a young child about your suffering. You don't point out everything that's wrong with her mother."

"You've never told me that."

"You haven't listened."

Now I've gone from glowering to glaring. "I've never

behaved inappropriately with Lola. I've behaved honestly. She asks me a question, I answer it. If I didn't, then she'd hate me like she hates Madeline."

"Then you should have let her hate you for a while. Sometimes that happens with kids. Sometimes you've got to disappoint them or be the bearer of bad news. Sometimes you've got to be a united front with the other parent instead of hanging her out to dry."

"Where the fuck is this coming from? Suddenly you're the parenting expert?" It's like he actually thinks this report is right.

"I co-parented four kids after my divorce. It wasn't always easy but they've all become great adults." Hugh folds his hands almost primly. "You behaved inappropriately with Wilfred, too. Telling him that story about Madeline and her dad. I told you that would blow up in our faces, and it has."

"I was telling the truth!" I say. "She went to court and said she wanted to live with her mother. But she didn't stop there. She lied and said that her father kept staring at her teenage friends' tits when he wasn't. She made her own father out to be a sexual predator. The judge had to award full custody to her mother."

"How do you know if he was staring at her friends' tits? Were you there?"

"No, but I could see how wrecked her dad was. She humiliated him."

"Or he was wrecked by shame over his own actions. You said you never even asked Madeline what was true." Hugh stares me down. "Did you? Or did you just believe her father?"

"I know when someone's lying."

"Everyone thinks they can tell. But you didn't know when Madeline was lying. What makes you think you could tell if her father was?" He shakes his head. "It doesn't matter one way or another. The reality is, you're fucked. This report is highly damaging, and it's going to hold a lot of weight with the judge.

Wilfred's recommending that Madeline be given primary custody and that, initially, you only see Lola every other weekend for supervised visits. No overnights."

"Supervised by Madeline?"

"Absolutely not. There's a list of approved agencies you can go through. It's just part of the divorce industrial complex."

"As in, I'm not allowed to be alone with Lola?"

"Not right away. Wilfred wants to make sure that Madeline and Lola have adequate time and space to try to repair their attachment bond." Hugh must be able to see my devastation because his eyes soften. "I know, this is hard to hear. But it's not a death sentence."

"Maybe not for you." Lola's what's keeping me together. Her and Sidney. Only I don't love Sidney. I love Madeline. For better or worse, it turns out.

"It won't be quick but if you demonstrate you can be trusted, you'll get more time with Lola. At some point, there will be overnights again and all the normal stuff. But you've got to keep your nose clean. The court is going to be watching pretty closely, and there are more reports in your future. I'd suggest you get yourself a therapist immediately."

I'm still reeling. This doesn't seem possible. "What about when Wilfred saw Lola and me alone? He must have seen how connected we are."

"He wrote that the two of you were enmeshed. Lola seemed like she was performing for your benefit, like she was overly alert and attuned to the impact she might be having on you. He said you see this sort of behavior in children who have severely mentally ill parents. She feels responsible for your well-being instead of it being the other way around."

"None of that's true. Lola and I have fun together, and we always have. She's not careful around me." How did Madeline pull this off? "Wilfred must have been bribed. Or he's got some kind of vendetta against me. What's our recourse? How do we bring him down?"

Hugh looks at me like he thinks I really might be severely mentally ill. "Your recourse is to stay out of Lola's relationship with Madeline. Focus on being the best father you can. Like I said, you keep your nose clean and you'll get where you want to go."

"You don't actually believe this report, do you?"

"Well, it's pretty persuasive."

"Madeline's persuasive. And she's beautiful, don't forget that. Wilfred must have been in her thrall." Not to mention how manipulative she can be, something that Lola's realized, but Wilfred seems to think I planted that in her impressionable little mind.

"His findings don't quote Madeline at all. He said she gave him a very detailed journal of the past months that was strictly facts and avoided drawing any conclusions, and that she avoided casting any aspersions during the interview. It sounds like she played it perfectly." Hugh sounds grudgingly impressed. "His findings were based on his interview with you, his interview with Lola, and his observations of Lola with each of you. Oh, and your psychological testing. I guess there was a lot of corroboration, too, from the collateral contacts. Like Lola's teacher, the soccer coach, some babysitters, Peter Tramboni—"

"He interviewed Peter Tramboni?" I realize my hands have been clenching and unclenching into fists. How did Peter Tramboni get on the list of collateral contacts, anyway? Madeline shouldn't have known anything about my falling out with Peter.

"Who would have thought that a titan of industry had the time to sandbag his former architect?"

For most of this conversation, I've been as shocked as I've been angry. But now it's pure rage.

What does a soulless piece of shit like Peter Tramboni have

to do with my fitness as a parent? Lola wants to be with me! She loves me more than anything, more than Madeline, certainly, and now she's going to be penalized for that? Living full-time with Madeline with only supervised visits with me? That's not in Lola's interest. All this is only in Madeline's interest.

Hugh should be incensed. He should be raging along with me, railing against this miscarriage of justice. But he's never cared about justice. He's just in it for the paycheck.

He's still talking, but I can't hear him. I've retreated into fantasy. I can see Lola on the stand in open court, pointing at me, saying, "I choose Daddy," while Madeline sobs uncontrollably. She'll finally have to face the error of her ways. It'll be her final reckoning.

"I've been worried about you for a while now," Hugh says. "I mean, you're so consumed with vengeance that you're about to lose your business—"

"No. You don't get it. You've never gotten it. I've been consumed by wanting my family back. You were supposed to get them back for me."

He shakes his head. "I never promised that."

"You knew the plan was to stall so I had more time to convince her."

"That was Plan A. We're on Plan D by now." Hugh's expression turns pitying. "I know this is a lot to take in, and it's not the result we were hoping for. But this is a long road. You and Madeline are going to have to deal with each other until Lola's eighteen, at a minimum. This might be the wake-up call you needed."

It was supposed to be Madeline's wake-up call. Instead, my daughter's being ripped away from me.

"Go home and cry it out. Then be a man and do what you need to do. Put on a brave face for Lola and make the best impression you can during the supervised visits. Over time, you'll extend an olive branch to Madeline, because if you want to speed all this up, it'll help to be back in her good graces."

I'd come in here today thinking that my bargaining position was about to be substantially improved, but now I'm finding out that Madeline is back where she loves to be: in total control.

I've lost. I'm lost.

Which means Madeline won. Of course she did. Because she'll stop at nothing. Apparently, she's as soulless as Peter Tramboni. Maybe she's fucking him now, too.

Lola cannot be raised by that woman. Whatever it takes, I can't let that happen.

I walk out while Hugh's still in mid-sentence. Without thought or volition, I start driving, and I find myself just where I need to be.

I storm into the office, past the waiting room where fortunately there's no receptionist to slow me down, throwing open the door to the inner sanctum. The guy is way too trusting. It must not have occurred to him to lock his door but it should have. I can't be the first enemy he's made.

Wilfred jumps to his feet but he's all of five foot six. He's no match for me.

"You can't be here," he sputters. The client he was talking to is staring up at me, owl-eyed and obviously frightened.

"You shouldn't be here," I tell her, and what I mean is that no one should be working with Wilfred, but she must take it as a threat because she scurries out.

"You're trespassing." His voice quivers.

"I have every right to face my accuser. You thought you could just write a bunch of lies and never be accountable?" I move in close, enjoying the fear in his eyes. "You're going to pay for this."

"Get out."

I stare him down. My fists are clenched again and I would

love to unleash some of the fury that's been building inside me for months.

He's staring back, and I feel like there's actually a challenge there. Will I prove I'm the animal he seems to think I am?

No, I'm not. Not yet anyway.

I back away. "You suck at your job," I tell him.

"Put it on Yelp," he says, and I almost laugh. I mean, I didn't know Wilfred was capable of humor. I'm not exactly sure what I'm capable of either.

I head home because that's where the bourbon is. I've barely walked in the front door when I get a call from Hugh. He's shouting and swearing.

"You fucking idiot! I told you to cool your jets! We had options. I could have put Wilfred on the stand and broken him down. Or I could have found you an expert to rebut the report. But now? There's no point. You've made yourself look like a lunatic. You're a menace to society and a danger to Lola!"

I've uncapped the bourbon and am swigging directly from the bottle. "You never said we had options."

"There are always options. But I'm not one of them. Not for you. Start looking for a new attorney."

He's already hung up so I can't tell him that his incompetence landed me here, that he's done nearly as much as Madeline to wreck my life. Lola's life, too.

And someone's going to pay.

SIXTY-THREE

MADELINE

"Congratulations." Esther slides the papers across her desktop, beaming at me like I've just won the lottery. Or more like she has. "You might want to frame that."

It's the judge's order. He's followed every recommendation from the custody evaluation, just like Esther said he would, but he's gone even further. I'm skimming rapidly.

"I knew you'd be pleased. Just look at all the humiliations that Greg will have to endure." She's actually crowing. "You'll definitely have to keep your eyes and ears open so that you can document any derogatory or unsupportive comments about you that Greg makes to Lola or to anyone else in the community. That way, we can really stick it to him since he'd be explicitly violating a court order. See there on page three? He has to pay for family therapy for you and Lola. He also has to write a letter to Lola, acknowledging that he's done and said things that have interfered with your relationship with her."

I scan the page. The letter has to say that he was wrong; that I'm not all bad and he's not all good; that we love her equally; and that I am in fact a responsible and loving parent. "Does he need to use this exact language?"

Esther nods with as much genuine excitement as I've ever seen from her. "Verbatim."

"It won't sound like him. Lola will know that the judge forced him." She'll think that I forced him. Or that I manipulated the judge into forcing him.

"That's the beauty of this whole thing. He's basically under a gag order. Totally hamstrung. If he says anything out of line to Lola, we haul him right back into court. He'll be charged with contempt. He'll get another year of supervised visitation."

She's so exultant, but I just don't know. "Is this really the way to get my relationship with Lola back?"

"It's the only way! This is one of the harshest court orders I've ever seen. The judge is putting Greg on notice. It says it right there on page six. If Greg is found to be in violation, he'll be held in contempt and there will be no leniency. Sanctions can include loss of time with Lola and financial penalties paid directly to you, along with my legal fees and court costs. Greg is in a vise, Madeline. His reign of terror is over."

Why aren't I happier? I don't need Esther to tell me that this is about as pure a victory as anyone can claim. Greg is being thoroughly emasculated and humiliated and denied what he thought of as his basic rights. He tried to destroy my relationship with Lola and now he's the one who—

I guess that's what it is, why I feel such ambivalence. Because even with all these restrictions, penalties, and sanctions, there's no guarantee that Lola and I will ever be okay. She might even hate me more since she'll think I'm blowing up the one parental relationship she did value.

"I didn't ask for any of this," I say. "I just wanted him to stick to our original agreement."

"This is so much better. You'll see that, in time." Esther seems a little disappointed in my reaction, like I'm an ungrateful child.

"There's something I've been wanting to clear up. It's been

on my mind since you shared the custody evaluation with me."
That was only a few days ago. Esther had been crowing then,
too, reveling in Greg's impending downfall. My response had
been more muted. I just kept thinking, *So Greg talked to my
father? Has he told Lola what my father said, and that's part of
why she despises me?*

Esther waves a hand. "That custody evaluation is a thing of
beauty. Nothing to clear up."

"But that part about my father, and how I lied to the
judge—"

"Let bygones be bygones. That's what I've learned. There's
no need to brood over the past." Her expression is dismissive.

She thinks it's true, I realize. She thinks I set my own
father up.

But she doesn't care. It's possible she's never cared about
me, or about Lola. All she wanted was the win, and now she's
got it.

I get to my feet clumsily. I hope I never see her face again,
but I'm not going to tell her that. I can't burn the bridge because
I still might need her someday. She is, clearly, a very good
attorney.

She smiles. "It's been a pleasure working with you, Madeline. Except for that blip with the boyfriend, you've been one of
my very best clients. It couldn't have been such a rousing
success without your top-notch documentation. You've got a
real eye for the telling detail."

"Thanks." Now I'm stumbling toward the door.

"I'll be in touch with next steps!" she calls after me as I race
down the hall.

Out on the street, I can't seem to catch my breath. I stand
under the building's canopy and text Tarek to say that I need to
see him ASAP, I'm freaking out, I won the whole case, I get full
custody, Greg has supervised visits, it's more than I could have
hoped for, more than I even asked for.

He texts back:

I can't do this anymore.

   What does that mean? You're breaking up with me over text?

We can do it in person if you'd rather.

I look back at our exchange and realize that he must have thought I was gloating. What I really should have written was that I'd gotten more than I bargained for.

I could try to clarify it but what would be the point? He's been trying to run away for weeks. This is definitely more than he bargained for. He's good with kids, sure, but that doesn't mean he wants to stand by me while I try to reconnect with my kid. If I even can. I developed a fantasy about him being Lola's stepfather when he never once said that's what he wanted.

I dismantled my life, and for what?

What have I done?

Another text comes in, this one from Greg, and it's not in the co-parenting app: *This isn't over.*

I look up and down the street, panicked. I don't see him, but someone could still be watching, maybe the same someone who alerted him when Tarek was at my house that time.

My breathing becomes even more shallow. I'm suffocated by fear.

Greg's been soundly defeated, that's certainly true. But what happens now, when he's got nothing left to lose?

SIXTY-FOUR

GREG

I'm not a loose cannon, and I can prove it. I didn't keep spinning out; I got strategic. I went to Antonio the PI and said, "In your line of work, you must know a lot of lawyers. Of all of them, who's the most brutal? Take no prisoners, no holds barred?" Antonio answered instantly. So I have my new representation and she is definitely not on Madeline's approved list.

Indigo is young but she's sharp as they come. She's no Dr. Vaughn, that's for sure. And she's the least judgmental person I've ever met. I was able to tell her absolutely everything, shamelessly, and at the end, she told me what we have to do. "It might sound cruel," she began, and that's where I cut her off. Nothing's as cruel as what I've already been through. I am fully on board with the play that she's drawn up. Indigo's the quarterback I've needed all along.

"What are you doing here?" Sidney asks. Her eyes dart back and forth in a classic what-will-the-neighbors-think. Then she waves me inside quickly.

She lives in a multimillion-dollar house in Piedmont, a tiny residential municipality entirely surrounded by Oakland. It's weird that she and Jared picked it since practically everyone else who does is in it for the better schools. They're the only ones on the block without kids. So maybe Sidney always knew, deep down, what she really wanted.

On the outside, the house is quaint and shingled, with four rocking chairs on the porch (each with a different colored cushion) that no one ever sits on. Inside, it's been completely gutted and modernized. Sidney's aesthetic is all sparkle and gleam, lots of natural light and white marble. We're in the foyer, which features a curving staircase that I've never used. I've only been here a few times for parties.

"Jared's in town," she whispers, looking mildly panicked.

"But is he home?"

"No."

"Unless he's got the place bugged, we don't need to whisper." The foyer seems like a grand setting for what I'm about to do. I get down on one knee.

"This is crazy," she says, but her eyes grow round and soft.

"I can't officially propose now, but I need you to know how I feel about you. I love you, Sidney." It's a lie, because I'm a husk of a man, incapable of love at this point but capable of many, many other things.

Her eyes moisten. "Oh, Greg. I love you, too. I think I have for a very long time. I just didn't want to admit it."

"I want a life with you. It'll be the three of us: you, me, and Lola. Until it's the four of us."

"You mean...?"

"Yes, I want us to have a baby. I'm going to build a new dream house, and this one will be on much firmer ground."

She pulls me to my feet and then clutches me to her in a hug. She's ecstatic, and I should feel terrible, leading her on like this. But I can't seem to feel anything at all.

I'm not going to sully my proposal, such as it is, with Madeline's name. I'll let a little time go by—very little—and then I'll make it clear that to have the future we're envisioning, there's one final matter we need to attend to. Sidney will help me defeat Madeline once and for all.

SIXTY-FIVE

MADELINE

Sidney's been here for five minutes, and it's felt like an hour. We're each waiting for the other to speak. But at least we have the view to occupy us, since we're outside on the main wrap-around balcony.

"You're sure I can't get you anything else?" I indicate her water with lemon. I'd prefer something stronger, myself.

"No, I'm good." She's a strange mix of antsy and feisty.

"Were you out of town? Is that why you haven't been returning my texts or calls?" I'm trying not to sound accusing.

"That's not it."

"I know I haven't been a lot of fun lately but I guess I thought a friendship as long and close as ours could handle a little—I don't know—benign neglect?"

Her eyes harden. "I don't think there's anything benign about what you've done to Greg."

I'm startled by not just her words but the ferocity with which she uttered them. "You don't know this yet but the custody evaluation completely vindicated me. It said that Greg has been intentionally and maliciously interfering in my relationship with Lola. That he's turned her against me, on purpose."

"Oh, I know what the custody evaluation said." I've never seen Sidney so cold. "Lola is entitled to her own opinion."

"I'm trying to tell you that it's not her opinion. It's Greg's. He's been shoving it down her throat."

Sidney pulls out her phone and starts scrolling on it, as if I'm boring her. Hurt and bewildered, not knowing what else to do, I mimic her. That's when I realize that I've missed a text from Esther. It's one word: *Emergency*.

"Excuse me, I'll be right back," I say. Sidney doesn't look up as I head back into the house.

As much as I'd love to avoid Esther for the rest of my life, I'm not about to ignore this. I call and she answers immediately.

"So my day started with a call from Hugh Warshaw," she launches right in. "He said that he'll no longer be representing Greg. It was clearly less than amicable but I'm not sure if Greg fired Hugh or it was the other way around. I told Hugh that since the case is settled, it's a good time for him to cut his losses. He agreed, but said Greg's new attorney has other ideas. He asked if I've ever been up against Indigo Reger, and I said no, I've never heard of her. He said, 'I know you think I'm dirty. She's the filthiest I've ever seen.'"

"But it's not going to matter, right?" The custody evaluator has spoken, and the judge has ruled. Indigo Reger has nothing to work with.

"I have contacts everywhere, and I spent the rest of the morning making discreet inquiries. Indigo Reger is filing a lawsuit against Wilfred for malpractice. Since Greg is suing Wilfred for millions in damages, of course Indigo's going to contest the custody evaluation and call for a new one. She'll probably try to get a new judge and start everything all over."

No. I can't survive another battle. "She'll fail, right? This'll just get thrown out of court?"

"I would have thought so except she's leaving no stone unturned. She's going after the collateral contacts, threatening them with lawsuits for slander. Some of those form the basis of Wilfred's findings and they might decide to recant rather than risk getting pulled into the muck. She's a piece of work, this Indigo." Esther sounds equal parts disgusted and admiring. "But I haven't told you the worst part."

"How can it get worse?" I glance outside at Sidney. I really could use my best friend right about now but I'm not sure where she's gone. She's still on her phone, and she's laughing. We're supposed to be having a summit about our entire relationship and she's watching TikTok videos.

"I'm talking about the personal betrayal level. Don't ask me how but I was able to get a copy of an affidavit from your oldest and dearest."

"Sidney?" My eyes fly toward the expansive glass window. Outside, Sidney still looks like she doesn't have a care in the world.

"The one and only. She's claiming to have witnessed multiple inappropriate conversations between you and Lola where you were the one trying to turn her against Greg. She's saying that there was an attempted parental alienation going on but it was being perpetrated by you."

"That doesn't even make sense! Lola isn't against Greg; she's against me."

"Sidney's saying you weren't very good at it. That, in fact, it backfired."

I take a deep breath. Can this really be happening? "What else did she say?"

"That you have a history of being seductive toward men in power, and that you were bragging about manipulating the custody evaluator."

"I couldn't even talk to her about the custody evaluation because she ghosted me!"

"Well, there's a notarized affidavit that says otherwise." Esther's tone is dry. You'd think she sees this kind of evil every day. "She also said that you manipulate and gaslight everyone in your life, including her, which is why it took her so long to come forward with the truth. Prior to the judge's decree, she'd felt a sort of twisted loyalty to you but when she realized that Lola was going to be exposed to your malevolent influence all the time, she knew she had to speak up. Her conscience insisted."

"So she lied under oath." I watch her through the glass. I know when the shock wears off, I'll be beyond furious but, right now, it's like the wind has been knocked out of me. "Why would she do that?"

"To help Greg. This breathes new life into his dubious legal arguments."

"Maybe she really does think I'm malevolent and that she's protecting Lola?" Now I get why she's been avoiding me. She couldn't look me in the face. "Because she's never been a fan of Greg's."

"Maybe she's had a change of heart," Esther says archly.

No way. Greg and Sidney? He chose me over her the very first night and I've never once caught him looking at her with even a scintilla of desire. Plus, she's happily married. But what other explanation could there be?

None of this makes sense. And it's about to start up all over again.

"We have to stop her," I say. "We have to stop them."

"I'm on it. Indigo will be filing some sort of ex parte motion soon and that'll give us more information. I know how to read between the lines. In the meantime, I'll gather as much intel as I can. What you need to do right now is trust no one. Keep your own counsel."

She's saying that I can't confront Sidney, much as I want to. Sidney's the one who invited herself over today. I need to find out why. Learn as much as I can while revealing nothing.

It's a tall order. I'm not an actress, and I'm literally shaking. Only Greg and my parents have ever summoned forth this much rage from deep inside me. Only people you love—people who are supposed to love you—can make you feel this brand of hatred.

Just look at her. She's drinking her water and staring out placidly at the view. She must think that her betrayal won't be made public for a while. But she knows I'm going to find out soon enough. So what's her end game?

I take two quick shots of vodka and suck on a lemon chaser. I close my eyes and try to center myself. First, I visualize Lola. I'm her only protector now. But that image just brings up more anger because I know she's with them. I try to replace the image with... nothing. Act like I'm in a yoga class, releasing all the tension, mind going blank.

I open my eyes and focus on Sidney. Namaste, bitch.

When I rejoin her, she says, "I'm sorry."

"What for?" I want it to come out light but it's almost strangled. I move the phone a little closer so that it'll record her every traitorous word.

"I'm sorry that I've hurt you so much. I can see it in your face right now. You've been through a lot and I never wanted to add to that."

"You have your own life. I get that you didn't just want to be at my beck and call." I need to pretend that her only crime was ghosting me, until she confesses. Which could very well be the reason she came here today. Maybe she came to give me a heads up about the affidavit, though I have no idea how she could even attempt to explain away all those lies.

"I've been busy, that's true." She looks away. "I've fallen in love."

"With Greg?" It just shoots out.

She nods, still not looking at me. "Unfortunately, yes. I mean, unfortunately for you, if you even care."

"What do you mean, if I care?"

"You haven't loved him for a long time. Honestly, I don't think you ever did."

I shake my head in disgust. "That's some self-serving revisionist history. You're just trying to justify what you've done. I mean, what have you done, exactly?"

"Like I said, we've fallen in love."

"So he's in love with you, too?"

She nods, seeming almost proud, which is revolting.

"When I asked you to stop seeing him, did you actually start seeing him, for real?"

"It wasn't that premeditated. I wanted to make sure he was taking care of himself for Lola's sake, and for your sake, too. I was trying to help him get over you. You were already under Tarek, which you lied to me about."

"I didn't lie. I just kept certain things to myself."

"Well, so did I."

"Disgusting." I'm talking about her, and him, and the whole situation. I can't believe I'm about to be going another round, only now it'll be two against one. Three, if you count Lola.

Her chin lifts defiantly though she's still staring at the view, not me. "Greg and I were finally friends. All these years, he and I just stayed on the surface level but all of a sudden, it was deep. We really connected."

"You came here today to get my blessing?"

"It's a courtesy call." She's fiddling with one of her chunky statement rings. That's when I realize she's not wearing her rings from Jared.

"Does Jared know?" I cast a discreet glance at my phone to ensure it's still recording.

"He and I want different things. I want a family and he doesn't. We always said we'd be together for as long as it made us both happy. He's upset, obviously, but he understands."

"So you suddenly want a family, and you want to take mine?"

"Well, you weren't using them." She isn't showing the slightest hint of shame. Does she really think that she's entitled to my leftovers? I know that divorce has changed Greg and me for the worse, but I never guessed it would have the same impact on Sidney.

"Jared might understand now but he's not going to be so forgiving later," I say. "How ugly is your divorce going to get once he finds out you've been fucking my husband?"

"Your ex-husband. You haven't wanted him for years. You haven't wanted him ever. Remember when I asked you about the sex and you called it 'technically proficient'?" It's like she's mocking me.

I stand up and walk toward the lip of the balcony. The rail is glass and shorter than it's supposed to be because Greg didn't want to obstruct the view. We had a few fights about that back in the day when Lola was little. In the end, our compromise was that she never came out on this deck; she had to use the lower one with the taller rail. This balcony's for company. For our precious guests.

I spin around to face Sidney. "I just don't get it. You told me for years that Greg was a narcissist."

"I never said that."

"Self-absorbed, then. I think you even said self-obsessed one time."

"He's an artist. Artists are like that."

"Oh, please!" I shout. "That's his propaganda. Lucas came over here spouting it, too. Greg's a puppet master, putting words in people's mouths." Like he did with Lola. "You're just one of his minions, running around and doing his bidding." Like that affidavit. Maybe I should feel sorry for her. "You'll do whatever he tells you. It's pathetic."

Sidney gets to her feet. She approaches me slowly as if I'm

some feral animal that might attack. Her voice turns low. "I can assure you, I'm not a minion."

"What are you, then?"

"I'm his next wife."

I can't help it, I laugh. "Where have you been? Haven't you seen how hard he's been fighting for me not to divorce him? At best, you're a rebound. You're a means to an end, a way for him to get even. But we're not even. I'm so far above him."

"You think you're far above everyone, don't you?" she sneers. "You're the most beautiful, and the smartest, and the most prepared. But you're also far more oppositional and competitive than you'd ever admit, which is why I acted like I wanted you to give Greg another chance. I told you to try harder at your marriage because then I knew you never would."

I stare at her, struggling to comprehend.

"Of course you'd never do couples therapy. You want to be the authority in any room. But you were willing to do co-parenting counseling because you thought you'd have the upper hand; you were sure you're the better parent. Only Dr. Vaughn turned out to be a real wild card, didn't she?"

Wait, could Sidney have sent us to an incompetent co-parenting therapist on purpose? Dr. Vaughn had seemed partial to Greg. Were Sidney and Greg in on this together since the beginning?

"The thing is, Lola's a genius at reading people. That's why she's always been so standoffish with you. For years, I've defended you. But with what you were doing to Greg, there was really no defense."

"What were you telling Lola during the divorce?" The heat rushes to my face.

"I didn't talk that much; I mostly listened, which is how I'm a far superior mother to you. I told her to watch carefully and trust her instincts. She's a smart girl."

So the parental alienation that was going on was, to some extent, Sidney's doing? "You've never wanted to be a mother."

"People change."

"So you want to be Lola's mother?"

"I want her to have a sibling, too. Hopefully, a boy." She suddenly looks beatific, as if she's imagining a little Greg running around.

"Have you always been this nuts?"

Her expression turns furious. "It's nuts for me to want a family? You're the only one who should get to have that?"

"You're talking about my husband and daughter."

"Your ex-husband. You threw him away. He could not have pampered you more or been more committed to your happiness but somehow that wasn't enough for you. You are the most narcissistic person I've ever met."

I'm speechless.

She advances on me, pointing her finger. "You cared more about Tarek than you did about Greg, or about Lola."

"That's not true." But I find myself taking a step back, both because of the aggression of her stance and because I've actually had that thought myself recently. I gambled on Tarek, and I lost.

Sidney can feel that the energy has shifted. "And I know what you did to your own father, too."

"Because my father told Greg, and Greg told you?"

"Of course he told me. Greg and I don't keep secrets from each other." She looks so smug.

"My father was lying, Sidney."

Sidney shakes her head. She doesn't want to believe me. She wants to think every bad thing about me is true so that she doesn't have to feel guilty for what she's doing.

I'm not going to tell her the truth, which is much more complicated than what Greg told Wilfred. This recording is her confession, not mine.

Greg said that I set up my own father, and maybe my

father's convinced himself that's what really happened. Maybe he doesn't remember ogling my friends, or maybe it was beneath his conscious awareness.

But I was sixteen and fed up. My parents had been separated for years and the divorce still wasn't settled, emotionally or legally. I was so sick of going between their apartments and hearing them spew hate about one another, trying to get me on their side.

So when my mom told me that my father was behaving inappropriately with my friends, I asked my best friend, who confirmed that yeah, my dad did seem sketchy and sometimes made her uncomfortable. I saw my opening. I was ready for the battle to be over, for custody to be decided once and for all.

Mom pushed for me to go before the judge with this "new information" and to say that I wanted to live with her full-time. On the surface, yes, she applied pressure and manipulated me. But that's not why I did what she asked. I did it for me. I needed an ending.

I didn't even care who I lived with. Like Wilfred said, I knew my parents hated each other more than either of them loved me. Sure, ostensibly I was what they were fighting over (they didn't have any monetary assets) but they could barely even see me through the haze of battle. They surely couldn't see what the battle had done to me, the way it had eaten up so much of my childhood and adolescence, from ages eleven through sixteen.

But I could suddenly see the finish line. So I went before the judge and I said what I had to.

Do I know the truth of what my father did or didn't do?

No, because some truths can never be known, absolutely. I do know that my father was wounded and stayed wounded. He continued to think he was the aggrieved party and that's why he told my husband I'd lied. It was payback. He wanted to hurt me.

I'm not sure why Greg sat on the information all these years, why he never asked for my version. It's not like he antici-pated we'd be having a divorce of our own someday. So he must have kept it to himself to protect me, and then later, he spied his opening. He thought he could see the finish line, just like I had. Only he told the wrong person. For Wilfred, it confirmed his low opinion of Greg.

It's not until this very moment that I realize Greg's behavior —sharing information with the intention of ending the pain— mirrors what I did when I was sixteen. And it's not until this moment that I can see how closely Greg and I have come to resemble my parents, with hatred overpowering love.

"Cat got your tongue?" Sidney taunts. She takes my speech-lessness for her victory. "You don't deserve your family, but I do." With that, she whirls around and heads back inside. Then she's gone, out through my front door.

Something ignites inside me. A wildfire, like the ones that have burned through this neighborhood before. I can't have done this to myself; it has to be her. Her and Greg. They're the ones, and they ought to pay.

I race after her, barefoot, and see that she's still sitting in my carport on her phone. She's probably texting Greg. Was that what was going on earlier? The two of them were laughing at me? They're delighting in bringing me low.

I'm debating whether to knock on her window or yank open the door. I can imagine pulling her out and onto the pavement, pummeling her while she begs me to stop. But then she revs the engine and starts backing out.

I run back in for my keys, not slowing down for my shoes. Then I'm in my car, following behind her. It's easy for me to stay right on her tail because she's driving slowly, like everyone does when they don't know these roads. Sidney, in particular, has a terrible sense of direction and as many times as she's come here, she still gets lost routinely. Since the GPS doesn't work, she's been known to have to double back three, four times. But she always makes the trek because she loves being in my house.

Does she think it'll soon be her house?

At that thought, I accidentally hit the accelerator and nearly graze her bumper. That's the first time Sidney realizes I'm there. Her eyes get wide in the rearview mirror, and she speeds up.

With roads this winding, and one lane masquerading as two, and all the switchbacks and blind curves, and how people have to yield to one another or face the consequences, it's surprising there aren't more deadly crashes. But they do happen.

I'm done backing up and rolling over. After everything that Greg and Sidney have done to me, I've got the right of way.

It's no accident that Greg and I never tried to fix our marriage, no accident that we wound up at each other's throats in co-parenting counseling, no accident that Lola hates me. Sidney might not be behind everything, but close enough.

That affidavit hasn't been filed with the court yet. Will it still be admissible if she's not around to be cross-examined?

This couldn't be going any better if I'd mapped out the route myself. In her panic, Sidney has been climbing higher and higher, toward the tallest ridge and the most dangerous blind curve of them all. So I gun it and...

As I brake, just in time, I watch Sidney's car hurtling over the side. I should be feeling something but it's just too much like a movie. I can't make out her face as the car flips end over end, a hundred feet at least, landing upside down in the ravine far below. From this vantage point, it's become small enough that I can almost believe it's not real, that none of this has been.

SIXTY-SIX

GREG

I've got a bad feeling as I pull into the carport. It's been hours and Sidney hasn't answered any of my texts. She hasn't called or shown up at my apartment. Being incommunicado is the opposite of her style.

It's turning out that Sidney is something of a clinger. I'm sure she'll relax when she realizes that I'm not changing my mind about the baby. I'm actually pretty excited at the prospect of being a father of two. I know I'll love that kid instantly, and I'll come to love Sidney. That's not how I did it with Madeline but maybe it'll work better if I reverse the order. If Sidney loves me more than I love her, then I'll never find myself in my current position again. No one's going to take my next child away from me.

I didn't even bother trying to text Madeline before coming here. If she knew I was on the way, she'd probably call the police. But as long as my name's on the deed, this is still my house.

"You sure you don't want to come in?" I ask Lola. She shakes her head vigorously, still buckled. That's the answer I was hoping for, since I don't want her witnessing my confrontation with Madeline. "I'll be right back."

I would use my key but Madeline's changed the locks. Instead, I ring the bell and prepare for a long wait.

Only Madeline opens the door right away. She looks like she's seen a ghost. Also, she's so pale she looks like a ghost. A ghost who's seen a ghost. Someone as terrified by what they've seen as by what they've done.

I know that exact feeling.

But I've never seen this from her before, and now I'm afraid. I follow her inside, and she doesn't protest. That's scary, too. "What happened?" I ask.

"The police must be on their way."

"I didn't break and enter. You let me in. Call them off, Lola's in my car."

"I didn't call them." Madeline wilts against the sofa. I can tell she's been crying a lot. I take a seat not too close to her, but not too far either.

"I don't understand. You didn't call the police but you think they're on their way?" My chest tightens, the fear growing more acute. "Sidney was here, right?"

Madeline nods and squeezes her eyes shut.

"So she told you then? About us?" I say. Madeline doesn't answer. "I'm sorry." I didn't expect to apologize but now, seeing how shattered she is, I feel like I have to.

"No, I'm sorry," Madeline whispers. Her eyes are still closed. "From the beginning, I never wanted to hurt you."

Really, another empty apology? "You didn't hurt me," I say, with a surge of anger. "You gutted me. You butchered me. You sliced me into a million pieces, slowly."

"I know." She's so quiet that I have to strain to hear. "I know."

For once, I can feel her remorse.

"I know, too," I tell her, with thudding sadness. She glances over, eyes bright with tears. We're feeling the very same thing. The devastation of what we've lost, and of what we've done. I've hacked her up, too.

"I just wish we could have had a nice divorce."

I almost smile. "I'm not sure there is such a thing." I think of Sidney's affidavit and how that's going to bloody Madeline some more. That can't be avoided but I can avoid taking any pleasure in it.

"I can't believe we turned into my parents. I knew better but... something just came over us."

"Yeah, you did me dirty, same as you did your father." My tone grows sharp again.

So does hers. "Is that what you told Lola?"

"No. I haven't said anything to her about your father."

"Well, that's good." She softens again. "I didn't lie in court. I just told the judge what I'd heard from my mom and from my best friend. All I wanted was for it to be over. Do you know what that's like?"

I meet her eyes and nod. I didn't expect this moment of communion; it's not why I'm here. "Did Sidney tell you everything?"

At Sidney's name, Madeline blanches.

"Did something happen between you and Sidney? Because I haven't heard from her all day."

"I thought she was texting you from the carport." For a second, I see the Madeline I've become accustomed to, the one who's always calculating, seizing an angle or an advantage. Then almost like a mask, it slips off. "It went really, really badly."

"What kind of badly?" The earlier fear returns. I think of Lola sitting in the car, of what I might have to tell her. No, Madeline would. She can't script me anymore. But whatever it is, it's big, and I have the sense that we'll all be dealing with the fallout.

"Esther had just told me about Sidney's affidavit, and then I was back outside on the deck and Sidney was telling me how I didn't deserve my family and that's why she did all those things to make sure you and I never got back together. But you know all that."

"No, I don't know." I stare at her, my brow furrowing. "What did Sidney do?"

"She kept telling me I should try harder to save the marriage because she thought it would make me do the opposite. She purposely sent us to the worst co-parenting therapist. She encouraged Lola to 'trust her instincts' and hate me." Madeline seems momentarily reanimated by her anger but then she slumps. "Not that it matters."

"What do you mean it doesn't matter?" Now I'm the angry one. "You're saying Sidney set us up, that she wanted our marriage to fail?"

Madeline nods, closing her eyes again. "But it doesn't matter."

"Why do you keep saying that?" Of course it matters.

Her eyes fly open. "I killed her, Greg. I killed an actual person. She was here, in our house, saying horrible things, and then she left. I got in the car to follow her. At first, I was going to, I don't know, confront her more, but then as I was driving, I was thinking about that affidavit and what it might do and what she'd already done. And you want the truth? I really, really wanted her dead."

Madeline's shocked me a lot these past few months, but could anything be more shocking than this?

There's a long silence.

"So Sidney's dead," I say slowly, "and you killed her."

"I ran her off the road. Then I came back here and waited for the police to show up. But they haven't yet so at some point,

I'm going to have to call them to confess." She dissolves into tears. "The only thing that's stopping me is Lola. She'd know that her mother is a murderer, and she'd be left with..."

"With me, yes."

"A father who can only see her for supervised visits." I can tell that the terror in Madeline's eyes isn't for herself. She's thinking only of Lola. "What's going to happen to her? Will she be sent to a foster home?"

"Bliss's family would take her in, if it came to that." But it won't. It can't.

"I want her to stay with you. I mean, at least you've never killed anyone."

"Oh, so you've noticed. I'm touched."

"Well, what do you want me to say? You've spent the last few months turning her against me. Now I'm going to spend the rest of my life—the rest of her life—in prison. She'll never forgive me, and can I blame her?" Madeline starts crying again. "Please take good care of her, okay? You're all she has now."

"Not yet I'm not."

The grandfather clock ticks away maddeningly. My brain's scrambled, and I need to pull myself together before I get back to Lola. Is Madeline thinking about Lola, too? Normally, Madeline would be chiding me for leaving her in the car so long. She'd tell me that people call Child Protective Services for less.

Then Lola opens the door and walks in. She looks back and forth from Madeline to me.

"What did you do to him?" she says to Madeline accusingly.

It's such a bizarre read of our body language that it jars me. The idea that Lola could walk in and see the two of us in our respective states and think that I'm the one who needs protecting makes everything come into sharp focus. What Hugh said, what Wilfred said, what Madeline's been saying—really, the only one who wasn't saying it was Sidney and she turned out to be some sort of psycho fatal attraction.

Everyone else recognized that I'd put Lola in the middle, and I refused to see it. But now Lola is literally standing between Madeline and me, and there's no way I can miss it.

I have a choice to make. I can try to undo some of what's been done, or bury Madeline once and for all.

JUDGMENT

MADELINE

How did we get here? I've gone over it a thousand times and sometimes I still wonder that. I know Greg does, too. But we've arrived at a narrative that works for both of us, mostly.

It was his idea to cover up the murder. He asked if anyone saw me on the road, and I told him I didn't think so. We got our stories straight and when the police came to see me the next day, I confirmed that yes, Sidney had been to my house. She and Greg had been there together to tell me that they'd fallen in love. Sidney drove off and Greg stayed behind so that he and I could keep talking. Arguing, actually. Screaming bloody murder at one another. Greg's now grieving the loss of the woman he was planning to spend the rest of his life with, and me? My grief is different, given the betrayal. The police seemed to understand that.

It worked, probably because no one would ever imagine that Greg would pretend to be my alibi after how contentious the divorce had become. Sidney had been alone in the car, she'd gotten lost (as she so often did), and, tragically, she took the wrong turn too fast.

Now at least Jared doesn't have to go through the pain of a divorce. And Greg and I are truly partners in crime.

We've had some dark nights of the soul separately and together, conducting a post-mortem of our marriage and our divorce. What's indisputable is that we were awful to each other because we were each convinced the other was the awful one. We became one big vicious dog chasing its own tail. Sure, we were manipulated by Sidney, and Dr. Vaughn was a disaster, and our attorneys had done us no favors, seeing as they reaped the rewards from us being at odds and assuming the worst of one another. But ultimately, Greg and I had driven ourselves (and Sidney) over the edge.

I seem to have gotten away with murder but I feel the weight of my actions every day. I can't escape the awareness that I was capable of such prolonged brutality, that I was capable of killing.

I know Greg's conscience is hurting, too. At various points, we've tried to justify and comfort each other, even briefly considering a reconciliation, but when we look into each other's eyes, we see our own reflections. We see our complicity.

I wish we could just blame Sidney because, after all, nothing we do will ever bring her back. She was pretty diabolical, wouldn't you agree? But in the end, she could only catalyze what was already inside us. She didn't create it. Maybe it's something in my DNA, and I truly am my parents' daughter.

Greg and I have made a pact to stay vigilant. We need to keep that tiger in its cage so that it never gets out again. We have to work together to make Lola a better person than either of us are.

We might have gotten away with the crime but we can't get away from each other, or ourselves.

Soon after Sidney's death, Greg and I went before the judge together, both pro se—meaning, representing ourselves. I said that I didn't agree with the custody evaluation, and Greg and I proposed our own parenting plan and financial settlement. As part of that, we would sell the house. We agreed that we both need a fresh start.

The judge was astonished and a bit skeptical but he signed off. "Take care of yourselves," he said, "and most of all, take care of your little one." We promised to do just that.

Throughout the legal process, we'd rewritten the story of our marriage, each coming to believe we were the one who'd been shafted, taken for granted, misunderstood, manipulated. But now when we look back, we can see that we willingly signed on for our roles. We struck a bargain that sustained us for a long time. He had grand visions and I provided the scaffolding so he could carry them out. He controlled many of the big decisions, and I controlled nearly all the little ones. It worked most of the time but we swept far too much under the rug. Were we selfish some-times? Of course. Did we make mistakes? Surely. But were we mistreated and misled? No, that was a fiction consolidated by an adversarial legal system.

When it came to the separation, we started out with decent enough intentions, especially where Lola was concerned, though we'd each been less than honest with the other. Our lies snow-balled, and misunderstandings could never be cleared up once the trust and goodwill were gone. We started to assume each other's bad intentions, always. We each wanted to win, at all costs. Sometimes we wanted to destroy each other more than we wanted Lola to thrive. The fact that I could so completely lose sight of Lola's best interests the way I did despite everything I'd gone through with my own parents is still a source of profound shame and regret. I imagine it always will be.

But now that I've walked in my parents' footsteps, I under-stand them in a way I never did before. Maybe someday, there can be forgiveness all around.

I'm not sure that Greg and I ever really operated as a true parenting team when we were married, but we do now. Greg wrote that court-ordered letter to Lola saying that he'd been wrong about me, only he did it from the heart. He actually meant it, and while Lola could see that, she still seems to worry that he's being bamboozled. She's not really warm to me but at least the door that had been closed is now ajar. We're not communicating exclusively by text anymore, so there's that. I'm learning to be less practical and more vulnerable, to show her my heart. The other night, she let me tuck her in. It's been a long time since I heard an "I love you" but I can be patient.

Greg finally admitted to himself as well as to me that he harmed my relationship with Lola, and it wasn't all by accident. He lives with that guilt. I live with my own, plus I can't help struggling with imposter syndrome. I'm trying to be a role model to my daughter when I'm really more of a cautionary tale. Meanwhile, Greg and I are bound together forever, committed to hiding the crime because that's what's best for Lola. But it has crossed my mind that I'd better not cross him.

Is he a narcissist after all or did he just play one in our divorce? I hope I never have to find out.

After Greg and Tarek, I've definitely got some trust issues. When it comes to men, I'm not sure I can ever trust my own judgment again. Greg and I have that in common. Neither of us can stomach the idea of dating. I try not to think of Tarek and the life we almost had. There's no point in fantasies anymore.

I guess in the end, Greg and I discovered that we truly deserve each other.

A LETTER FROM ELLIE

Dear reader,

I want to say a huge thank you for choosing to read *The Custody Battle*. If you did enjoy it, and want to keep up to date with all my latest releases, just sign up at the following link. Your email address will never be shared and you can unsubscribe at any time.

www.bookouture.com/ellie-monago

I hope you loved *The Custody Battle* and if you did I would be very grateful if you could write a review. I'd love to hear what you think, and it makes such a difference in helping new readers to discover one of my books for the first time.

I love hearing from my readers—you can get in touch on my Goodreads page.

Thanks,

Ellie Monago

g goodreads.com/elliemonago

ACKNOWLEDGMENTS

In publishing, as in life, sometimes a reboot is required. You need a change in perspective and approach, and if you're lucky, you retain the most devoted members of your old team while simultaneously adding strong new members. With this particular book, I've been exceedingly lucky.

I'm so grateful for everyone at Bookouture. At the helm is Harriet Wade, my editor, and she's truly all a writer could ask for: supportive, enthusiastic, astute, a top-notch collaborator, a great communicator, a lovely person. Not to mention, she's my efficiency twin. I also want to express my gratitude to Natalie Edwards, my more recent editorial collaborator, who's already proving to be invaluable. I've been in traditional publishing before and can really feel the difference with the Bookouture model. I have every confidence they're going to get me where I want to be, and that I'll have fun doing it. I already am.

A million thanks go to the incomparable Sophie Hannah for pointing me in this direction.

And to my abiding team (which includes Jenny, Tara, Avie, Lisa, my parents, and my husband, Darrend): You've never lost belief or faith, never questioned whether I'm meant for this work, and always shared in my excitement for the next project. Because of all of you, there's always a next project. I couldn't appreciate you more.

PUBLISHING TEAM

Turning a manuscript into a book requires the efforts of many people. The publishing team at Bookouture would like to acknowledge everyone who contributed to this publication.

Audio
Alba Proko
Sinead O'Connor
Melissa Tran

Commercial
Lauren Morrissette
Jil Thielen
Imogen Allport

Data and analysis
Mark Alder
Mohamed Bussuri

Editorial
Natalie Edwards
Sinead O'Connor

Copyeditor
Donna Hillyer

Printed in Great Britain
by Amazon